The Ghosts of Summer

Alex J. Milan

Copyright © 2021 by Alex J Milan.

All rights reserved. No part of this publication may be reproduced, stored in or introduced into a retrieval system, or distributed or transmitted in any form or by any means, including photocopying, recording, or other electronic or mechanical methods, without the prior written permission of the publisher, except in the case of brief quotations embodied in critical reviews and certain other non-commercial uses permitted by copyright law.

Publisher's Note: This is a work of fiction. Names, characters, businesses, places, events, locales, and incidents are either the products of the author's imagination or used in a fictitious manner. Any resemblance to actual persons, living or dead, or actual events is completely coincidental.

Original cover painting courtesy of Getty Images/iStock.com/sbelov

Formatting by Polgarus Studio

ISBN 978-84-09-26820-7 (print)
ISBN 978-84-09-26821-4 (ebook)

It has been a pleasure to work with the same team who helped me to produce my first novel, The Last Carriage. I would once again like to thank Jessica Espejo Hernández for her work in producing the cover and Polgarus Studio for preparing the text for publication. My thanks also go to all the people who have given me encouragement and support.

Author's note

This book was written during the challenging and uncertain year of 2020. The book, however, is set in the pre-pandemic world of 2019, allowing a certain level of escape from our current reality for me and, I hope, also for you.

Whereof what's past is prologue;
What to come, in yours and my discharge.
William Shakespeare,
The Tempest, Act 2, Scene 1

Part 1
London, England
July 2019

Prologue

Millie woke before sunrise after another restless night. She could no longer remember the last time she had slept well. Friends had told her it was her age and that they had the same problem; people in their sixties needed less sleep, they said, but she knew it was nothing to do with that. Not that she could tell them the real reason.

She got out of bed and went to the wardrobe. Standing on tiptoe on a chair and trying to ignore the pain in her knee, she retrieved the box from the back of the top shelf. She returned to the bed, placed the box on her lap and removed the lid. The ghosts of the past rose to meet her as she had known they would. The regrets never really disappeared; they just got tucked away, hidden from view.

Resisting the temptation to look through the other items in the box, she took out the small envelope balanced on top of the other contents. She removed the letter inside and carefully unfolded the delicate, pale pink sheet of paper.

Villa Iris, Andraxos, Greece
29th May 1975

My dearest Emily,

I have recently returned to Andraxos for the summer. Opening up the house was something of an ordeal, but now things are rather more orderly. I am not ashamed to admit that these past six months without your Uncle John have been difficult, to say the least. Whilst I was in Sydney, I seemed able to stay afloat; there are always distractions in a big city, I suppose. Now I am back here, I sense his loss even more acutely. My mind keeps drifting back to 'last summer we did this', 'last summer we did that', all in blissful ignorance of what the winter would bring. I had always been most content to return here, but bittersweet memories have tempered the experience this year.

Sadly, I will not have the chance to visit you there this year and as it has been so long since we last saw each other, I was wondering if you would like to come and spend some time here with me. I would so enjoy your company, and I am sure you would enjoy some sunshine. It will transport you away from that gloomy London weather for a while so that has to be a good thing.

Don't worry, I will not expect you to be my constant companion but, goodness knows, some young life around the place would not go amiss.

Do write soon and let me know if you can visit.
Your loving aunt,
Sylvia

Millie's hand traced the outline of her aunt's precise, elegant handwriting as she thought about the sequence of events which had been triggered by that letter. How could anyone have predicted what would result from such an innocent suggestion? She knew she would have to account for those consequences but not yet. Not quite yet. It had been a long time coming, but she still had a few hours left. The only question now was how high a price she would have to pay for finally confronting the truth.

Chapter 1

The twentieth of July, the day Millie had been dreading, had finally arrived. It seemed strange that she would fear her beloved granddaughter's eighteenth birthday; the day when Eva would become an adult, but with days of endless promise still ahead of her. But Millie knew Eva. After all, she had been the one who had raised her. Eva had been waiting for most of her eighteen years for answers, and Millie instinctively realised that Eva would have chosen her birthday as the day when she would no longer accept evasion tactics. Millie also knew she had the right to answers or at least as many as she could give her.

She glanced at the clock on the wall in the kitchen – almost 8 a.m. Eva was not an early riser. In that way, if in no other, she was a typical teenager so Millie thought she had a few hours left. She made coffee and gazed out of the window. A squirrel appeared out of the early morning mist drifting across the lawn; it was alert, checking for danger. She inspected the cake she had made for Eva's birthday and wondered what the day would bring. When she looked up, the squirrel had gone. It crossed her mind that it, too, had perhaps sensed something was about to break.

She heard a floorboard creak overhead and felt her stomach somersault in response. It was almost time after all.

* * *

Eva had woken up early. It was unusual for her, but she felt the inertia of her teenage years was slipping away. Adulthood, so long just a port on a distant horizon, was coming into sharp focus, but she knew she would not truly be able to move forward while she was still anchored in the past.

With her exams behind her and the long weeks of high summer stretching ahead before she began university, her life, to a casual observer at least, would have appeared to be entering a calm, untroubled period, but appearances could be deceptive.

After spending her life asking questions, she had resolved that this was the day when she would finally discover the truth about her mother's disappearance and her grandmother's past. She knew she would refuse to accept the stalling and diversionary tactics which had met every previous attempt. Whatever the cost, by the end of the day, she would know the truth.

* * *

'Happy birthday, darling,' said Millie, greeting Eva with a kiss on the cheek and an offer of coffee, which Eva accepted. She was happy to wait for the caffeine to kick in before she started.

They sat at the table in the kitchen, both cradling cups of

coffee. Millie felt the tension but also an unnatural stillness of the kind encountered just before a storm unleashes itself. She said nothing, hoping the moment might pass, yet still wondering what she would say if it did not. She looked at Eva, who was sipping her coffee and twisting her silver necklace through her fingers; the necklace she never took off, which had once belonged to the mother she could not remember.

Eva took a deep breath and prepared to launch into her carefully planned speech, but just as she did, her phone started to ring. They both looked across at it; Tom, Eva's boyfriend.

'Don't you want to answer that?' Millie asked, glimpsing a ray of hope that this might be the distraction which would save her for at least another day.

Eva shook her head and waited for the ringing to stop. When it had, she switched the volume off, turned it face down and looked at her grandmother. 'Millie, I need to know.'

'Know what, dear?'

'It's no good. I need to know what happened to my mum, and I need to know about your past. They're linked somehow. I just know it.'

'Eva, you're imagining …'

'No, I am not.' Eva's hand slammed down on the table, and the sound split the air. Millie stared at her hand, and the silence which wrapped around them was loud and painful. Such an outburst was out of character for the steady young woman Eva had become, but Millie knew this was the culmination of years of frustration, half-truths and obfuscation; it had finally arrived – the moment when she would start to pay.

Eva resumed more calmly. 'I am not imagining the fact that I know nothing about my mum. I am not imagining the fact that, unlike all of my friends' grandmothers, you never talk about your past. I am not imagining the fact that every time I ask you a question about the past or my mum, you find a way to avoid giving me an answer. All of that is definitely not in my imagination.' She could hear her voice rising in indignation and broke off.

Millie started to protest but was cut off. 'No, Millie. This has to stop now. I love you, and you can't tell me anything which will change that, but I need to know. I can't live the rest of my life like this. Enough is enough.'

Millie sighed and circled the top of her coffee cup with her finger, back and forth, caught between which direction to go in. She glanced over at the birthday cake on the kitchen counter. She realised she would not be saved by talk of birthday celebrations. 'There's no way back from the truth, Eva.'

'I know, Millie.'

'And I don't know everything either. You will have to accept that. Just as I've had to.'

'All I ask is that you tell me what you do know.'

Millie looked at her and saw the confidence of youth. Eva was a young woman who had yet to experience the pain of the fork in the road and, even worse, what came after the decision had been made and the road had been taken; the agony of wondering what would have happened if the other path had been chosen. 'Last chance to change your mind.'

'I won't. I want to know every detail. I need to know.'

'Perhaps you're right. Perhaps it is time.'

And so she prepared herself to tell Eva the story of her life, to tell her what she had done, and what she had allowed to happen. It was time to break the dam of guilt and hope the flood did not destroy Eva's life.

Chapter 2

'Wait here.'

Millie got up, and Eva heard her going upstairs. She wondered if this was to be the prelude to yet another evasion tactic, but before long Millie was back, holding a box in her hands, which she placed on the table between them.

'What do you think of when someone mentions the 1970s?'

Eva shrugged. 'I don't know really. It's 50 years ago. Flares? Abba?'

Millie smiled. 'Well, yes, but there was more to the 1970s than that. It was a very different world to the one you know. In the summer of 1975, I was eighteen. Just the age you are now. I used to think it was a more innocent time, but that's not really true. I was more innocent. Looking through the lens of hindsight, it's easy to think it was a better time too, but it wasn't really. The 1970s had their fair share of problems, but at eighteen my main concern was getting a ticket to see Led Zeppelin and wondering where my next packet of cigarettes would come from.'

'Wait. What? You smoked?'

'Yes. Don't look so shocked, darling. It wasn't unusual back then. I soon gave up when –, but I'm getting ahead of myself. Where was I? Oh yes, just like you, I had finished school, and I was due to start university that autumn. I didn't have a summer job, but I was far from alone in that respect, and I was lucky because my parents didn't put too much pressure on me. Anyway, I spent my days idling around until a letter arrived from my Aunt Sylvia, my mother's sister. I have it here. It's dated May, but I didn't get it until the middle of June.'

She opened the box and took the letter out. 'Aunt Sylvia. What a character she was; a true British eccentric. She and her husband, my Uncle John, spent their summers in Greece and their winters in Australia. Uncle John was Australian, you see. Well, I had nothing else to do so I decided to go.

'My parents didn't mind. I think they thought it would be good for me and for Aunt Sylvia. Uncle John had died the previous winter. Well, here's the letter. You can see for yourself.' She handed the letter to Eva, who read it intently.

'She sounds so sad in that letter, but very sweet,' Eva said, as she finished reading the letter.

'Yes, she was lovely. She was also very correct, but she had a twinkle in her eye although I didn't see it so often that summer.'

'But why didn't she…?' Eva shook her head. 'Never mind.'

'Tell me.'

'I was going to ask you why she didn't just email you or

send you a message. Then I realised that wouldn't have been possible.'

'Yes, that would have been a bit difficult back then,' said Millie. 'We didn't have any of that technology. She didn't even have a landline in Greece. The electricity was sometimes hit and miss, too. We spent more than one evening by candlelight.'

Eva shuddered. 'How did people manage?'

'I actually don't know,' said Millie, considering the point. 'I honestly can't remember how we did some things before we had laptops, smartphones and the Internet. Yet we did get things done and what I do remember is that we managed perfectly well, and we seemed to have more friends and more time. Our lives weren't ruled by these things,' she said, waving a hand in the direction of her phone, which sat beside Eva's on the table.

Eva considered the amount of time she spent using her phone, updating all of her social media accounts and contacts, the uploading of photos, the posting of updates and the anxious quest for likes. She wondered fleetingly if her grandmother had a point, but life without it seemed unthinkable. The pressure to be connected, to be visible, was too strong, but sometimes the loneliness of a life so often lived through a screen, with the expectation to appear permanently happy and perfect, was just as hard.

'Anyway, what was I saying?' asked Millie, cutting across Eva's thoughts.

'Sorry? Oh yes, you were saying you didn't have anything to do that summer so you accepted her invitation.'

'That's right. Well, my parents paid for the flight, which

I imagine would have been quite expensive. Travelling was so different then. I remember packing summer clothes – beach dresses and the like – but my mother insisted that I wore smart clothes, as she put it, to travel in. I was glad actually because when I turned up at the airport that was exactly how everybody else was dressed. There was none of the nuisance you get these days either when you almost have to get undressed to pass through security. I understand it, but it's just so undignified.

'Anyway, I digress. The flight was an adventure. I had never been on an aeroplane before. I had a reasonable meal and smoked half the way. Can you imagine doing that now? When we landed and I had retrieved my suitcase, I went outside and, my goodness; I had never experienced anything like it. The light. It was … golden and yet white; so white it seemed to burn everything. It was almost brutal in its beauty and intensity. Totally unlike the light here. And the heat was something I'd never experienced before either.

'I had to get from Athens airport to Piraeus and then take a ferry from there. I'd never done anything so adventurous in my life. It was great fun. And then there was the ferry journey itself. It was all so exciting and new.'

'It must have been so wonderful,' Eva said.

'Yes, it was. My aunt picked me up at the port on the island in a battered old car, and we set off through a landscape which was totally alien to me. Enchanting, though. Her house was outside the main town on a dirt track, perched on a hillside above the Aegean. Although I was eighteen and thought I was extremely grown up, I felt like a child again.'

'When we arrived, I just stood and stared at her house. It was like something from a fairy tale. It was totally whitewashed, blinding in the sunlight of a late June afternoon. The door and shutters were painted a deep blue, the shade of the sea. And from the front gate to the door she had fashioned a tunnel with bougainvillea growing over it. It was ramshackle but all the more charming for that. It was like a sensory overload – the colours, the heat. It was cooler inside of course, and my room had a view over the sea. Aunt Sylvia happily left me alone to settle in. I stood at that window for what seemed like hours and not just on that day either.

'Aunt Sylvia was true to her word and left me to my own devices. I explored her house and garden with glee and wandered off through the tracks in the woods and down to the beach. There were no hotels – it was a wild, unspoiled land.

'I slipped into a routine of sorts. I slept deeply, had breakfast with my aunt and then spent my days swimming, walking or exploring. Occasionally, I helped her out in the garden. My aunt had an orchard full of orange, lemon and almond trees and a garden full of flowers. I didn't know much about gardening back then so I didn't help her too often, but that was fine. There were no rules there. Not that my parents had that many rules, but in Greece I was totally free. It was unlike anything I had ever known before.'

'It sounds magical,' Eva said. 'What an amazing experience.'

'It was. You have to remember that Greece seemed so far away and so different in those days. Nowadays, people head off much further afield, and Greece is just a hop down the road. I started to learn Greek before I went, and then I started speaking a bit of broken Greek when I got there. Mainly because I couldn't find anyone who could speak much English, apart from my aunt of course. It's not as difficult to pick up a language at that age. I'd struggle now, I'm sure.

'On some days, I would just walk into the village. It took about half an hour along the tracks – there were no paved roads. People would stare at me curiously, but I never felt threatened. On the contrary, I felt like I was some sort of celebrity. Everyone seemed to know I was the niece of the British woman up at the "big house", and they were intrigued. Nowadays, tourists are two a penny there I'm sure, but that was then. A different world; my special world.'

'I wish I could have experienced that. Everywhere is becoming so samey now,' Eva said wistfully.

'Yes, it is, isn't it? But you must remember that tourism brought money to Greece, and people needed that. Poverty and isolation aren't romantic.'

'No, of course not, but I would love to have seen the world back then. Do you have any photos there?' Eva asked, indicating the box.

'Yes, I do.'

Millie rummaged around in the box and drew out a handful of photos. She looked through them. 'Oh, good grief.'

'What? Let me see.'

'This is me. It was taken in London.' Millie turned it over

and looked at the date on the back. '1974.' She passed it to Eva.

Eva studied the photo. Millie was wearing a halter neck top, miniskirt and knee high, white boots. Her hair reached almost to her waist and was adorned with a bandana. 'You must have been seventeen then?'

'Yes, that's right. What a fright I looked.'

'I think you looked great.'

Millie smiled at Eva. 'These are some of the photos I took in Greece. I don't have many. It was expensive to get film developed back then.' She passed them to Eva.

Eva looked at the photos of Millie's past; a window into her world back then. Even though the faded colours were overlaid with a faint sepia tone, Eva could sense the vibrancy they had captured. Millie in front of what had to be the Villa Iris, posing under the tunnel of bougainvillea she had described; Millie on the beach and in a small harbour town. She came to one of Millie with an older woman. They were standing on a whitewashed terrace brimming with pots, which overflowed with flowers. The Aegean sparkled in the background.

'Is this Aunt Sylvia?'

'Yes, that's her.'

'Can I see the others?' Eva asked.

'Not just yet. I need to tell you more first.'

Millie took a deep breath. She knew she had to continue before her courage failed her, and she descended into obfuscation again.

'I was telling you about exploring the island. One day

when I went into town, I stopped for an ice cream. I took it down to the harbour and sat there with my feet in the water, watching the boats coming and going. I remember I started to feel quite sleepy, and then I sensed a shadow. I looked up, and there was a young man staring down at me.'

Eva was listening with rapt attention. She had a feeling they were getting close to the heart of things now, and she refused to allow herself to interrupt and risk being blown off course again.

Millie had stopped, hoping for an interruption, but when she realised one was not to be forthcoming, she willed herself to continue. 'I stared back at him, and then he smiled at me. That smile – I can remember it so clearly. I had never seen anyone so handsome.'

She looked so sad that Eva wanted to tell her to stop, but she was so close now, and she had to know.

'He sat down beside me, and asked me if he could share my ice cream. He could speak English although not very well. Somehow between his English and my Greek, we managed to communicate.'

'Did you let him?'

'Oh yes. I was melting faster than the ice cream.' Millie suddenly remembered she was talking to her granddaughter and blushed. 'Sorry, dear.'

'Don't apologise Millie. Go on. Please.'

'His name was Dimitris, and we became inseparable after that day.' Millie picked up the rest of the photos and handed them to Eva.

Eva looked through them, silenced by the photos which

transported her to another era. Millie, her grandmother, as a young woman, the same age as her. She was learning about a completely new side to the woman who had always been there for her; a woman with hopes, dreams and feelings beyond raising her granddaughter. A real, fully rounded person. It was if a light had been switched on, and she could now see the whole person. She stopped as she came to a photo of a young man.

'Dimitris,' said Millie and turned away.

Eva studied him. Old photos had always seemed melancholy to her; a frozen moment which could never be recaptured, and after what Millie had told her, these seemed even more so. He was as handsome as Millie had said, and the way he was smiling at the unseen photographer could not be misinterpreted. It was a look filled with love. Eva thought about her boyfriend, Tom. She wanted someone to look at her like that, and Tom was not that person. She dragged her thoughts away from him and back to the photo. An unexpected tear stung her eyes and when she looked up at Millie, she saw the same sadness reflected back at her.

'Could you move on to the others, dear?' Millie asked.

'Sure,' said Eva.

'I don't want to see any more of them. Just have a look yourself.'

'OK.' Eva finished looking at the photos and handed them back to Millie, who carefully put them back in their envelope and then into the box.

'Do you want to hear the rest of the story?'

'Yes, please.'

'Dimitris showed me a side of the island that the few tourists who visited ever saw. I remember the trails through the pine forests and olive groves. One led to a lookout point and, from there, you could see the whole of the town and the harbour, the islet in the bay and, out on the horizon, the darker blue shadow of the next island. Everything seemed so small and insignificant from there. That became one of our places. I would tell Aunt Sylvia I was going for a walk, and we would meet there. In the cool of the evening, we would walk on the beach below the house and swim. It was difficult because I thought my Aunt Sylvia, liberal as she was by the standards of those days, wouldn't have been happy to know I was spending so much time with him, or any boy come to that, and he was sure his family would have had something to say about him spending his days with "the British girl".'

'But that didn't stop you?'

'No, of course not. If anything, it made us more determined to be together. It was the two of us against the world. Add that to the setting and first love … well, it was a heady combination. Many things change over the years but some things never do. I think it would be much the same these days.'

'Probably. No, totally. It sounds crazy romantic.'

Millie managed a smile. 'That describes it pretty well. We were crazy about each other, but the summer was starting to draw to a close. The idyll of those months was coming to an end, and we became more serious, less carefree. He decided he was going to tell his parents about us. I don't know what we were thinking really. Was I going to pass up on the opportunity of going to university, which I'd worked so hard for? Did he think I could live there and fit in with his family or that he could live here and adapt to life in England away from his family? Did he think he could live with the guilt of abandoning his responsibilities? I don't suppose we were thinking at all. Well, we were, but only about how to stay together.

'The day before I was due to leave, we decided that I would tell Aunt Sylvia while he was telling his family and then meet on the beach below the Villa Iris that night to talk about what had happened.

'My aunt wasn't overly happy, but she wasn't as disapproving as I'd expected either. Then again, I didn't tell her quite how serious I was about him. She said I had to treat it as a summer romance and go back to my "real life", as she put it, at the end of summer.'

'She sounds pretty open-minded for her time.'

'She was in many ways.'

'What happened when Dimitris spoke to his family?'

'That was a different story. They said they were sure I was a nice girl, but a British girl wouldn't be suitable. They had already planned his future for him, and that included the person he was going to marry.'

'An arranged marriage?'

'Yes.'

'Couldn't he have refused?'

'I suppose so, in theory, but you have to remember life was different then, and Greece was even more different. He was the eldest son and as such was expected to carry on the family business, marry the girl who had been chosen for him to form an "advantageous union" and eventually take on the responsibility of caring for his parents as they got older. Those weren't choices, they were obligations.'

'It's hard for me to imagine,' Eva admitted.

'Yes, it was difficult for me too.'

'So did you see him that night?'

'Yes, we met as agreed down on the beach below the house. We talked, we realised it was going to be impossible for us to be together, we cried.' Millie twisted the sleeve of her blouse.

'Millie?'

'This is not the sort of thing a grandmother shares with her granddaughter. We … we spent the night there.' Millie looked away from Eva and out into the garden. 'My whole life pivoted on that night, and my life has continued to revolve around it ever since.'

Eva sensed her grandmother's acute embarrassment and said simply, 'What happened after that?'

'Sylvia drove me back to the port the next day, waved me off on the ferry to Athens, and I never saw him again.'

'No, Millie. That's so sad. I wouldn't have been able to cope with that. What did you do when you got back?'

'I was devastated, but I started university that autumn. I thought that perhaps, given time, I would start to forget him just a little, just enough, and then I found out I was pregnant.'

'With mum?'

'Yes, of course.'

'And then?'

'Well, being an unmarried mother in those days was scandalous. As I said, it was a different world. I refused to say who the father was to protect Dimitris and also my aunt. I knew my parents would blame her for not keeping an eye on me, and I didn't want to cause a rift between my mother and her sister. I also didn't want to risk my aunt writing to Dimitris and his family. He had had his choices made for him. There was no point in stirring things up.'

'Were your parents angry with you?'

'My darling, angry doesn't even come close. Incandescent, I'd say. My father wouldn't speak to me for months. My mother came round, but only because she could see how much I was struggling with the abuse I was getting.'

'Who was abusing you?'

'Almost anyone and everyone. People we knew would stop and look at me in the street and whisper to their friends. My tutors and supposed friends at university made their feelings very clear. In the end, I couldn't take anymore, and I dropped out of university, saw my pregnancy out at home, and then devoted myself to looking after your mum. I managed to get my degree later on. As I said, my parents were furious, but I was luckier than some. A lot of girls who got into trouble, as they used to say, were sent away and forced to give up their babies. '

'But that's so cruel.'

'Yes, it is. At least that didn't happen to me.'

'Didn't you want to tell Dimitris about mum?'

'Yes, more than anything. But if you think Britain was

conservative back then, you can't imagine how it was in Greece. They hadn't been willing to accept me before. I was sure appearing with a baby wouldn't have made things better. And, as I said, Dimitris had responsibilities. I didn't want to add to them. No, I agonised over it, but I was convinced I was doing the right thing by not telling him.'

'And you never thought about how things might have turned out if you had told him?'

'My darling, at some point, everyone wonders what would have happened if they had done things differently. It's one of the hardest things to come to terms with. The what if.'

Eva thought about that for a while. 'Did my mum know about her dad?'

'Yes, she did. I told her after we'd moved out of my parents' house. She was still young when I told her, and she just grew up with it. She was surprisingly accepting.'

Eva shook her head. 'But if you told mum, why did you never tell me any of this?'

'The stigma of those early years with your mum branded me. I wasn't ashamed of your mum, please don't think that. I loved her with all my heart, and I was so proud of her, but when you are told and shown every day that you have brought shame on your family, when doors are closed to you, it cuts deep. Wounds like that never truly heal. Some events are so intense that it's like a white heat branding your soul. I had no choice but to tell your mum, but I felt it defined her in some way, and I didn't want that to happen to you. I suppose I also thought I could avoid reliving the whole thing again.'

'It's all just so wrong.'

'Which part?' Millie asked, expecting Eva's censure.

'Taking someone's child away. Making someone feel ashamed for having a child in the first place.'

'Yes, but life moves on; the world changes. Fortunately, sometimes it changes for the better.'

'What happened to Aunt Sylvia?'

'She died the year after I went to stay with her. I don't think she ever really got over my uncle's death. She never knew about your mum. My parents weren't in a rush to tell anyone who didn't have to know and, as I said, I had my own reasons for not wanting to tell her.'

'And there was never anyone else for you?'

'I went on a few discreet dates. I married when your mum was three.'

'You were married?' One by one, truths were being revealed. She had never thought about it before, but it surprised her nonetheless.

'Not for long. I wanted to give Helena a father figure and give her a name, as we said in those days. Not good reasons for getting married so, of course, it didn't last. Passion might not last a lifetime, but if there is none to start with …' Millie trailed off.

Eva thought about Tom again. There had never been any passion with him. They had been friends since their early teens and had somehow drifted into being boyfriend and girlfriend. Everyone teased them about being perfect for one another. Eva had started to feel she was the only one who wasn't so sure about that. She heard Millie draw breath to start again and turned her attention back to the conversation.

'The split was amicable. Howard and I both realised we had made a mistake. You can't keep believing in something which doesn't exist.'

You can't keep believing in something which doesn't exist. It was a strange thing to say, and yet it made perfect sense to Eva who had tried so often to conjure feelings of love and longing for Tom and come up empty. In fact, empty was the perfect word for how she had felt lately, and yet she was loath to let go. Tom had been so sweet when they had first got together, but as they had got older and changed, they had not changed together. Eva still wanted to believe that the kind, sweet Tom was still inside, and his moodiness and selfishness were just part of a phase. If they split up and the phase passed, then what? Perhaps she just needed to be patient. She wished she understood herself and Tom better.

'Deciding to go it alone – that can't have been easy back then, going by what you've told me,' Eva said.

'Life doesn't revolve around being in a relationship. I hope I've shown you that. I had Helena, and after I got my degree, I was able to pursue a fulfilling career. Eventually I moved here and made friends who didn't know about my past. I just never met the right man, or rather I did, but it wasn't meant to be.'

'Do you think you can only fall in love once?'

'I didn't allow myself to take the chance and find out. In retrospect, I believe that's another reason I married. It sounds so dreadful to say it, but I thought it was a safe option. Marrying someone I liked but didn't love, I mean. I knew I wouldn't get my heart broken.'

'Do you regret not taking another chance?'

'In some ways, but I made my choices and regrets don't help.'

'What happened to Howard?'

'He married again. As far as I know, he's had a good life.'

'And your surname is your married name?'

'Yes, but only because it was such a bother trying to change everything again. He didn't mind and neither did I so I left it. As I said, there was no animosity.'

Eva took a deep breath. 'And what happened to mum?'

'I told you I don't know everything.'

'But you know something.' Eva looked at Millie, searching for the truth. 'You do, don't you?'

'Something, yes.'

'Then please tell me whatever it is you know. We've come this far.'

'I think it's better if your mum tells you in her own words.'

Eva stared at her.

'I have all the emails she sent me when she went to Greece. I printed them off.'

Chapter 3

Millie retrieved an A4 envelope from the box, took out a sheaf of papers and handed one of them to Eva.

6 August 2005

Dear Mum,

I've just arrived, and I'll write more tomorrow – it's been a very long day. I can only get online and write emails at the computer in reception, and there's only one for all the guests to share so I'll write when I can, but I can't promise exactly when it will be. Anyway, I just wanted to say I'm sorry we left things the way we did. I hate the fact that we argued. The last thing I wanted to do was fall out with you.

You know that when I had Eva, everything changed. I started to think about where I had come from. I realised I needed to know about my father's side of the family but not just for me. I want to be able to tell Eva where she comes from. Since we lost her dad, that feeling has been growing stronger. I might be wrong to do this, but I'd like to be able to tell her about him and Andraxos.

I admit I'd also like to see my dad – and that is just for me. Even if it isn't possible to speak to him (I know you don't want me to), I'd love just to see him and know what he looks like now and also see where he lives.

Please don't be angry with me. I love you both. Thank you for looking after Eva. Give her a big kiss from me.

Lots of love,
Helena, xx

'Why did you argue?' Eva asked.

'Because I didn't want her to go. I didn't want to risk Dimitris finding out about her, and I didn't think any good would come of going there just for a look around, and in that I was to be proved right. How I wish I had been wrong.' Millie sighed and looked at the papers on her lap.

Eva looked at the email again and the mention of her own father. 'How old was I exactly when my dad died?'

'Three.'

Eva thought about the man who, like her mother, she knew only from photos.

'What was he like?'

'He was a lovely man; the type of person who could light up a room just by walking into it. He doted on you and Helena. Losing him was such a tragedy. It threw your mum off balance.'

'He died in a fire, didn't he?'

'Yes, he got out, but he went back in to try to save someone.'

They both fell silent at the thought of that until Eva finally said, 'Can I look at the next one?'

Millie nodded hesitantly and then handed all of them to Eva.

'Are your replies here too?'

'No. You can see them if you want to, but you'll need the laptop for that. I never deleted them. But I printed these off to show to the police when I was trying to convince them they needed to investigate.'

Eva looked at Millie waiting for her to say more.

Millie nodded at the pages in Eva's hand. 'Let your mum tell you. As best she can.'

7 August 2005

Dear Mum,

Is Eva OK? I was so worried last night that she might be anxious if she woke up, and I wasn't there.

It was too dark, and I was too tired, to appreciate it last night, but I'm in a beautiful room overlooking the Aegean. I can understand why you loved it here. It's a corner room so it could even be the room you stayed in! It's the most gorgeous place I've ever seen. Everyone at the hotel is very kind and friendly. I haven't got much else to say at the moment so I'm going to have some breakfast now.

I'll write again soon.

Lots of love to both of you,

Helena, xx

'I don't understand,' said Eva. 'I thought you stayed with your aunt at her house, not in a hotel.

'Yes, I did. Sylvia left the house to my mother in her will, but she was keen to dispose of it as quickly as possible. She just saw it as a potential headache to have a house abroad so she sold the place to a local family, and they converted it into a hotel. I thought staying there was just compounding an already bad idea, but Helena wanted to see the place.'

Eva turned the page.

7 August 2005

Dear Mum,

The breakfast this morning out on the terrace was lovely. I haven't done much today apart from going for a walk down through the pine trees to the beach. I'm still getting used to the heat, and I don't think there'll be much happening on a Sunday. That's my excuse anyway! Tomorrow, I'm going to go into town and well, I'm not sure really. I'll let you know.

I love you both. Please give Eva a big cuddle from me.

Helena, xx

8 August 2005

Hi Mum,

I went into town today as planned. It's so pretty with all the boats in the harbour. The light here is extraordinary – it glows. Well, you know – I don't know why I'm trying to describe it to you! I think there are more tourists and hotels here now than when you came here, going by the way you described it to me.

Lots of love to both of you and a big cuddle for Eva,

Helena, xx

8 August 2005

There was someone waiting to use the computer while I was writing the last email so I couldn't say everything I wanted to. I was so determined to track down my dad when I set off this morning, but my nerve failed me. I know I cannot go on like this with only two weeks here so I will try again tomorrow. Please don't be angry with me.

Love,

Helena, xx

9 August 2005

Hi Mum,

Well, I'll get straight to it. I've made progress. I haven't spoken to him, but I know where he is. His family has a farm up in the hills on the other side of the town to the Villa Iris. Finding out was a complete fluke. I went to a bar in town, and on impulse asked if they knew Dimitris Petrakis and then someone said that I must want to buy some of their farm produce. I went along with it and got the address. I suppose I'll have to go over there tomorrow or what have I come for?

Please write and tell me what Eva is doing.
Love to both of you,
Helena xx

'Didn't you know where Dimitris lived?' Eva asked.

'The shop wasn't there in my time, but I knew they had a farm just outside of the town. I never went there for obvious reasons. I confess I didn't tell Helena. I thought that way she might not find him.' Millie paused. 'Don't look at me like that, Eva. I know how that sounds, but I thought what I was doing was for the best.'

Eva was not sure she could follow Millie's logic and went back to the emails.

10 August 2005

Hi Mum,

I spent all night thinking about what I should do. When I was at home it all seemed so clear. I would come here and just catch a glimpse of him. If the circumstances felt right, I would introduce myself and somehow everything would be fine. But it's not going to be that easy, is it? You were right. Every action has consequences.

Anyway, I ended up getting up late, and I wasn't in a good mood so I decided to wait until tomorrow to go to the farm. Instead, I walked and walked, trying to think what I would say to him, but I don't feel as if I'm any further forward. You would think after years of wondering and waiting, I'd have

worked it out by now, wouldn't you?
 I hope everything is going well there.
 Love and a big hug for Eva,
 Helena, xx

12 August 2005

Hello Mum,

I'm sorry I didn't write yesterday. Every time, I went to reception, there was someone using the computer and there were other people waiting. I hope you weren't worried. I don't have much to report.

Please keep sending me updates about what Eva is doing.

I miss you both.
Love,
Helena, xx

13 August 2005

Hi Mum,

I'm still shaking as I'm typing this. I've spoken to my half-brother. His name is Nikos. I went to the farm on the pretext of buying something from the shop. I got Nikos talking about the history of the place – it seems to be his favourite subject – and managed to work round to his father's role in developing the farm shop. Well, our father, I should say. That was so strange – talking to my half-brother and he had no idea. I almost told him who I was, but I couldn't get the words out.

Anyway, he happened to mention that Dimitris was in Thessaloniki. It would have looked weird if I'd asked how long he'd be there, and I needed time to think. I don't know what to do now, but I'm tempted to go back and talk to Nikos again. I know you don't want me to, but I'm not sure I can stop myself.

I love you both.
Helena, xx

14 August 2005

Hi Mum,

I went back to the farm today. When I told Nikos who I was, he didn't believe me at first, but eventually he seemed to realise nobody would make up a story like that. What would be the point? I told him everything, and he got angry and said I shouldn't have gone there. But, to cut a long story short, he finally agreed to meet me again in a few days as long as I don't go back to the farm, and I don't speak to anyone else about all this in the meantime.

I suppose it's a question of waiting until I meet him again. Perhaps, he'll have calmed down by then. I don't want to cause any trouble. I just want to see my dad.

Love,
Helena, xx

15 August 2005

Hi Mum,

I can't write much. There are people waiting to use the computer. I wish I hadn't come here, and I just want to get home. I've spent the day sitting around, doing nothing. I don't know what to say apart from I miss you both so much.

Helena, xx

16 August 2005

Hi Mum,

Nikos has contacted me. I'm going to meet him again tomorrow. Maybe coming here wasn't a waste of time after all. My emotions are all over the place at the moment. Let's see what tomorrow brings.

Love and big hugs to Eva, xx

17 August 2005

Hi Mum,

Nikos cancelled our meeting. He said he'd changed his mind and went back to that 'you shouldn't have come here' theme. I realise you were right and coming here was a stupid idea. I should have listened to you. This is not my world. I thought I could be a part of it, but I was wrong. Perhaps if dad had been here it would have been different. Or perhaps it's better just to have dreams – that way they can never be shattered.

I'm counting the days until the flight. I'm even

thinking about leaving the island now and spending the rest of my time on the mainland. Even the cheapest hostel in Athens sounds tempting at the moment or I might be able to get on an earlier flight. I don't want to be here anymore. The only thing I want is to be at home with you and Eva. Give her a big hug from me.

Lots of love,
Helena, xx

17 August 2005

Hi again,

I don't have anything new to tell you. I just wanted to write to you as it's the closest I can get to what I really want – which is to be able to talk to you and give Eva the biggest hug imaginable.

I'm going to try to find out about ferries so I can leave here tomorrow and get back to Athens. I can't wait to see you both. Saturday still seems so far away.

Love,
Helena, xx

Eva finished reading and realised that her hands were shaking. Reading her mother's words would have been poignant in any situation, but to read of her increasing anxiety and unhappiness was painful. She flipped the page and realised she was back to the beginning; there were no pages left.

'Where are the others?'

'There are no more,' Millie said. 'I never heard from her again. That's why I printed her emails. I took them to the police here after I had gone for two days without hearing from her to try to convince them that something had happened, and that they needed to investigate. It was only when she didn't turn up for the flight the day after that on the twentieth that they started to take me seriously.'

'What happened after the police did listen to you?'

'They contacted the Greek police. The Greek police investigated, but their theory was that she had gone back to Athens early, as she had mentioned she might do in her email, and then disappeared there. They said there was no evidence that anything had happened to her on the island. Eventually they said they had no further avenues of enquiry to follow, and there was no evidence of a crime having been committed.'

'But surely there would have been lists of the passengers on the ferries? They would have at least been able to tell if she'd made it to Athens?'

'You would have thought so, but I don't think things there were that organised back then. Life wasn't as documented as it is now. Anyway, I kept on at the British police to do something, but they said it was outside of their jurisdiction, and there was nothing more they could do. Everyone, in Greece and here, was very kind but nobody seemed able to get anywhere.'

'So that was the end of it?'

'I was told that if any evidence came to light, they would reopen the enquiry but, effectively, yes, that was the end of it.'

'But didn't they question Nikos?' As she asked the question, Eva saw a shadow pass across Millie's face, but it vanished so quickly she wondered afterwards if she had imagined it.

'I don't believe so.'

'But that doesn't make sense. Mum mentioned him in her emails.'

'I don't really know, dear. It was a very confusing and emotional time.'

'It doesn't sound like they did enough to try to find her. How were you able to accept that?'

'I've never accepted it. Losing Helena tore a hole in my heart which has never healed, but I had to think of you. I knew if I didn't pull myself together, I would lose you too or at least be useless to you. I had to pick up the pieces and carry on.'

'I don't know how you did that. I would have been a wreck.'

'I thought about what losing you would mean, and I resolved that I would have to pack all my pain away and focus on doing the best for you that I could. There are many reasons I've never told you about the past. Telling you what happened with Dimitris ... well, it's not the sort of thing grandmothers and granddaughters talk about. Then I thought that if I started talking about your mum, I would fall apart again. So you just grew up knowing your mum wasn't around. When you were younger, it was easier because you didn't question things; you just accepted that was the way it was. When you got older, it became more difficult.'

'We had some blazing rows, didn't we?'

'Yes and a fair few doors got slammed as I recall. I thought it was just part and parcel of those mid-teen years, and it would all blow over.'

'Why didn't you just tell me this then when I started asking questions?'

'It's hard to explain. As I said, I didn't want to go through it all again, and I thought I was protecting you. I didn't want my burdens to become yours. I thought it was a phase, and you would get to the point where you just accepted it again as you had when you were a child and that you would be able to get on with your life. That seemed better to me than dredging everything up again.' Millie sighed. 'The more I try to put it into words, the less I feel able to explain it.'

'I searched for information about mum on the Internet years ago.'

'I suppose I should have expected that.'

'I didn't get anywhere. It seems what happened to her wasn't newsworthy.' Eva's words were touched with bitterness.

'Not everything was online then, and I didn't go out of my way to encourage the press. Perhaps I should have done and tried to create more headlines, but I'd already learned how judgemental people could be.' Millie hesitated and went back to the box. 'Here you are,' she said, handing Eva a yellowed newspaper cutting.

The mother of a British woman who went missing while on holiday in Greece has appealed for information regarding her whereabouts. 'Helena was due to return from Greece five days ago, but she didn't get on the flight. She has never disappeared before and this is completely out of character,' said her mother, Millie Taylor, 48, from London. 'Helena has a young daughter, and we both want her safely back at home with us as soon as possible.'

Chief Inspector Welsh added that Helena had been staying at the Hotel Villa Iris on the Greek island of Andraxos and her mother had last heard from her by email on Wednesday 17th August. She had been due to fly home on Saturday 20th August. 'If anybody was on holiday there and saw her or spoke to her, please contact the police. Any information, no matter how trivial, could prove vital to the investigation. Helena Johnson is 29 years old, 5 feet, 6 inches tall, with long, dark brown hair and brown eyes.'

The Greek police confirmed an investigation had been opened but nobody was available to comment further.

The article was accompanied by a grainy picture of her mother. Her long, dark hair framed her face and her smile was bright and full of hope. Eva stared at it for a long time before finally asking, 'And nobody had any information?'

'No, quite a few people had unkind comments to make, though.'

'About what?'

'It brought some very unpleasant people out of the woodwork; people who didn't even know us. Comments along the lines of "What was she doing going off on holiday on her own when she had a young child back at home?" Things along those lines and much worse. It was like reliving what had happened when people found out I was pregnant.'

'That sounds just like today.'

'The problem with some people is that they love to have an opinion. Not knowing the facts doesn't stand in their way.'

'Can I see what else is in the box?'

Millie handed it over. She thought she had already done the hardest part and that perhaps they were over the worst. A glimmer of relief filtered through her. She watched as Eva sifted through the contents: another letter from her aunt, saying how thrilled she was that Millie would be going to stay with her; two postcards, showing the harbour from different angles; pressed flowers, long ago turned brittle and faded, and underneath everything else, a bracelet made of tiny shells. Eva picked it up. 'This is beautiful,' she said. 'Did you get it in Greece?'

'Dimitris made it for me.'

Eva thought she should be able to come up with a fitting comment, but as she couldn't think of anything, she carefully put everything back in the box. When she had finished, she looked at the open box in front of her and started threading her necklace through her fingers as she always did when she was preoccupied or wrestling with a decision.

'I'm going.'

'Going where?'

'To Andraxos.' Eva got up to go to her room.

No, Eva, darling. You can't,' Millie called after her. She debated getting up and following her to pursue the matter further, but before she could decide what to do, Eva reappeared with her laptop.

'What are you doing?'

'I'm going to look for flights,' said Eva, as she entered her password.

Millie felt as though the ground beneath her had become unsteady, and the relief died. She had always instinctively believed that nothing good would come of telling Eva, but this was one outcome she had not anticipated. 'You can't.'

'Why not? I know you've told me everything that you know, and I appreciate it, I really do, but it's not enough.'

'And what would be enough?'

'Seeing where my grandfather's side of the family comes from.'

'Just what your mum said.'

'Perhaps meeting them.'

'What? No, you can't possibly meet them. Everything would come out then. If you want to see the island that's one thing and quite bad enough, but you can't meet them. I cannot stress that enough. You'll destroy too many lives.'

'I might be able to find out what happened to my mum.'

'How do you think you'd find out now when the police couldn't at the time?'

'I don't know, but I could at least try.'

'You think I didn't try? You think I didn't do everything I possibly could?' Millie could feel anger rising within her. 'No, there's absolutely no way. You might even be putting yourself in danger.'

'I have to try.'

Millie recognised Eva's mule-like stubbornness, which she had inherited from her, but persevered anyway. 'This is totally impractical anyway. Flights and accommodation are going to be prohibitively expensive at this time of year. Besides, you need to be here to get your exam results,' she said , scrambling for any potential reason to change Eva's mind and stop everything from unravelling.

Eva started tapping on the keyboard. 'I can get my results without being here in person.'

'What about Tom? I thought you were going away with him in the summer.'

Eva snorted. 'I've spent the last two or three months trying to get him to make a decision. I could still be waiting by the time I start university.'

'Are you happy with Tom, dear?'

Eva looked up, caught off guard by the question and the sudden change of tack. 'We've been together for what seems like forever.'

'I know how long you've been together. That wasn't what I asked you.'

'Yes, of course. We're fine.' Millie heard Eva bite down on the word "fine" and was fairly sure what that meant. She wanted to pursue it, but Eva had resumed her work on the laptop.

'I can't just up and leave anyway.'

Eva looked up at her. 'I'm not expecting you to come with me.'

'Well who would you go with then if not me or Tom?'

'I can go on my own.'

'No, Eva. There's no way. I know all you young people go off doing things on your own these days, but not there.'

'Then come with me. Because one way or another I am going.'

'I can't. There's the business for one thing.'

'Jenny and Peter can take care of that. You always say summer is a quiet time, and they can contact you if there's a problem.'

'Who would look after the garden?'

'The neighbours will come and water the plants,' said Eva, by then barely paying attention.

Millie watched Eva, her face illuminated by the glow of the screen. Her every objection being brushed to one side and the constant tapping and clicking suddenly irritated her. 'Will you just stop that?'

'No, I won't.' Eva could hear the defiant tone in her voice.

'Eva, I am pleading with you not to do this.'

'And I am telling you I'm going to do it.'

'No.'

'Why not? What are you so afraid of?'

'I'm afraid of losing you; just the way I lost your mother. I'm afraid you will go there, and you'll never come back again.' Millie hit back.

Eva's anger evaporated as quickly as it had flamed. 'I'm sorry. I don't want to upset you, but I need to do this.'

'That's exactly what your mum said to me, and look where that got us. I'm begging you to leave this be. Please Eva, leave the past where it belongs.'

Eva reached across the table and took her grandmother's hands in hers. 'I don't want to argue you with you. You've been the one person who has always been here for me, and you mean the world to me, but please try to understand that I have to do this. I want to know about where that side of my family comes from, and I want to know I've tried to find out what happened to my mum.'

Millie was silent for a moment as she weighed her options. 'In that case, I'm going with you. I can perfectly well understand that you'd prefer not to have me following you around, and I swore I'd never go back, but that's the way it will have to be. I can't lose you too.'

'OK, if we're going to do this, let's do it together. Shall I book the flights for two people?' Eva released Millie's hands and held one out, inviting Millie to shake it.

'Flights for two,' Millie nodded and shook Eva's hand. She made an effort to smile.

'We can leave the day after tomorrow,' said Eva, looking at the screen again.

'So soon?' Millie had at least hoped she would have time to try to prepare for the ordeal ahead. 'You have to go to school.'

'In theory, but I've finished all my exams so nothing much is happening. They're running a course for the last few days called Preparing for Independence.'

'What on earth is that all about?'

'Managing money, how to wash your clothes, how to cook, stuff like that. Some of them think it will be useful.'

'Don't people know these things?' Millie asked, looking astonished.

'Apparently not. They obviously haven't had a Millie in their lives.'

'Even so, I don't want you to get into trouble. Not after you've worked so hard.'

'Trust me, I won't,' said Eva. 'And look at these flight prices. If we go in term time, it's £200 less each than if we go once the school holidays start.'

'What about accommodation? It's bound to be terribly expensive,' Millie said, aware she was grasping at straws again.

'Do you want to stay at the Iris? Assuming it's still a hotel.' Eva asked, scrolling through another page.

'No, definitely not. And I will not be moved on that point.'

'No chance of that anyway. It's £150 per person per night.' Eva started clicking again. 'Hold on.' More clicking ensued. 'How about this?' She turned the laptop round and showed Millie a flat to rent perched above the main town with views of the terracotta rooftops framing the harbour beyond.

As Eva scrolled through the pictures, Millie's memories rushed back. 'It looks lovely,' Millie forced herself to say.

'Two bedrooms, two bathrooms. Walking distance to the harbour and local amenities. Affordable too. Look, it's free until the twenty-third of August. That would give us plenty of time, and there's a discount if you take it for more than three weeks.'

'A month? I was thinking of a week.' Millie thought about the prospect of being there for so long, and it filled her with dread.

I've got some money saved. Is it OK with you?'

'I suppose so.'

'I'll book everything then. Can you let me have your passport, please? I might need it for the booking.'

'Yes,' Millie got up slowly, suddenly feeling much older. Her heart was heavy, but she knew the journey she had sworn she would never make again was now inevitable. The last person she ever wanted to see again was Dimitris; even talking about him had opened up old wounds. She wondered how she would manage a month there, but she could see no way out unless she allowed Eva to go alone, and that was unthinkable.

The fracture which had run through her life was opening up again and now threatened to engulf both of them.

Chapter 4

Eva carefully took the dress which Millie had given her out of its box. She had had her eye on it for ages. It was her first little black dress; a dress for a woman, not a girl. She inspected herself in the mirror and thought perhaps it did suit her. She was her own harshest critic, but this dress seemed to melt away all the imperfections she usually saw when she looked at herself.

As she brushed her hair, it occurred to her that she bore more than a passing similarity to her mother in the photo she had seen earlier. It unsettled her although she was not sure why. Picking up her bag, she went downstairs. She saw Millie in the garden, inspecting her beloved plants and deadheading the occasional faded bloom in the amber light of early evening.

As Eva watched Millie through the window, she felt guilty for pushing so hard for the trip to Greece. She knew she had hurt her. She hadn't wanted to, but the need to know about her mother had overridden every other consideration. She felt she should say something about that but couldn't find the right words.

She stepped out into the garden. 'I'm leaving now, Millie.'

'You look beautiful. Are you pleased with the dress?'

'I love it. Thank you again.'

'Don't mention it, dear. I'm happy I was able to get you something you really wanted. Have fun.'

'It's only a quiet dinner with Tom. I told him I wanted to keep it low key.'

'Why?'

'Too much on my mind – what with waiting for exam results and thinking about mum a lot lately. If I had a big celebration, I'd be expected to be the life and soul, and I'm not in the mood for that.'

Eva realised she had not told Millie everything. How could she say that she had never truly felt that she had fitted in with her peers? Yes, she had friends, but most of her friendships felt shallow. She had always been more comfortable around older people. She thought it was to do with being an only child and living with Millie. She didn't mind, but thought Millie might feel she had failed her if she said that.

'Well, I'll say good night then.'

'OK. I probably won't be late, though.'

Eva disappeared, and as Millie heard the front door shut, another door, one to her past, opened up. She sat down on a bench and trailed her hand through the thyme planted beside it, put her hand to her face and breathed deeply. The smell of the thyme stirred other memories from long ago – the scent of pine trees, dust and heat. The breeze rippling through the olive trees, feathering them with silver; the touch of a hand reaching for hers; his hand brushing her face; his mouth against hers. It was all too much. She could go for days, weeks, sometimes months, without consciously thinking of him, decades had come and gone, but when she thought of him, it was as though no time had passed at all.

She willed herself back to the present and watched the shadows lengthen and trace their arc over the garden. As she felt the chill of the evening moving in, she stepped back into the kitchen. She looked at the box on the table, still open, its secrets spilled and stories told, never able to be withdrawn, and beside it the emails confirming their flights and accommodation. She picked up the booking confirmation. Andraxos. She had sworn she would never go back, but now her hand had been forced. She could never have allowed Eva to go there alone. If Eva had booked a flight just for herself, Millie would have been booking the next seat, but still she wished she could have convinced her not to go.

She found the photos of Dimitris, and the emotions she tried to keep locked away washed over her again. Each time they hit her was like the first time; as if they had only parted the day before. Over the years she had tried to convince herself that she had had the life she had wanted, but at times something crept through the gaps and she was transported to the island, whether she wanted to be or not.

She thought about the edited version of the truth she had told Eva earlier in the day and felt the guilt eating into her. There had been no lies as such, but she had not told her the entire truth either. What did they call it? Lying by omission, that was it. She wondered now whether by trying to protect

Eva, she had put her in danger.

When the moment had come for her to act and set the future on a different course, she had found she was even more unprepared than she had expected. Now she was somewhere in uncharted waters; a strange territory where a newly edited version of the past had been added to the existing layers of truth and lies, and she had no idea where it would all lead. She no longer knew the right or wrong thing to do. Instead she had a sense of being carried along by events over which she no longer had any control.

On impulse, she sat down at Eva's laptop and opened a map of the island. She found the Villa Iris. Looking at the house at street level, she saw that the dirt track from the villa to the town was now a paved road. The entrance looked completely different; the tunnel of bougainvillea had been ripped out and a sweeping driveway led to the house. Guests had posted pictures from around the grounds, which were also barely recognisable. They were encroaching on her place. Millie knew she was being irrational, but that just made her more irritated.

A sense of longing which was almost unbearable crept into her bones; a longing for a person she could never be with again and a time in her life which could never be recaptured; a time she could never return to and yet never quite escape. She had worked so hard to live in the present, to look to the future and to make a success of her life and help Eva to do the same, but now the past was coming back to reclaim her. There was an inevitability about it which she found disturbing. Perhaps it really was never possible to outrun the past.

She thought about Eva and the parallels between the past and the present were too strong: both eighteen, both about to go to university, both with a free summer ahead, both headstrong. Millie slipped into a space where past, present and future crowded around her, threatening to collide and, in the ensuing chaos, tear everything apart.

* * *

'Hey,' Tom said, as Eva got in the car.

'Hey yourself,' said Eva. 'Have you booked a table?'

'Yeah, but I forgot to bring some money. I need to go home.'

'Sure. Oh, I have some news. Millie and I are going to Greece.'

'What? When?'

'The day after tomorrow.'

'When did that get decided?'

'Earlier today.'

'You could have spoken to me first. I thought we were going to go somewhere together.'

'We still can. It's not as if I'll be there all summer.'

'It would have been nice if you'd talked to me about it first.'

'I've been asking you about the summer for ages, and you couldn't make your mind up.'

'You could still have told me first.'

'Tom, I want to spend some time with Millie before I go to university. Don't begrudge me that.'

'I can't understand why you want to spend so much time with the old girl.'

'Tom, please don't talk about her like that. She's my grandmother, mother and mentor all rolled into one. I don't know what would have happened to me without her. You should understand that.'

'Mentor?'

'Yes,' said Eva awkwardly. She hated the way it sounded as though Tom was mocking her, and it did sound a little strange, but Millie truly felt like that to her.

Tom grunted in response, and the rest of the journey was conducted in silence. Eva considered his tendency to sulk whenever they had even the most minor of disagreements one of his less endearing qualities. Eventually, Tom pulled into the driveway. 'Are you coming in?'

'You're only going to be a minute, aren't you?'

'You might as well come in. The reservation is for a bit later.'

Eva shrugged. 'OK.' She got out of the car and hoped Tom might comment on her dress. When he didn't, she stopped him. 'Tom.'

'What?'

'Look at me.'

Tom turned around. 'Yes, what?'

'My dress. Do you like it?' She performed a playful twirl in front of him.

'Turn around again more slowly.'

Eva complied, hoping he might say something complimentary.

'Have you put on weight?'

Eva looked at him, crushed with disappointment. 'No. It's new.'

'Oh right. Yes, very nice. Come on.'

Eva trailed after him, tugging at her dress. She knew Tom's mother had a mirror in her bedroom. She would go straight upstairs and take a look. If it was that bad, at least in a restaurant they would be sitting down, and nobody would really be able to see her. She thought perhaps she could take it back to the shop if she was careful with it.

As they walked into the house, an explosion of noise and light surrounded them and Eva heard shouts of "Surprise!" and "Happy Birthday".

Eva tried to mouth her displeasure at Tom, but he had gone ahead and was busy saying hello and slapping his friends on the back. She said a few hasty hellos and then headed for the stairs as fast as she could, more anxious than ever to check her dress. Before she was able to reach the stairs, she was waylaid by more people wishing her a happy birthday. She forced herself to smile and thanked them all for being at the party.

As soon as she could, she escaped to the bedroom where she took a long look at herself in the mirror. Her earlier confidence that the dress flattered her had evaporated. She stood there, wishing more than anything that she could go home and change. Or better still, just go home. She cursed Tom under her breath and wondered why he would never listen to her or respect her wishes. There was a knock at the door and Amy appeared.

'There you are. I've been looking for you everywhere.'

Eva fiddled with her dress. 'I was just on my way down.'

'Come on.' Amy tugged at Eva's arm.

'Before we go, I need you to do me a favour.'

'What's that?' Amy asked.

'Will you pick up my exam results for me?'

'If they'll let me, but why can't you do it?'

'I'm going away, and I won't be back in time.'

'Where are you going?'

'Greece.'

'Half your luck. I'm going to be stuck here all summer.' Amy rolled her eyes at the thought of it. 'Going with Tom?'

Eva shook her head.

'Who then?' asked Amy, looking surprised.

'Millie.'

'Millie? Why do you want to go on holiday with your grandmother?'

'It's a long story, and I can't get into it now, but if I drop a letter off at your house tomorrow saying you can pick my results up, will you do that and send them to me?'

'Yes, sure. Now can we get back to the party? Please?' Amy grabbed her friend's hands and pulled her out of the sanctuary of the bedroom.

Eva reluctantly let her friend lead her back to the party. She had a couple of drinks, but she couldn't relax. She looked around and noticed barely anyone she knew. As Amy melted away into the crowd, she headed for the kitchen, hoping for some relative peace but stopped dead at the door. Tom had his back to her and was pouring drinks while Isla, her closest friend apart from Amy, had her arm around his waist. She turned back before they saw her, wishing she could be anywhere else. She hurried upstairs and retreated into Tom's room. She could not get into the mood for a party, particularly after the scene she had witnessed in the kitchen. She thought she could probably leave without anybody noticing, but then there was a knock at the door, and Tom appeared. Eva glared at him.

'Isn't it great?' Tom yelled, over the music, which was vibrating through the floor.

Eva shrugged.

'I'm glad I found you. I wanted to spend some time alone with you.' He took a drink from a bottle of beer.

'You should have thought of that before you organised the party,' muttered Eva.

'What's that?' Tom asked, but it was clear to Eva that he was not interested in her answer. He moved towards her and started to kiss her.

'Don't Tom. I'm not in the mood.'

'Why not?'

'Because you organised a party for me when I specifically told you I didn't want one. Then you started going on about my trip with Millie as if we'd had something planned and I'd let you down, and after that you insulted her. Then you told me I looked fat and now, to top it all, you want to have sex with me at this party, which I don't even want to be at, where anybody could walk in.'

'I was only trying to do something nice for you.'

'Something nice would have been going out for dinner, which is what I said I wanted to do. But then Isla wouldn't have been around, would she?'

'Meaning?'

'Nothing.' Eva was still trying to make sense of the scene in the kitchen. She wondered if she could have misinterpreted it.

'You're so ungrateful. I went to a lot of trouble to pull this off.'

'I'm ungrateful? For not enjoying a party I told you I didn't want? Unbelievable.'

'I don't get it.'

'No, Tom, you never do.'

'And what the hell is that supposed to mean?'

'You don't listen to me. You don't get it, and you don't get me.'

'What the …? That sounds like a line from some sort of self-help book, Eva.'

'So now you're making fun of me?'

'If you say so,' said Tom, taking another swig from the bottle.

'OK, now it's my turn. What does that mean?'

'It means I obviously can't do right for doing wrong so, yeah, whatever you say.' Tom stormed out, leaving Eva staring at the door he had slammed shut behind him. She sat down on the bed and, in a pause in the music, heard a whimpering sound coming from underneath her. She knelt down and found Dylan, Tom's dog, cowering under the bed. 'Dylan, come here,' Eva said.

Dylan edged towards her and as she sat down on the floor, he crawled into her lap. 'I guess Tom really doesn't think about anyone else, does he?' Eva said, scratching him behind the ears.

* * *

Eva closed the front door quietly. After she had left Dylan with Tom's neighbours, she had headed home. She saw a light coming from under the sitting room door and felt obliged to say hello to Millie although all she wanted was to go to bed.

'Hello dear. How was your evening?'

'Tom had organised a surprise party for me, and then we had a big argument.'

'About the party?'

'About everything and nothing.'

'One of those.'

'Is that normal?'

'Oh my darling, what's normal when it comes to relationships?' She paused. 'But I assume you made it up when he brought you home.'

'I got a taxi.'

'I'd have picked you up.'

'I just wanted to get away as soon as I could. I didn't want to wait. Anyway, I thought you might be asleep.' Eva slumped in the chair. 'Millie, do you think I look OK?'

Millie looked at her in astonishment. 'Yes, of course. Why on earth do you think you don't?'

'It doesn't matter why. I just want to know what you think.'

'Well, you look lovely,' said Millie, and it was the truth. She had always believed appearance, beyond looking presentable, to be fairly low in importance on a list of desirable attributes, preferring to stress to Eva the importance of kindness and education, but she knew she was fighting an almost impossible battle against the tide of social media, which ranked looks above all else. She was thankful that Eva did not spend hours perfecting selfies in front of the bathroom mirror so she supposed she had had some success. Nevertheless, Eva had blossomed into a beautiful young woman, one who filled Millie with pride and worry in equal measure, when she saw the way men looked at her when they were out together.

Her curiosity piqued, Millie repeated the question. 'Why?'

Eva shrugged, dismissing the question. 'It doesn't matter. I'm just glad we're leaving tomorrow.'

'Tomorrow? Is it that late already?'

Eva glanced at her watch. 'It's nearly 1.30, and we can't get away soon enough as far as I'm concerned.'

Millie thought how at odds they were over the trip. Eva couldn't wait to go whilst she was dreading it, but there was no point in rehashing everything which had been said.

Eva saw the anxiety etched on her face. 'Don't worry, Millie. Everything will be fine.'

Millie got up and kissed her on the top of her head as she passed her on the way upstairs.' I hope you're right. I'll see you in the morning.'

Part 2
Andraxos, Greece
July – August 2019

Chapter 5

The plane taxied out onto the runway. 'Are you sure we've got everything?' Millie asked.

'Yes, but it's a bit late now if we haven't.'

'And Amy has all the paperwork she needs to get your results?'

'Yes, relax Millie. You know I went to her house earlier today with the letter and my student ID.'

'I just don't want you to miss out on your place at university.'

'Neither do I.'

'I still wish we were safely back at home.'

Eva reached across and squeezed her grandmother's hand. 'Really Millie, it will be OK. You'll see. Anyway, changing the subject, there's something I'd like to know.'

'Oh?' Millie wondered what was coming next.

'Why do I call you Millie instead of grandma?'

Millie breathed a sigh of silent relief. That at least was an easy question to answer with no dangerous traps ahead. 'You were learning to speak, and you heard my friends calling me

Emily. You tried to say Emily and came out with Millie, and it just stuck. I liked it so much that I started encouraging other people to use it as well. Besides I was still quite young to be a grandmother so I didn't mind.

'OK.' Eva settled back into her seat. It was a small point, but one that had been on her mind since everything had bubbled to the surface.

'Have you spoken to Tom?'

'Not since the party, no.'

'I don't like to interfere, but don't you think you should have contacted him?'

'He hasn't contacted me.'

'Even so, don't you want to clear the air?'

'I don't know what I want, Millie.'

'That puts a different complexion on things. I thought you were happy with Tom,' Millie said, hoping to coax Eva into talking about what had happened at the party.

'Can we just leave it for now?'

'Yes, it's not really my business.'

'It's not that … I just don't want to think about it right now.'

'Fair enough.' Millie opened her book and while she tried to keep her mind occupied, Eva closed her eyes and slept until the sun rose and filled the cabin with light.

* * *

'Good morning, this is your captain speaking. We have just started our descent into Eleftherios Venizelos airport in Athens, and we expect to land on time. If you would like to adjust your watch, it is currently 9.15 a.m. local time. The weather in Athens is sunny and currently twenty-one degrees Celsius with a high of thirty-four degrees expected later today so wonderful holiday weather. On behalf of all our crew, we wish you a pleasant stay in Athens, and we hope to have the opportunity to welcome you on board again soon.'

Not soon enough, thought Millie. She wished she could share in the enthusiasm of the pilot and her fellow passengers, not least the excited Eva who was peering out of the window, not wanting to miss a thing. Millie had tried to sleep, but every time she had come close to dozing off, a memory had punctuated her thoughts. On each occasion, she had turned to find Eva fast asleep, apparently able to switch off from her own concerns about her relationship with Tom.

As they landed, Millie turned to Eva. 'Do you mind if we let the others fight it out before we get off, dear?'

'Not at all,' said Eva. She looked at her grandmother and noticed the shadows under her eyes had deepened. She felt the pull of guilt again and a sense of her own inadequacy. She wondered if she would ever learn the gift of saying the right thing.

They watched as a scrum ensued with everyone keen to be off the plane first, and then Eva and Millie followed. They collected their bags and walked out into the early morning sunlight and a blanket of heat. On the bus to the port at Piraeus, Millie observed Eva. She was glued to the view, taking in every detail of her surroundings. That had once been her. The similarities between their two situations struck her afresh, forming a tapestry woven from the past and present, which made her uneasy.

Eva nudged Millie. 'I can see the coast. Those beaches look really good.'

'If you like those, wait until you get to Andraxos.'

They got off of the bus in Piraeus, and the heat hit them anew. Now, though, that was combined with the clamour of traffic, vendors calling out to each other, and advertising hoardings, which all competed to be the biggest and brashest. They negotiated their way around cars and mopeds parked wherever a space had been found and held their breath as they crossed the road to get to the port. The rough and tumble of early-morning Piraeus after an overnight journey was an overload for the senses.

Eva hurried off to get the tickets and then bounded up to Millie. 'Here you are,' she said, passing her one. 'And I think that could be ours,' she added, as a huge ferry headed towards the port.

The memories were starting to pull further at Millie's fraying edges. The tear which had opened up in the fabric of the world she had constructed was straining and threatening to rip apart. She looked at Eva who was overflowing with excitement and could no longer imagine how the journey they had embarked on would end.

They watched in silence as the ferry docked and then found their seats. The ferry moved out of the port again, its new cargo safely on board.

'I'm going outside, Millie. Do you want to come with me?'

'No, I'm going to stay here.'

'OK.'

Eva stood outside, hanging over the railings, watching the boat cut through the water. With the sun warming her skin and the breeze ruffling her hair, she felt a sense of liberation she had not experienced in a long time. She had been so preoccupied with studying for her exams, wondering about Tom and thinking about her mother, that there seemed to have been little time for anything else.

She watched as the ferry made stops on its passage across the Aegean, depositing and collecting more passengers. Finally, she found a seat on a bench and as the sun moved over her face and she succumbed to the rhythm of sea, she started to doze. She was woken by shouts from the crew and got up to see what was happening. On the horizon, she was able to make out an indistinct purple-blue shape. She glanced at her watch and her heart started to pound. It had to be Andraxos. She wanted to go and get Millie and persuade her to join her, but she was transfixed.

Inside the cabin, Millie looked out of the window and saw Andraxos drawing closer. The place she had sworn never to return to, for reasons beyond those she had shared with Eva. She should have been honest with her. Why had she not learned from the past? With every push of the ferry through the water, the weight of her guilt seemed to bear down on her further. She had been wrong not to tell Eva everything. It had not been too late back in London after all, but now it was.

Back on deck, Eva watched as the land took form and

hazy outlines became real places. The indistinct was forced to take shape, forged in the furnace of the violet-white Greek light.

The ferry entered the natural amphitheatre of the harbour, which seemed to welcome them into its embrace. The slender cypress trees on the hills behind the town pierced the sky and framed a town of white and pastel-hued houses topped with terracotta roofs. Crowning the rise on which the town sat, was a white church with a gleaming blue dome, which caught and reflected the light.

It seemed to Eva a joyful place, full of possibility and promise, and the sense of excitement she felt was palpable. The loudspeaker announced the ferry's imminent arrival, and Eva forced herself to turn away and head back into the cabin to help Millie with their bags.

Millie stood up and sat down again just as suddenly as the ferry protested against its moorings.

'Are you OK, Millie?'

'Yes, I just got up at the wrong moment. I'm fine. I'm not quite used to the heat yet either.'

'It is pretty warm.'

They queued patiently and were soon on their way off the ferry, Eva jumping off and Millie departing rather more sedately and cautiously. They stood on the quayside as the crowd around them started to drift off to their homes and hotels. Eva got her phone out and consulted the map.

Millie looked around anxiously, afraid someone might recognise her. How ridiculous, she thought. She barely recognised herself in the photos she had from all those years ago. As she took in the harbour, the memories of her youth flooded her mind: the carefree days when she had wandered those streets, enchanted by the island; sitting by the harbour and the shadow of Dimitris falling over her. Fitting, she thought. She had lived in the shadow he had cast over her life since that day.

'We'll have to walk. Will you be OK?'

'Yes, of course. I'm not an invalid.' Millie felt testy. This had been her place long before Eva or Helena had come along, yet now Eva seemed to be taking charge.

'Sorry.'

'They set off away from the waterfront into the narrow lanes between the houses where there was some relief from the heat. They climbed a steep staircase street, and Millie felt her knee hurting again. She gritted her teeth; she would not tell Eva that her arthritis was troubling her or allow it to slow her pace.

They paused at the top of the staircase, and Eva consulted her phone again. 'It should be just round the next corner. Wait here. I'll go and see.'

Millie waited; glad to have a moment to get her breath back and allow her knee to recover a little. She looked around her. The world seemed to be sleeping in the hush of a summer afternoon, disturbed only by the insistent buzzing of the cicadas. It was the same place she had kept safe in her dreams, and yet it was also not the same, in ways she could not yet define.

Eva reappeared and made her jump. 'I've found it. It's not far.'

They continued on their way and arrived in front of a white apartment building with a courtyard surrounded by low white walls, topped with iron railings. They stopped at the blue wooden gate, Eva pressed the intercom, and a young woman came to greet them.

'Hello. You must be Millie and Eva. I'm sure you are tired after your journey. Let me show you to your apartment.'

She led them inside and the cool enveloped them. 'It's so nice in here after the sun,' she commented.

They followed her up the flights of stairs. 'We have two apartments each on the first and second floors, but you have the top floor all to yourselves. You're lucky – we had a last-minute cancellation. There are a lot of stairs, but it means you have the best view.'

She unlocked the heavy wooden door to the apartment and took them inside. The door opened on to a large living space, with a sitting room to the left, a dining table in front of the windows which were straight ahead and a kitchen to the right. The walls and tiled floor were white and the dark wood furniture stood in stark contrast to them. 'To the left you have a bedroom and bathroom and the same to the right,' she said indicating. 'But first I must show you this.'

She walked to the long, white, muslin curtains. 'Come,' she said beckoning them. They complied, and she drew the curtains back. They stepped out onto the balcony and saw the view they had seen on the internet just two days before. 'Welcome to Andraxos', she with a broad smile, which Eva returned, while Millie looked rather more uncertain.

'Is this your first visit here?'

'Well, actually –,' Eva began, but Millie spoke before she could continue. 'Yes, it is.'

'I'm sure you'll love it. Here in the kitchen you have tea and coffee and some other bits and pieces. My name is Violeta. If you need anything, please tell me or one of my family. We live in the house just across the courtyard.'

'Thank you. We'll let you know if there is anything,' Millie said, ushering her to the door as politely as possible.

Violeta left, and Millie closed the door behind her and leaned against it.

Eva was aware of Millie's discomfort but, for want of anything better to say, offered, 'She seems very friendly.'

'Yes, I'm sure she is. I just need some time alone. Which room would you like?'

Eva was unused to this side of Millie; a side which seemed slightly antagonistic. 'I don't mind,' she said.

'Neither do I.'

'In that case, I'll take this side and you take that one?'

'Fine.'

Eva watched as Millie picked up her suitcase and trudged past the sofa towards the left-hand side of the apartment. She hoped she might turn round and give her a smile and reassure her that everything was fine, but she did not. As Millie closed her bedroom door behind her, Eva sensed a rift had opened up between them and felt lonelier than she had ever done before. She realised how much her grandmother meant to her and began to understand what she had asked of her.

She picked up her bag and went to her room. At any other time, her heart would have lifted at the sight of the corner room. With windows on two sides, the room was flooded with light, and there was a small balcony just big enough for a table and two chairs. To her right was her own bathroom, a luxury she would normally have relished.

She put her bag down on the luggage rack and opened it. On top of the things she had packed, she found her black dress, carefully folded. Millie must have put it in there. She unfolded it and looked at it. It held only bad memories of the party, and she wished Millie hadn't packed it. She hung her clothes up and dug out the emails from her mother, which she had smuggled into her bag.

I've spoken to my half-brother. His name is Nikos.

Nikos. The name burned on the page in front of her. *Nikos Petrakis*, she murmured. *What did you do? What do you know?*

She tucked the emails away again, showered and went to sit out on the balcony, wondering what Millie was thinking over on her side of the apartment.

Millie slumped down on the bed. She knew she should try to do better, but the lies, the fear, the anxiety had all been too much on top of a long, sleepless night of travel. *I must pull myself together. I'm here to protect Eva, and how can I do that if I fall apart?*

She had been strong when she had discovered she was pregnant, and for Helena when Eva's father had died, and then once more for Eva when Helena had disappeared. She knew she would somehow have to find that strength again, but it seemed too much. She retreated to the shower and felt calmer although no less weary by the time she had finished and put on some clean clothes. She closed her eyes and when she woke up, found a few hours had passed.

Eva and Millie opened their doors at almost the same moment.

'About earlier,' Eva started awkwardly.

'What about earlier, dear?'

'I felt, I mean you were … I know you aren't happy about this, and I'm sorry.'

'I was just tired after a bad night.'

'But you don't want to be here, do you?'

'In an ideal world, no. But we are so let's try to make the best of it.'

'I'm sorry.'

'Stop saying sorry and let's go out and find somewhere to eat.'

They retraced their steps and found Violeta in the courtyard, who waved them over.

'Please come and have a drink,' she said.

'Aren't we going out to get something to eat?' Eva asked Millie quietly, impatient to start seeing Andraxos and hungry, in almost equal measure.

'Not yet. It would be rude to decline.' She raised her voice a notch. 'Thank you.'

They sat down at the table and Violeta poured glasses of lemonade. 'It's homemade,' she said.

They tried it and savoured the sharp, refreshing taste.

'Where in England are you from?' Violeta asked.

'London.'

'I want to go to London. It would be a good chance for me to practise my English.'

'Your English is already perfect,' said Eva. 'Did you learn at school?'

'Yes, and I practise a lot with my grandfather. Ah, here he is.'

They turned and saw a man of about Millie's age walking towards them. 'You must be our new guests. Welcome.'

They introduced themselves in turn. 'My name is Konstantinos, but you can call me Gus. Not such a mouthful.'

'OK, that is easier,' said Eva with a big smile. 'But why Gus?'

'That's what everyone used to call me in Australia.'

'Australia?' said Millie, thinking of her aunt and uncle and feeling her stomach turn and contract.

'Yes, I lived there for many years.'

'What took you there?' Eva asked.

'It was due to chance as are so many of the things that happen to us in life.'

Millie heard Eva asking Gus what had happened and wished again that they were safely back at home in London.

'There used to be a couple who spent their summers up at the big villa just outside the village, the Iris. It's a hotel now. I met the husband, and I did some odd jobs for him after I'd told him how hard it was to get a job here on the island. He was Australian, and he fixed me up with some contacts. Before I knew it, I was on my way there with a job offer.'

Millie and Eva exchanged glances. They knew who he had to be talking about. Eva opened her mouth to speak and felt a warning squeeze around her knee under the table.

'What was his name?' Eva asked, fairly sure it was a safe question; one which even Millie would sanction.

'John. It was because of him and the job that I was able to save money and buy this place. He changed the course of my life. In fact, he did so much for me that I named my son, Yiannis, after him. Completely against the tradition here, which is to name children after their grandparents, but my parents recovered in the end.' He smiled.

'Did you ever meet John's wife?' Millie asked, feeling as though someone had prepared a noose for her, and she was now stepping forward to accept it. Every time she thought she had reached the worst point, telling Eva about the past, confronting her memories, travelling to Andraxos, she was proved wrong. Within hours of arriving on the island, she had unwittingly walked straight into a connection with her past.

'A few times when I was up at the villa, but most of my conversations with John were conducted at the local coffee shop, and that was strictly for men only. What was her name? Sophie? Stella? No, Sylvia, that was it. She seemed like a kind lady.'

'How long were you in Australia?' Millie asked, deciding to change course.

Gus sat back and thought about it. 'I left in 1974 and came back in 1985. Eleven years. That's a long time to be away from home. Of course, Australia was a big adventure for me, but there I lived to work, here I worked to live when I came back. There was too much order over there. Here there is too much chaos, but a little chaos is good. Too much organisation can be bad for you. Don't misunderstand me – Australia is a fine country, apart from the fact that nearly everything can kill you.' He broke off and smiled. 'But for all its problems, there is nowhere like Greece, and more so, there is nowhere like Andraxos. He turned to face the setting sun, and they followed his gaze; it was dipping behind the distant hills, bathing the town and the sea beyond in a golden glow.

1974, thought Millie; the year before her trip to the island. She thought she was safe and wondered if she might be able to allow herself to relax a little.

Violeta eventually turned their attention back from the sunset to the lemonade and as they sipped their next drink, she told them more about her family. 'My grandfather owns the place as he told you, but my brother and sister run it, and I help in the school holidays. I deal with the English-speaking guests, my brother speaks Italian too so he deals with Italian guests and my sister, well, she is like a butterfly – she lands here and then she lands there – a little French, a little German, but never too much of any one thing.'

'I wish I was better at learning languages,' said Eva.

'All you need is time and opportunities to practise,' said Violeta. 'How are you two related?'

'Millie is my grandmother,' said Eva.

'That is so nice that you can travel together. I suppose your parents are working?'

Eva thought about the contrast between Tom's reaction, and even Amy's, compared with Violeta's towards her travelling with her grandmother. She could also feel the tension radiating from Millie. 'They died when I was very young. I'm sorry, but I prefer not to talk about it.'

'Of course. I'm sorry too.'

They lapsed into silence for a while, which Violeta broke by asking them where they were going for dinner. 'The taverna round the corner is run by my dad – that's Yiannis – and my mum, Maria. If you are too tired to go down to the harbour, it's convenient. And the food is very good of course.'

Eva looked at Millie who replied, 'That sounds like a good idea. I'm certainly tired after the flight and the ferry journey.'

'If you would like to go, I can show you the way,' Violeta offered.

She led them out of the gate and down the narrow street. As they lost their bearings, Violeta said, 'Remember it's right, right and then left to get there. Here we are.'

Millie and Eva looked at the taverna set on a small square. It resembled every picture-postcard view of the perfect Greek taverna, nestled under heavy vines with blue, wooden chairs with woven rush seats and white tables decked with blue and white gingham tablecloths. The hand-painted sign proclaimed the name – Mythos Taverna. The square was surrounded by small shops except for the right-hand side of the square, which was occupied by a whitewashed, blue-domed church.

'Is that the church you can see from the ferry?' Eva asked.

'Yes, it is.' Violeta led them into the restaurant. 'Now where would you like to sit?'

Eva had been about to suggest a table on the square, but Millie was already indicating a table set as far back from view as possible. Violeta seated them and went to find her father.

'I don't like this,' said Millie.

'It'll be fine,' said Eva. 'I can't see what the problem is.'

'No,' Millie replied and managed to load a single word with more meaning than Eva would have thought possible.

Violeta returned with her parents. 'Mum, dad, these are our new guests – Millie and Eva.'

'I am delighted to meet you. My name is Yiannis.'

'And I am Maria.'

'I should go,' Violeta said, checking her watch. 'We have some more guests arriving soon. Enjoy your meal.'

Yiannis brought them drinks and menus, and Eva suddenly realised how hungry she was. 'I think I could eat one of everything,' she said, looking at the options on offer. The thought of tzatziki, stuffed vine leaves, roast chicken and desserts drenched in honey made her feel ravenous. Then she remembered Tom's remark about her weight, and her appetite subsided. 'Are you hungry, Millie?'

'Not really. I'll just have a salad.'

'OK. I'll have the same.'

After they had ordered, Eva looked at Yiannis's retreating figure. 'They are a lovely family, aren't they? Isn't it amazing to think Yiannis is named after your uncle and that Gus knew them?'

'For pity's sake, Eva, will you keep your voice down?'

'I was hardly shouting.'

'No, but we don't need anyone hearing comments like that.'

'No, of course not. Sorry.'

Their salads were eaten in a subdued silence, punctuated by polite smiles and assurances that everything was perfect whenever Yiannis appeared to ask if there was anything else they needed.

'What do you want to do, Millie?' Eva asked, after they had finished their meal and paid the bill.

'I think I'll call it a night.'

Eva had been tempted to suggest a walk down to the harbour but thought better of it. She could go along with what Millie wanted for the first night at least. 'Good idea,' she said. 'We'll start exploring in the morning.'

As they let themselves into the courtyard, they saw Gus. 'I hope Yiannis looked after you, and you enjoyed your dinner,' he said. 'Will you come and have a coffee?'

Millie had had enough of being sociable for one day, but smiled and accepted the invitation. They sat with Gus and sipped the thick, sweet coffee.

'What are your first impressions of our island?' Gus asked.

'I think it's beautiful,' Eva replied, enthusiastically.

Gus smiled. 'And you, Millie? May I call you Millie?'

'Yes, of course. Well, yes, from the little I've seen. As Eva said, it looks lovely.'

Andraxos is a wonderful island. Of course, it's my home

so I'm biased. However, it's not on the main tourist route. What made you choose to come here?'

Millie felt the same sensation she had experienced earlier when Gus had mentioned her aunt and uncle; a sensation that she was trapped in a situation which would take her wherever it saw fit. She willed Eva not to say the wrong thing in the silence which opened up as she tried to find a suitable reply. She heard Eva's voice, and closed her eyes.

'We chose it for that reason. We wanted to visit an island where there weren't too many tourists,' Eva said.

Millie took a deep breath.

'I also wanted to learn more about Greece and its culture and lifestyle,' Eva continued brightly.

Millie felt the floor opening up again.

'Why is that?' Gus asked.

'Eva has always been interested in history and culture, haven't you dear?' Millie said, recovering herself sufficiently to say something which had not been true up until a few days ago. Her face was angled away from Gus, and the look she gave Eva almost froze her.

'Oh yes,' said Eva, trying hard to sound earnest. She topped it off with a lie of her own. 'History was always my favourite subject at school.'

'Well, if you have any questions, I will be happy to answer them.'

'I'm sure we've taken up enough of your time already,' said Millie.

'Time is one thing I have. I stopped running against the clock many years ago.'

'You are fortunate,' Millie replied.

'Do you work?' Gus asked.

'I do, and I often feel as though I don't have enough time, but I enjoy my work.'

'Then you are also fortunate. Not just to enjoy your work but to have work. So many people here in Greece lost their jobs and homes during the crisis.'

'I understand it was a very bad time.'

'Yes. It wasn't only a financial crisis, though. It was a crisis of everything we believed in. I know what the world says about us. We are lazy, we have only ourselves to blame. But those people do not know us, they do not live here. They just come here and see what they want to see, or they pick up what passes for news in most of the media. They do not live our reality. They do not see our lost generation – the ones who left and the ones who stayed.'

'People are always quick to give their opinions,' Millie replied.

'Very true.'

'But things are getting better here now, aren't they?' Eva asked, wanting it to be true.

Gus tilted his head slightly. 'For now perhaps but there are still many problems. One unexpected crisis and everything could …' He clicked his fingers. 'One thing is for sure. It's not over yet. A reckoning will come one day. It always does.'

'How right you are,' said Millie, aware that her own reckoning had only just begun.

Chapter 6

Eva rolled over in bed, woken by the sound of a rooster crowing. She groaned and pulled the pillows over her head, trying to muffle the noise, but it was no good. The rooster had won the battle, and Eva dragged herself out of bed. Out of habit, the first thing she did was check her phone. There were no messages from Tom and nothing of much interest on her social media. She liked a few posts, and then she showered, dressed and went into the main room where she found Millie, who was also up but not dressed.

'Did you sleep well?' Eva asked.

'Not really. And you?'

'I was fine until that rooster started.'

'Yes, that's something to look forward to every morning,' Millie said. The forced early start to the day had obviously not helped to improve her mood.

Eva watched as Millie made coffee. 'What would you like to do today?'

Millie sat down and handed Eva a cup. 'I think I might just stay here and get acclimatised. I can enjoy the sun from the balcony, and I brought some books with me. It's been a long time since I've had the luxury of just being able to sit and read and not worry about watching the clock.'

Eva's desire to get out and start exploring was starting to edge ahead of her desire to keep Millie happy. She toyed with what to say and whether to go out on her own, but looking at the tension and tiredness written across Millie's face, she couldn't bring herself to leave her alone. 'A quiet day sounds like a good plan,' she said and thought that a day spent sunbathing on the balcony didn't sound so bad. There were plenty of days ahead to explore and find out about her family.

* * *

As one day turned into two, Eva felt the walls closing in. By the evening, she decided it was time to tackle Millie.

She took a deep breath and launched in. 'I need to talk to you.'

'About what?'

'Looking for my grandfather.'

'Oh. That.'

'Yes. I know how difficult this is for you, but we're here now. And I didn't come here to sit in this apartment for the next month.'

'No, I know you didn't, but things have been moving so fast. It was only a few days ago that we were at home, and the idea of coming back here was the last thing on my mind. I'm still coming to terms with all of this.'

'Millie, I feel … that is … I want to see him, even if I

don't tell him who I am, and I want your blessing.'

Millie sat back and looked at Eva. 'If you really wanted to take my feelings into consideration, we wouldn't be here, would we?'

The words stung Eva. 'I thought we'd agreed.'

'No, you decided and pushed me into an impossible position.'

Eva cupped her face in her hands and massaged her temples. 'I knew you weren't keen on coming, but I thought once we were here …'

'You thought what?'

'I don't know. I suppose I thought you'd feel better once we'd arrived.'

'Well, I don't and now you know.' Millie stood up. 'I think I'll go to bed.'

'Wait, please.'

'What is it now?'

'How about this? I won't look for him until you tell me that you're OK with it.'

'You're assuming I will be happy with it at some point. What if I'm not?'

'We'll cross that bridge when we come to it.'

Millie shrugged.

'And as we're here, why don't we try to make the best of it? You said as much yourself the night we arrived.'

'That's what I'm doing.'

'By making the best of it, I mean going out and seeing some of the island.'

'I've already seen the island,' Millie reminded Eva. She

heard the sharpness in her voice and hated it.

'Yes, I know, but I haven't, and I would like to see it. Preferably with you. Will you just think about it? Please?'

Millie nodded so slightly it was almost imperceptible. 'I really am ready for bed.' Eva watched her disappearing into the shadows of her darkened room. She felt the distance between them opening up further and the loneliness bit deep.

* * *

The following morning, Eva returned to the apartment with some supplies from the local shop, feeling more cheerful than she had done since the day they had arrived.

'Violeta's invited me to go for a drink with her.'

Millie looked at Eva but didn't respond.

'You don't mind, do you?'

'Not as such, she seems like a very sweet girl, but I'm worried about what you might say. You nearly put your foot in it the first night we arrived.'

'How?'

'When Violeta asked us if we'd been here before, what would you have said, if I hadn't interrupted you?'

Eva was silent, recognizing she had been on the verge of saying the wrong thing.

'Then when we met Gus, I was so on edge thinking about what you might say.'

'But I didn't say anything out of place.'

'You came close when you started saying you were interested in learning more about the history and culture of

Greece. I'm not sure he hears that too often from tourists, particularly the younger ones, and then there was what you said in the restaurant. You have to remember that Violeta and her family have – or at least had – a connection with ours. It's all too close to home for my liking. One careless word and … I don't know. I like her, but I don't like the situation.'

'I promise I'll be careful.'

'Well, it's not as if I can stop you anyway.' Millie shrugged, and Eva thought again how defeated she seemed. Ever since they had arrived, all the spark and sweetness had drained out of her. And Eva knew it was her fault. If she hadn't insisted on the trip, Millie would be at home happily running her business and tending to her garden. Yet she couldn't find it within herself to say sorry again when she was not sorry that they were there.

'When are you going?'

'Tomorrow morning after Violeta has finished cleaning the rooms. What shall we do today? Perhaps we could go down to the harbour. Take one of those boat trips?'

'I don't think so. You go if you want to, but I'm quite content here with a good book and a cool drink.'

'You've barely set foot outside since we arrived.'

'We've already had this conversation, Eva.'

'You don't even want to go into the centre, do you?'

'No.'

'Why?' Eva asked.

'I think you know the answer to that.'

'Not really.'

'I don't want to run into Dimitris.' That would have been bad enough but even worse, Millie thought, would be meeting Dimitris and his wife. That would have been too much. 'I can't expect you to understand.'

'I do, but you can't stay in here for the next month.'

'Probably not, but I'm not ready yet. And from what I saw when we got off the ferry, it's changed. I prefer to remember it the way it was.'

'I'd like to go out. I'm starting to feel restless.'

'I'm not stopping you. I know you want to see the place.'

'OK, I'll see you later.'

Eva got up to leave and as she reached the door, Millie's words stopped her. 'Eva, please be careful.'

Millie watched the door close and felt the anxiety crawling over her. It occurred to her that if only she could bring herself to leave the apartment, she might be able to control the narrative. She would have to find a way to get over her dread of going out. Sitting there left her with no option but to see where Eva's actions took them and that, she was sure, would be unwise.

Eva wandered through the streets, feeling relieved to have escaped. Her brief trip to the shop had given her a taste of the world beyond the apartment, and she wanted to explore more of the town. The apartment was beautiful, but it had started to feel claustrophobic, in no small part due to Millie's mood. After sitting around for so long, she relished exploring the lanes. Her progress was slow as she stopped to take pictures of the houses with their blue shutters and the purple bougainvillea pouring over walls and framing the staircase streets.

She rounded another corner and found a row of tourist shops. She browsed the array of souvenirs, and finally found a simple, silver ring which she bought and put on. It would be something to remember the island by.

She glimpsed the sea, a small wedge of blue sparkling between the houses, and found the steps leading down to the main road running around the harbour. The road was ringed with bars, restaurants and more souvenir shops.

She wandered the length of the harbour, enjoying the warmth of the sun on her skin. She looked around the shops, stopped for ice cream and studied the information about boat trips. She was impatient to start doing things. She started to feel hungry and stopped to look at the menus outside the restaurants.

A waiter approached her. 'Some lunch?'

Eva glanced at her watch. She was tempted, but Millie had been on her own for a long time. Reluctantly, almost resenting the fact she felt she had to return, she declined the offer and slowly walked back to the apartment. As she let herself into the courtyard, she met Gus.

'Hello Eva.'

'Hello Gus. What have you got there?' Eva said, peering at the photos he had scattered on the table.

'I started thinking about John after our conversation the other night so I dug some old photos out. I'm taking a walk down memory lane.'

'Can I have a look?'

Gus looked at her in surprise. 'I don't think they'll be of much interest to you.'

'I like old photos,' said Eva. 'May I?'

Gus moved round, making space for Eva.

'Who's this?' Eva asked.

'That's John.'

Eva picked up the other photos and started looking through them, immersing herself in a world lost in time. She came to a photo of John with a woman. She looked at Gus, sure it was Sylvia, but unable to say as much.

'That's Sylvia,' he said. 'I had forgotten I even had a photo of the two of them.' He picked it up and looked at it more closely. 'You know, I thought your grandmother reminded me of someone. How strange is that?'

Eva felt the blood surging to her head and pounding in her temples. 'Do you think so? I can't see it myself.'

Gus evaluated the photo again. 'Perhaps you're right. It's probably my eyesight.' He laughed and offered Eva a drink. They sat with their drinks, looking through the photos, and Gus told her some of his anecdotes about the old days in Andraxos. Eva finished her drink and set her glass down.

'What am I thinking? You don't want to listen to the stories of an oldie like me.'

'That's not true. I really enjoyed them, but I suppose I should get back to Millie.' Eva looked up at the building and felt her heart sink.

'And it's time for lunch,' Gus added.

Eva took the stairs slowly and felt the tension as she opened the door. They ate in near silence and then retreated to their rooms, occupied with their own thoughts; Eva to contemplate her lost mother and Millie to mull over the glimpse she had caught from the window of Eva and Gus sitting in the courtyard, deep in conversation. She wondered what they had been talking about and why Eva had failed to mention it over lunch.

Chapter 7

Violeta led Eva through a maze of narrow, whitewashed alleyways which eventually opened up to reveal a small, sunlit square with a bar on one side and a coffee house on the other. They settled themselves at a table outside the bar and ordered their drinks.

'I'm so happy to have a chance to speak English beyond the usual things I need to explain to our guests.'

'But you speak English with Gus, don't you?'

'I do, but it's nice to speak to someone of my own age. I love my grandfather, but it's different. I can't talk to him about everything. Isn't it the same with you and your grandmother?'

'Not really. I can tell her anything.'

Violeta's eyes widened. 'Anything?'

Eva laughed. 'Well, almost anything.'

'That is unusual or perhaps it's a British thing?'

'It's unusual. We're very close or we had been until recently.'

Violeta looked at her, waiting, and Eva wanted to say so

much more. The urge to confide in someone, even a virtual stranger was almost overwhelming, but she saw Millie's face in her mind's eye and chose her words carefully.

'You remember I told you my parents died when I was young? Millie brought me up.' As she spoke, she wondered again what had really happened to her mother. She had long ago decided that she had to be dead because even that seemed better than the thought she might have abandoned her. That was one of those things she could not even share with Millie because if her mum had abandoned her, she had abandoned Millie too.

Violeta reached across the table and patted Eva's arm. 'So it's just you and your grandmother?'

'Yes.'

'I can understand why you are so close then, but you said it has changed?'

'Yes, but I don't know why. Maybe it's just because I'm getting older and becoming more independent.'

'How old are you?'

'Eighteen. It was my birthday a few days ago.'

'Happy Birthday.'

'Thanks. How old are you?'

'Seventeen. Next year I have to decide whether to stay here or go to Athens to attend university.'

'What do you think you will do?'

'I want to go to university, and I want to experience living in a big city. Not just Athens – I want to see the world.'

Eva heard the slight edge of uncertainty. 'But?'

'My heart is here.'

'I can understand why you love it here.' Even in the few days that Eva had been there and with the little she had seen of the island, she had realised it was a place that got under your skin, seeped into your blood and would always claim a part of you. She wished she could share with someone that Andraxos truly was a part of her.

'And there is someone special here,' Violeta continued.

'Your boyfriend?'

'Actually he doesn't know how I feel about him, but I'm sure we are meant to be together.'

Eva thought about Tom. A year or so before she might have thought they were destined to be together, but now things were so much less certain.

'Why haven't you ever told him how you feel?'

'I want him to tell me first.'

Eva wondered if Violeta's conviction that her feelings were reciprocated was misplaced.

'Do you think he would go to Athens with you?' Eva asked.

'No, he's an island boy through and through. He'd probably be willing to leave for a holiday – reluctantly – but he wouldn't live anywhere else. I understand in a way. Andraxos is my home, and I will come back here, but I want to do other things first. Like my grandfather. He went off to see the world, and then he came home again.'

'Relationships aren't easy.' Eva paused. 'Can you choose who you want to marry?' As soon as she had said it, Eva realised it must have sounded like a strange question, but she had been thinking of Millie and Dimitris.

'Yes, of course. It's true our families always have an opinion about who is suitable – or not – and they certainly have something to say if they think the person is not suitable. They are also all in each other's lives, especially here on a small island, but we don't have arranged marriages. Why do you ask?'

Eva shrugged, trying to look as casual as possible. 'I was just curious. I don't know much about Greek culture and traditions.'

Violeta appeared to accept her explanation. 'It was different in my grandparents' time, but now I am happy to say we can choose. Do you have a boyfriend?'

'That's a good question. I honestly don't know. Things were … difficult before I left.'

'If it's meant to be, it will all be fine. Don't you think?'

Eva thought about Millie and Dimitris and about her shifting, uncertain feelings for Tom. 'I really don't know, Violeta.'

'What are your plans? Are you going to university?' Violeta asked, looking to change the subject.

Eva nodded. 'I'm waiting for my results. If they are good enough, I'll go.'

'What did you study?'

'Maths, further maths, physics and art.'

Violeta whistled softly. 'Those are some tough subjects and an unusual combination.'

'I want to be an architect,' said Eva, by way of explanation.

'You are lucky. I don't know what I want to do.'

'See the world,' said Eva smiling. 'And I think you are

very lucky to be able to call such a beautiful place home.'

Violeta beamed at her. 'What are your plans while you're here?'

Eva thought about what she had planned and what she could safely say. 'I'd like to see as much of the island as I can, go to the beach, swim, walk … that's about it.'

'I can recommend a place. I think you and your grandmother would both like it.'

'Where do you have in mind?'

'The Villa Iris.'

Eva stared at her.

'The place my grandfather mentioned the other day,' Violeta added.

Eva sat up, her heart beating faster. 'Yes, I remember, but we're not guests there.'

'It doesn't matter. We know the owners so I can clear it with them for you to go to the pool there – it's amazing. Then there's the beach below, which is stunning. You should definitely go there while you're here.'

'How do you know the owners?'

Violeta smiled. 'I can tell you come from a big city. Everyone knows just about everyone here. Or they know someone who knows the person. But actually the owners are …' She scratched her head. 'I don't know even in Greek what the word is. Antonis, the current owner, inherited it from his father and his wife's aunt is a cousin of my grandfather.

Eva tried to visualize the family tree but got nowhere. 'I haven't got a clue.'

'Me neither, but anyway if you would like to go, let me know.'

'And you've been there?'

'Oh yes. We normally have a big party there at the end of the season. It has the most beautiful views. You can't imagine until you see it.'

'I would love to go,' said Eva, aware that Violeta truly could not imagine just how much she wanted to visit the place.

Violeta checked her watch and sighed. 'I must return to work. Do you want to stay here or come back with me?'

'I'll come back. I want to see how Millie is.'

'Is she unwell? If you need a doctor, please tell me.'

'No, it's not that. It's just, she's … I think she's a bit tired after the journey and with the heat.'

They walked back to the apartments. 'I really enjoyed our chat, Eva.'

'So did I,' said Eva, feeling sad. If she had grown up there, or had at least grown up having contact with Andraxos, she had a feeling she and Violeta would have been good friends. She seemed so much more down to earth and genuine than many of the people she called friends back at home.

Eva climbed the stairs to the apartment, her heart heavier with each step. Apart from the fact that she had enjoyed spending time with Violeta, the truth she almost did not want to admit to herself was that, for the first time she could ever recall, she had enjoyed not being with Millie. She turned the key and went inside to find Millie sitting on the sofa, reading a book.

'Hi.'

'Hello, dear. Did you enjoy yourself?'

'Yes, it was good, thanks.'

'I'm pleased.'

'And I didn't say anything I shouldn't have,' Eva said, hoping to pre-empt an interrogation.

Millie nodded and put the book down. 'I know the last few days haven't been easy. And I was worried about this morning.'

'And I understand why, but you need to trust me. I've taken in what you said to me.'

'I'm sure you have. What are you going to do for the rest of the day?'

Eva thought about Violeta's offer to get them permission to go to the swimming pool at the Iris, but decided it was not the right time to mention it or the fact that there were ties between Violeta's family and the owners of the Iris. She was not sure there ever would be a right time. She thought that if Millie found out about that it might be too much for her. The connection between Gus and her own family had already affected her deeply.

'Let's take it easy this afternoon. Tomorrow, though, I thought we might go for a walk around town. I know you said you didn't want to, but you really can't spend the next month sitting here. I know you, and this is not you.'

Millie sighed. 'I am starting to feel like a prisoner in here.'

'But you don't have to be. Come on. You might even enjoy yourself once you get out.'

Millie hesitated.

'Please?'
'Tomorrow?'
'Yes.'
Millie hesitated. 'All right, tomorrow.'

* * *

Millie put on an enormous sun hat Eva had never seen before and sunglasses. She felt slightly ridiculous as though everyone would know she was trying to hide as much of herself as possible, but it was the only way she could face venturing out. She was relieved when Eva made no comment about what she was wearing, and they walked through the winding lanes of the town, gradually descending to the road which ran around the harbour. Millie stopped and took in her surroundings.

'Is it very different?' Eva asked.

'Yes and no. I thought it had changed completely, but the bones of the place are the same. It's just on the surface that it's different.'

Eva thought about that and wasn't sure if she was the lucky one or not for having no memories with which to compare the place.

They looked at the shops Eva had visited before and, as they walked further on, Millie came to a halt. She looked around her as if checking something.

'What is it Millie?' Even with her sunglasses on, Eva could see Millie's expression had changed. She watched as Millie walked to where the water washed against the stone harbour wall. She hesitated, wondering if joining her was the right thing to do. She waited for Millie to move away and when she didn't, she walked over to join her.

'Was it here that you met?' Eva asked.

Millie nodded and they stood quietly, watching the reflections shimmering on the water's surface. Eva had no idea what to do so she reached for Millie's arm and linked hers through it. She felt Millie pat her hand and thought that perhaps they hadn't drifted so far apart after all.

* * *

'Where do you want to have lunch, Millie?'

'I don't mind. Which one do you like the look of?'

'This one looks nice. Is that OK with you?'

Millie nodded, and they walked over and sat down. The waiter brought them menus. 'It's all in English.' Millie said. 'And there are pictures,' she added, with a hint of disdain.

'That's helpful, isn't it?'

'It was more fun when you had to guess what you were ordering.'

As the waiter brought them their food, Millie asked, 'Have you spoken to Tom yet?'

'I sent him a message the day we got here saying we'd arrived.'

'And?'

'And nothing. He read it, but he hasn't replied.' Behind her sunglasses, Eva screwed her eyes up and scanned the horizon. She wasn't sure how she felt about that, but she was starting to wonder if she was suffering from injured pride more than injured feelings.

'It's not my place to interfere, but you should resolve this, Eva. One way or another.'

'You're right. I'm just not sure how I feel at the moment. I was hoping a change of scene might help, but it hasn't yet.' Eva paused. 'What do you think of Tom?'

Millie shifted in her seat and poured herself some more water. Eva knew her well enough to realise she was playing for time.

'Millie?'

'He's always been very polite to me.'

'Millie, come on.'

'I shouldn't influence you.'

'I'm asking you for your opinion, though.'

'All right. I used to think you were a good match, but lately, when you've seen him, you seem … strained afterwards. I might be completely wrong, but if I'm not, that doesn't seem positive.'

Eva mulled over Millie's comments. 'You're right. I kept thinking it was just a phase, but he's changed. I've changed.'

'But not together?'

'Exactly.'

'You don't have to stay with Tom if it's not working.'

'I keep feeling I should be able to make it work, though. If I can't, doesn't that make me a failure?'

'Eva, you were very young when you started seeing Tom. Many people don't stay with their first boyfriend forever – particularly when they start going out together at fifteen.'

Eva fiddled with her necklace. 'It's just …'

'Just what?'

'I lose everyone who matters to me; except you. Everyone leaves. Nothing, nobody … sticks. Maybe it's me.' The words tumbled out before Eva could stop them.

There was a silence while Millie came to terms with what Eva had said and wondered why had she never known she felt that way. 'Darling, that's really not true. I can promise you that your mum and dad both loved you dearly. They didn't choose to leave you.'

'OK, maybe not dad. But mum?'

Millie looked down at the table, trying to think of something to say. She felt her jaw muscles tighten so much that the pain stung. 'She would never have chosen to leave you.'

'But she's not here, is she?'

'No, but not because she didn't want to be.'

'How do you know?'

'I know – knew – my daughter,' said Millie and looked away.

Eva took off her sunglasses and started wiping her eyes. 'Sorry, I'm being stupid.'

'No, no, you're not.'

'I don't want to be a failure.'

'You're the furthest thing from a failure I can imagine, Eva,' said Millie. 'You are kind, intelligent, the most wonderful granddaughter I could ever have asked for.'

'Stubborn, headstrong …' Eva said.

'Yes, well, that too.'

Eva managed a weak smile.

'But you get those traits from me,' said Millie, 'so I can't really complain.'

'What should I do?'

'About Tom?'

Eva nodded.

'Do you remember what I said to you before we left home?'

'Which part?'

'You can't keep believing in something which doesn't exist.'

'Yes. I thought of Tom when you said it.'

'Then you have to decide if that's what you're doing. Think about it. When you have the answer to that, you'll know what to do.'

Chapter 8

Eva woke up the next day full of resolve. Over breakfast, she took a deep breath and said, 'Millie, I thought we might go to the Villa Iris today. I really want to see it.'

'You know how I feel about that, Eva. Besides, it's a hotel. It's not open to the general public.'

'About that,' Eva felt the nerves starting. 'Violeta can get us permission to go there and use the swimming pool.'

'How's that?'

'She knows someone who works there. She suggested it to me the other day.'

'You were talking to Violeta about the Iris?' A hint of accusation was apparent in Millie's tone.

'No, not really. She mentioned it to me. She said she thought it was a place we'd both like. She was only being nice.' Eva chewed on her lip, frustrated by Millie's reaction.

Millie wrestled with her feelings; a part of her wanted to see it one last time and another part of her couldn't even contemplate the thought. She remembered how strongly she had reacted just to seeing it on a laptop screen. Then she thought about how much it meant to Eva, and the balance swung in favour of going.

'I suppose we could. After all, I don't have to stay if I don't want to.'

'Exactly. The moment you feel uncomfortable, we can leave.'

'It's a long walk as I recall. I think we should take a taxi.'

It was only when they were on their way that a thought occurred to Eva. Violeta had talked about the complex relationship between her family and the owners of the villa. What, if by some twist of fate, it was someone in Dimitris's family who had bought the place? She would be leading Millie directly to them with no warning.

She looked at Millie's profile, taut with tension. She could not bear to add to it, but now she had lied, and she was ashamed of that lie and frightened of the consequences. What had happened to her? To them? They had always been so close and so open with each other and now things were changing, and she didn't know what to do. Before she could decide whether to say anything, the taxi had stopped.

'Villa Iris,' said the driver.

They got out of the car, and Millie took in her surroundings. Even though she had thought she was prepared, nothing could have readied her for the moment. More work had been done to the place since the photos she had seen online had been taken. The low, ramshackle stone walls, which had always threatened to crumble, had been replaced by professionally built walls which towered well above head height, keeping prying eyes at bay, but a pair of wrought iron gates stood open. The villa itself was pristine; the walls shone white, and the deep blue shutters were perfectly aligned.

'Are you ready, Millie?'

'I don't know.'

'I'll go and let them know we're here. Take your time,' said Eva. She went ahead, and Millie followed slowly behind her.

Eva was busy chatting to the receptionist by the time Millie arrived so she slipped past them and took the opportunity to have a look around. Inside everything was different as well; modern, crisp and sleek. The days of her aunt's comfortable but eclectically furnished home were long gone. She went up the stairs and found a door at the end of the corridor to what she thought must have been her room when she had stayed there.

'Excuse me,' she said to the cleaner. 'Is anyone staying in this room?'

The woman consulted a list. 'No. They arrive later.'

'Could I see the room, please?'

'Why?'

'I'm thinking of staying here, but I'd like to see the room before I decide.'

The woman looked at her curiously but produced a key and let Millie in. 'Tell me when you finish.'

Millie walked into the room, taking in the luxurious surroundings. She went to the window and looked out at the view of the sea. It was unmistakably her room. Despite the many things which had changed, the view had not, and seeing it took her back in time.

Her hands gripped the windowsill as her mind was filled with memories of her time there and then, years later, the emails she had received from Helena during her stay. She remembered how she had been so concerned about Helena that she had considered leaving Eva with a friend and travelling to Andraxos. What had stopped her? Had she put her own feelings before the needs of her daughter? She felt tears starting to burn her eyes and pressed at them with the heel of her hand. She would not cry, not here, not now, not when she had to face Eva.

Her thoughts drifted again to her younger self gazing out at that same view for hours on end. She recalled the evenings she had come back to her room after meeting Dimitris, hugging herself and their secret close to her heart, not daring to say anything to her aunt until it was no longer possible to avoid the issue.

She heard someone behind her. 'Have you finished?'

'I'd just like to take a few photos.' Noticing the woman's expression, she added, 'To show to my friend.'

She took photos of the view and the room, stopping to absorb each aspect and corner of the room, knowing she would never go back. One return visit had been more than enough.

She slowly made her way to the door, her hand pausing to touch the door frame as she went; one final moment of contact with her past.

'Thank you.'

'You're welcome.' The cleaner locked the door behind them and went back to work.

Millie went downstairs and found Eva waiting in reception for her. The receptionist was nowhere to be seen.

'Where have you been?' Eva asked.

'I went upstairs to see my old room.'

'Oh.'

'What's the matter?'

'I would have liked to see it too,' said Eva.

'I've taken some photos of it.'

'I suppose that's something. Anyway,' said Eva, brightening up, 'we can go to the pool.' Eva went ahead again while Millie continued to linger in her memories as she slowly followed her down the path and around the house. The courtyard garden was still there, but it had been revamped and turned into a stylish bar. It was not a change for the better in Millie's opinion.

They went up the steps which led to the pool area, and Millie felt her knee complaining again. She saw Eva's ease of movement and wished she was still blessed with the unappreciated gifts of youth. The terrace Millie remembered had been converted into the pool area. It was where the photo of Sylvia and Millie had been taken before she had met Dimitris and everything had irrevocably changed; a time when her life had still been uncomplicated. All the flowers and pots and the creaky charm had been eradicated, replaced by a swimming pool surrounded by expensive sun loungers draped with towels and people.

'It's beautiful,' said Eva.

'Different from my time,' Millie responded, feeling as though someone had taken a bulldozer to her memories as well as to the place itself. 'You have a look around.'

Millie left Eva and went over to the low wall running around the pool area. She looked over it and the sight of the bay far below restored some calm to her. Eva appeared at her side. 'Do you want to use the pool?'

'No. I think I might go down to the beach. You stay here.'

'I can come with you.'

'No, you stay here. I'd like a little time on my own down there. Meet me there after your swim.'

Eva watched Millie leave and felt that perhaps she should follow her, but Millie had said she wanted to be alone. She shed her inhibitions enough to venture into the pool for a swim and then had a drink at the bar but felt unable to relax. She looked up at the villa beyond the tourists idling in the sun. She thought of the time Millie, and later her mother, had spent there and wondered what secrets its walls had been privy to. That there was more to learn was the one thing she was certain about.

* * *

Millie left the chatter at the pool behind her, walked back down the driveway, crossed the winding, coastal road and headed into the pine trees. She stopped in the shade, relieved to be away from the Iris. It held more memories than Eva knew, including one of her lies by omission.

She remembered the morning of her departure all those years ago. She had crept back to the house at first light and hurriedly showered and dressed. While she had waited for

Aunt Sylvia to get ready, she had gone to sit on the bench at the entrance to the bougainvillea tunnel, willing Dimitris to come back, willing him to say his parents had relented, willing the world to smile kindly on them.

She recalled the man who had rounded the corner; she had expected him to pass by on his way down to the beach, but he had stopped and was scrutinizing her.

'Emily?'

'Yes.'

The man grunted. 'The girl with Dimitris.'

Millie wasn't sure how to respond to that. 'Who are you?'

'The father of Dimitris.' He moved closer to her. Unexpectedly, he grabbed her arm and dragged her to her feet.

'Go away and don't return.' His hand moved from her arm to her throat. 'Do you understand?'

Millie tried to nod, shaking too much to say anything.

'Go. Today.'

'I am going.' Millie managed to say through the grip he had on her. 'Today.'

She felt his hand loosen. 'Remember I know where your aunt lives.'

'This is nothing to do with her.'

'Don't make it to do with her.'

'OK, OK,' Millie said, hoping to placate him.

'Then you understand,' he said, releasing her. 'There is nothing here for you. Good bye, Emily.'

In the shade of the trees, Millie tried to calculate how old he would be now. In his eighties, she thought. Maybe he was not even still alive, but the image of the man who had barred the way to her future danced in front of her eyes. She could still feel his hand around her throat and smell the aroma of cigarettes, which carried on his breath. She pressed her back against the trunk of one of the trees, finding reassurance in its solidity.

The fear she had felt at that moment had never really left her. The island had gone on to claim Helena, and now she was afraid for Eva as well. She thought once more that she should have told Eva about her encounter with Dimitris's father. She hadn't because that would have led to Eva asking questions and wanting to investigate whether he had had something to do with Helena's disappearance. For her own reasons, she had made the choice not to mention it to the police when Helena had disappeared, just as she had made the choice not to say anything to Eva, and now she had to hope she had done the right thing.

When Millie had recovered, she scrambled and slid down the slope and emerged from the pine forest onto the beach. The geography at least was still the same; a long, soft, sandy beach cradled between rocky headlands smothered with pines.

But, as with the Villa Iris, everything else had changed. There were no big hotels, but sun loungers had been laid out with a notice indicating the price for renting them, and a path leading away from the beach was marked with a signpost to a guesthouse, the roof of which was just visible through the trees. She felt the now familiar stirring of resentment that people had intruded into her place.

She watched as a young man worked his way around the

loungers, collecting payment for them and another group of tourists appeared from the direction of the guesthouse. They were laughing and chatting, and Millie sighed; it seemed she was to find no peace there either. She walked down to the shore, took off her shoes and walked alongside the sea, allowing the water to lap at her feet. As she reached the far end of the beach, she looked back and surveyed the scene. By most standards it was quiet, but compared to her memories, it was far too busy.

She looked over to where Dimitris had met her that last night. She saw the two young people they had been, holding each other, crying, refusing to believe there was no answer and then the crushing reality that it was the end of their time together. She rubbed at the tears streaking her face and, as she forced herself to look away, she noticed a little shack at the other end of the beach, tucked close into the pine trees.

She cautiously approached it as though she expected to see Dimitris serving drinks there, but there was just one young man, not much older than Dimitris had been back then. She took a seat at the bar and ordered a glass of ouzo.

'With water?'

'A little.' Millie watched as the ouzo turned cloudy and held up her hand up to signal it was enough.

The barman slid the shot glass and a small plate of olives across the bar.

Millie knocked it back and felt the punch in her stomach as it settled there. She looked back at where she had spent the night with Dimitris and ordered another one. Another one followed that.

'Are you OK?' The barman looked at her with concern.

'Yes, I am OK. Why would I not be OK?' asked Millie, no longer able to suppress the irritability she felt. Since she had arrived, Eva had done little but ask her if she was OK and now this stranger was starting. She caught his look. 'Sorry. Yes, I'm fine.'

She heard her phone. 'Hello Eva.'

'Hi. Where are you?'

'I'm at the bar on the beach. They serve exceptionally fine ouzo.'

'You're drinking shots?'

'Yes, I am drinking shots, and I am about to drink another one.'

Eva heard Millie ordering another one and noticed that her voice did not sound entirely steady.

'I'm on my way,' said Eva.

Eva scrambled through the trees and got to the beach bar as fast as the deep sand would allow.

'Millie, are you OK?'

'For crying out loud, will everyone stop asking me that?'

Eva took a step back. This wasn't her beloved Millie. What had she done to her?

'I'm sorry,' said Millie, annoyed that she seemed to be spending as much time apologizing as people spent asking after her wellbeing.

Eva cautiously took a seat at the bar.

'Do you want ouzo?'

'No, thanks. I'll have a beer, please.'

They drank in uneasy silence. Eva racked her brains for something to say which wouldn't be wrong, which wouldn't further fuel the fire she had lit, but could think of nothing, and they finished their drinks without uttering a word.

'Perhaps we should head back to the apartment?' Eva finally suggested.

'Yes, I think that's a good idea,' said Millie, climbing down from the bar stool and almost falling in the process. Eva caught her and only just stopped herself from asking Millie if she was OK.

'I think the heat has got to me,' said Millie.

Eva privately thought it had more to do with the empty shot glasses lined up on the bar, but restrained herself from saying anything. She had never seen Millie drunk before and didn't want to think about what had prompted her to down shot after shot.

They made it back to the road, and Eva sat her down while she called for a taxi. When they arrived in town, she helped Millie back to the apartment, keeping her fingers crossed that nobody would see them. In that respect at least she was lucky. They made it upstairs to the apartment, into Millie's bedroom and to the bed.

Eva looked at Millie, who had fallen asleep the moment her head had touched the pillow. She gently took her shoes off and propped another pillow under her head. She knelt beside the bed and examined the face of her sleeping grandmother. She had done this to her, she had brought her to such a state. She would never forgive herself, and yet she knew she would carry on regardless in her quest to learn more about her family. Visiting the Iris had made everything much more real. It had become something she could not abandon, whatever the cost.

Chapter 9

Eva eyed Millie over coffee. It had been a late start to the day. Millie had woken up feeling as though she had been run over, and Eva had barely slept either. Eva had the sense not to ask Millie how she was feeling or even to make any reference to the previous day.

'I was thinking it would be nice to have a quiet day,' said Eva. 'We could go to the Mythos tonight. Or stay in and make something to eat?'

'A quiet day sounds ideal.'

Millie resumed her place on the sofa with a book, and Eva settled herself on the balcony. She thought about the events of the previous day and then further back to what Millie had said to her about Tom when they had been at the restaurant. It had been a week since she had sent him the message saying she had arrived, and she had heard nothing from him. He seemed to be taking his talent for silence to new heights.

She flicked through her social media accounts, caught up on her messages and liked some posts because she thought she should although they all suddenly seemed strangely boring. They had lost their compelling nature. Her finger hovered over Tom's name on her messenger app. Finally she tapped his name and saw he was online. She felt annoyed that he was there but was still ignoring her.

She started typing and after several failed attempts at something meaningful, settled on *Hi*. Neutral, safe.

She watched and waited. He was still online. Finally he started typing.

Hello.

Eva thought for a moment. He wasn't giving her much to work with either.

What are you doing?

Hanging around with Josh and Matt. I had an interview for a summer job, got it, but then it fell through.

Sorry to hear that.

Yeah, sure.

Really, I am.

I expect you're having more fun than me.

What, Eva wondered, was she supposed to say to that? It occurred to her that at one time she might have suggested they plan a trip together when she got back to cheer him up, but she realised she didn't want to go anywhere with him. She thought again about Millie's words; about believing in something which didn't exist. Tom was still online. He seemed to be waiting.

She considered phoning him but thought better of it. At least if she wrote to him, he wouldn't be able to shout over her. She started to type again. *Things haven't been great between us lately, have they?* She felt her hand start to shake but sent the message anyway. She saw that he was typing. The reply seemed to be taking forever.

Not really. It had taken so long for him to type his reply that she had expected something much longer.

I've been thinking about that a lot since I got here.

And? Tom replied, leaving Eva looked at the single word, cursing the fact it was impossible to read his tone. Was it concerned? Offhand? She had no idea.

With university coming up, we'll be spending a lot of time apart. Eva sent the message and then wondered what she had done. If she wanted to split up with him, she should have the courage to say so outright, not dance around the issue. She could hear Millie telling her the same thing. She started to type again. *Do you think it would be better if we split up now? You know long-distance relationships are difficult at the best of times.*

You want to have this conversation now? Like this?

I know it's not ideal, and I'd rather do it in person, but I won't see you for nearly a month. It's not fair to you not to talk about it now.

Is that what you want?

A tear rolled down Eva's face, but she recognised she was mourning the end of a stage in her life, more than she was regretting the end of the relationship. *I think it would be for the best. We don't make each other happy anymore. I understand if you want to talk about it when I get back, but I need to be honest with you now.*

There was a long pause. Eva waited, hoping for

something although she was not sure exactly what. Tom's reply appeared. *Fine.*

Five years as friends; three of those as girlfriend and boyfriend; summarised by one word – fine.

Do you want to meet and talk when I get back?
I'll think about it.

Eva wasn't sure whether that was sarcasm or not. *OK. Let me know.*

She saw him disappear. She put her phone down on the table and thought about what had just happened. She felt she had handled it badly and breaking up as they had done was far from the best way to go about things, but she knew she couldn't have carried on with the lie any longer.

As she reflected on what she had done, she slowly became aware of her phone buzzing incessantly. She picked it up; messages were flooding in. Tom had already made news of their breakup known and had managed to cast her as the villain. A tangled maze of messages starting with '*OMG …*', '*You'll never guess …*' and '*Have you heard…*' combined with judgements on the situation and demands for information from Eva.

The messages started to blur before her eyes, and she was suddenly sick of the constant pressure on her to explain herself and be in contact all the time. She got up to take her phone inside.

Millie looked up as she came in. 'Can we talk?'

'Sure.' Eva threw her phone onto the armchair and sat down on one of the dining chairs by the window.

'About yesterday –'

'Millie, it's fine. You don't need to say anything.'

'I think I do, dear. I don't know what came over me. It was going to the Villa Iris. And then the beach. It was all just too much, but you should never have had to see me like that.'

Eva felt a shift in the delicate balance of their relationship and a sense of responsibility she was not sure she was ready to take on. She was slowly learning more about Millie as a person, rather than as a grandmother. She was unsure how to address it. She wondered what she would say to a friend of her own age. 'I guess I might have done the same thing. As a matter of fact I feel like doing it now.'

Millie temporarily forgot her predicament. 'What? Why?'

'I broke up with Tom.'

'When?'

'Just now; on the phone. I handled it badly, and I know I should have waited to do it in person, but I just couldn't go on pretending. You can't believe in something which doesn't exist, right?'

Millie nodded and feeling the room start to spin, stopped. 'I hope I didn't convince you to do something you didn't want to do.'

'No, I wanted to do it. If anybody has been making someone do things they don't want to do, it's been me. I know you told me to stop saying sorry, but I am sorry. Truly, Millie. I'm not sorry we came here, but I'm sorry for the effect it's had on you.'

Millie patted the sofa cushion. 'Come here.'

Eva slumped down beside her. 'Do you think we can lay our ghosts to rest?'

'I don't think I'm really in a fit state to consider that at the moment.'

They looked at each other; Millie with her hangover and Eva glum and despondent. 'What a pair we are,' said Millie.

'Yup,' said Eva and rested her head on Millie's shoulder.

* * *

The afternoon passed quietly. Eva had managed to avoid looking at her phone for hours, but in the end she could no longer resist. She deleted all the messages without even bothering to read them properly but stopped when she came to Amy's.

Breaking up like that – not cool. What were you thinking?

Eva started typing. *You don't have to tell me. I already feel bad about it.*

Amy appeared immediately. *Why didn't you tell me what you were going to do?*

I didn't plan it. It's complicated. Anyway, you're supposed to be on my side.

Yeah, well, Tom's making you out to be the bad guy.

I've seen the messages.

Just warning you.

Thanks.

Eva was about to put her phone down when another set of messages started cascading in. Some asking why again, others accusing her of being mean to Tom. One from Tom's sister caught her attention.

I always knew I didn't like you. Now I know why.

Eva stopped to digest that and rubbed a tear from her eye.

'What's the matter?' Millie asked.

'Tom's painting me as the one in the wrong for breaking up with him.'

'I suppose that was to be expected.'

'You think I deserve it? Eva asked.

'No, I know why you did it and I understand, but this is what I told you about people – everyone has an opinion, and they don't need possession of all the facts to form them.'

'I feel like everyone is turning against me.'

'It'll blow over. By the time you get to university, it – and they – will all be a distant memory.'

'I hope you're right.'

'In the meantime, a piece of advice. Turn your phone off for a while. Take a break from it.'

'Perhaps you're right,' said Eva as the phone started to vibrate in her hand yet again. She switched it off and prepared a salad. They sat at the dining room table and although Millie only picked at her food, the atmosphere between them was more companionable than it had been since they had arrived.

By the time they had finished and washed up, Eva was starting to feel restless again.

'I need to get out Millie.'

'It's getting a bit late to go exploring, isn't it?'

'I just need to go for a walk. Burn off some nervous energy. Do you want to come with me?'

Millie, who still felt queasy when she made any sudden movements, declined. 'Just be careful, Eva.'

'I'm pretty certain this place is way safer than London.'

'Yes, I'm sure it is, but that's not what I'm worried about.'

'Millie, I promised you that I'm not going to start looking for my grandfather. Not without telling you and certainly not at this time of night. I just need to get out.'

'All right. I'll see you later.'

Eva emerged into the courtyard, and the warm night air wrapped around her. She walked through the dimly lit upper town and found her way to the stairs leading down to the harbour, where bright lights blazed from the bars and restaurants. It was not a long walk from where they were staying, but it was a world away in atmosphere.

She enjoyed the fact that all the shops were still open and stopped off to browse. She got to the end of the harbour and was about to start retracing her footsteps when she saw a young man sketching portraits. She was in no rush to go back and was happy to have found an excuse which could keep her out a little longer. She wandered over and joined the small crowd watching him.

As his customers came and went, Eva noticed how he charmed the crowd and put his subjects at their ease. He smiled a lot, and Eva found herself comparing him with Tom, who had rarely smiled in recent times. She moved a little closer as the group of people around him started to thin out, and she was finally able to see his work; he was as talented as he was good with people. She was so absorbed with looking at the work he was producing that she had not realised most of the people around had drifted away, comparing the sketches they took with them.

He finished the portrait he had been doing and said something to her in Greek.

'Sorry, I don't speak Greek,' Eva replied.

'I asked you if you would like me to draw you,' he said in fluent, lightly accented English.

'Oh no, thank you. I don't think so.'

'Why not?' He spread his arms in a good-natured, what-have-you-got-to-lose gesture.

Eva's honest reply would have been that she was sure she would not like the finished result. When she uploaded photos onto social media, she either avoided being in the photo or positioned herself in such a way that she could not be seen clearly. Those thoughts and the lack of confidence from which they stemmed were not ones she wished to share with a complete stranger. She didn't even share them with her friends. She realised she still hadn't answered his question.

'It's getting a bit late,' she said weakly.

He looked at his watch. 'Ten. That's not late. Not in Greece.' He gave her a heart-stopping smile, which made her want to stay and run in equal measure.

'I don't know.'

'I do. Please. Sit down. If you don't like it, there is no charge.'

Unable to think of any other excuses, Eva sat down. She estimated that he had done the others in about fifteen minutes so at least the ordeal would be over quite quickly.

He started to draw her, and she noticed him examining her. Time slowed down; people stopped to watch and moved on again; the lights at the bar behind him went out. She chanced a glance at her watch – 10.30. He would be finished soon.

'Don't move yet,' he said.

Eva switched her gaze from somewhere past his shoulder to his face. He had moved from looking at her intently to whatever he was putting on the paper in front of him. He looked back up at her and their eyes met. He smiled at her and despite her misgivings, Eva found herself responding.

He carried on with his work, and Eva took the opportunity to study him. Far too attractive for his own good, she concluded. She chanced another look at her watch. 10.40. What was taking him so long?

'Nearly finished.' He added a few finishing touches to the paper. 'Here you are.'

Eva took the paper, dreading the caricature which awaited her, playing up all her worst features. She braced herself to look at it. When she did, she felt a strange sensation wash over her. He had made her look beautiful yet it still looked like her, a contradiction she could not make sense of. More than that, he seemed to have captured something beyond her appearance, but she could not identify exactly what he had done. She felt that at last someone had really seen her. He had reached inside her and seen her spirit. She shook herself – of course he would have produced something beyond a simple representation of her, he was an artist.

'Do you like it?'

'Yes, thank you. How much do I owe you?'

'No charge.'

'But it took you ages. You said no charge if I didn't like it, but I do. I must pay you.'

'No, put your money away,' he said, seeing her reach inside her bag. 'Drawing you was my reward.'

Eva blushed and managed a thank you.

'What's your name?'

'Eva.'

'That's a beautiful name.'

'Thanks,' Eva felt herself blushing an even deeper shade and was thankful it was dark. 'What's your name?'

'Mitsos, but you can call me Jim if you prefer. That's what the American side of my family calls me. How long are you staying here?'

' Four weeks. I've been here for a week already.' She saw what appeared to be a spark of interest in his eyes.

'So I will see you again.'

'I don't know. Maybe.' Eva felt awkward and wondered why she could never find the right words.

'I'm here quite often.'

'OK, well, yes then. Probably.'

'And if I'm not here, I'm probably working at that bar over there – the Mimosa.'

'Right.'

'Good night, Eva. Remember where I am.'

'Good night.'

Eva forced herself to move away although she could have stayed and just looked at Mitsos for hours. Walking back to the apartment, the streets had fallen quiet, but she felt completely safe.

The apartment was in darkness when she returned. She went to her room and lay down on the bed. She rolled over onto her stomach and reached for the cardboard roll which contained her picture. She pulled it out to study it and as she did, a piece of paper fluttered to the floor. Mitsos had written his name and a number on it, and Eva felt the first stirrings of something she had never experienced before.

Chapter 10

As Eva packed her beach towel and book away at the end of the afternoon, her thoughts turned again to Mitsos. He had intruded on them frequently during the course of the previous two nights and days since she had met him. Sometimes she thought he had really liked her; sometimes she considered he had just been flirting to see how she would react and would be doing exactly the same on every other evening with every other passing female. She wondered how many of them had received his phone number. She decided she might take a walk down to the harbour just to see what he was doing. If she saw him flirting with other women, it would be so much easier to forget about him. And forgetting about him was something she wanted to do. He had made her feel vulnerable, and it was a feeling she hadn't liked.

As she had expected, Millie did not want to go out so Eva was free to go back to the harbour alone. She walked around, feeling increasingly nervous and finding excuses to stop and examine every souvenir and T-shirt in great detail. Finally, she spotted Mitsos. He was slightly angled away from her so she was in the perfect position to observe him. She took a seat in the nearest bar and ordered a drink.

The first customers she saw him with were children, and she watched as he put them at ease, playfully teasing them and handing them their sketches. There was a sweetness about the way he interacted with them which touched her. Other customers came and went, and she ordered another drink.

An older couple thanked him and went on their way, and then Eva's attention pricked up. A young woman was asking him about prices. She sat down, and Mitsos went to work. He completed the sketch in the usual quarter of an hour. The portrait was handed over, money exchanged hands and the woman disappeared. There had been no additional conversation. Eva watched as Mitsos started reorganizing his materials. He had not flirted with her or given her a second look as she had walked away. She found herself feeling guilty for watching him.

She glanced at her watch and was surprised to see how late it was. She thought she should get back to check on Millie and felt that kernel of resentment again, followed by a wave of annoyance at herself. She paid and as she got up and was assessing the best way back to the apartment without walking past Mitsos, she saw him walking towards her.

'Eva,' he said, his face lighting up.

'Hello.'

'You remember me?' He smiled, which did something to Eva's insides she could not quite identify.

'Mitsos, wasn't it?' Eva asked, as casually as she could.

'Yes.' He looked at the empty glass on the table. 'Are you leaving?'

Eva nodded.

'Why don't you stay a while longer? I need to pack my things away, and then I can have a drink with you.'

'OK, I suppose I could have one more.'

'Great. Wait here.'

Eva waited until he was busy with his packing and pulled out her phone to send a message to Millie.

Hi. Just to let you know I'm fine. I know you worry.

Thank you. Where are you?

Having a drink down in the harbour and people watching.

What time will you be back?

I'm not sure, but I won't be late.

OK. Be careful.

Don't worry, I will be. See you later.

Eva put her phone away. In all the years they had lived in London, Millie had never told her to be careful as many times as she had in the last few days. She put that out of her mind as she started to feel nervous about what she would find to talk about with Mitsos.

He came over, and they ordered drinks.

'What do you think of Andraxos?'

'It's very beautiful. I wish I could stay here longer.'

'You still have three weeks you said?'

'Yes,' said Eva, surprised he had remembered.

'Then you have a lot of time to explore. You can come with me, and I will show you the island. The island away from the tourists.'

'But I'm a tourist too,' Eva said with a smile.

Mitsos looked at her and seemed to be evaluating her. 'You are different.'

'How?' She wanted to challenge him and not appear to fall for flattery.

'I don't know, but you are.' He paused. 'Where are you from?'

'England. London.'

'And you came here alone?'

'I came with someone, but she normally stays in the apartment.'

'It's strange to come here and stay inside all the time.'

'Yes, but she has a stressful job. She wants to rest.'

Mitsos shrugged as if there was nothing to be done about it, and Eva realised there wasn't. 'So effectively you are here alone?'

Eva recalled how alone she had felt at times since she had arrived. 'I suppose I am.'

'When can I take you out to see the island?'

'I don't know.' Eva realised she had never been in a similar situation before. Her relationship with Tom had prevented her from the need to deal with any of the trials of dating or getting to know a new man. She wasn't sure what she was supposed to do or say.

'You have my phone number?'

'Yes,' Eva admitted, 'but not on me.'

Mitsos gave her his number again and asked her to put it in her phone. 'Will you call me?'

Eva did as he asked.

'Good. You can contact me when you want to go out.'

'OK.'

They paid the bill and got up. 'I will walk you back,' said Mitsos.

'No, it's fine.'

'I would prefer to.'

'I'll be fine, honestly,' said Eva.

'An independent woman,' Mitsos remarked, but when Eva looked at him she saw no sign of the mocking tone Tom had used so often.

'That's me,' she said, as lightly as she could manage.

'Well, good night, Eva.'

'Good night, Mitsos.'

Eva walked home, going as slowly as she could as though the magic of the evening would evaporate as soon as she walked through the door of the apartment. Mitsos seemed like a genuine person. She wondered if she could really trust him and if she could, where that would lead. And if it led anywhere, what would she tell Millie?

* * *

Eva forced herself not to contact Mitsos the following morning although the temptation at times proved almost too strong to resist. She didn't want to appear too interested in him, and she was still unsure about whether he was just on the prowl for a tourist to have fun with. She was also well aware from Millie's experience that even if he was genuine, it could lead to complications. She sighed and wondered why things had to be so difficult. Nevertheless, by the time the evening came, she found she could no longer resist the urge to see him.

With Millie still determined to remain cocooned in the apartment, Eva was able to leave the apartment without any questions. She looked for Mitsos by the harbour, but he was not there. She was surprised by how disappointed she felt but then remembered he had told her about his job at the Mimosa.

She decided to go to the bar and got as far as the entrance when she started to feel nervous. She walked past the bar and further down the harbour road and took a seat on a bench.

The evening had washed the blues and greens of the day away. People started to emerge from their hotels and onto the decks of their boats. She walked around the harbour once more but Mitsos was nowhere in sight. She turned back and decided it was finally time to see if Mitsos was in the bar.

She walked in and when she saw Mitsos, she felt a surge of excitement. She started to make her way to the bar, planning what she might say to him. She didn't want to seem too enthusiastic, but, on the other hand, he had told her where to find him.

As she got closer to the bar, she saw him move out from behind the bar and put his arm around the shoulders of a young woman who had been standing on the other side. He didn't see her, but she watched as they headed out of the door. They stood by the waterfront. His arm was no longer around her shoulders, but their body language suggested that they were entirely comfortable in each other's company.

Eva was rooted to the spot. She remembered seeing Isla

with her arm around Tom in his kitchen. Her excitement drained away as she called herself an idiot and a fool. Millie may have had a genuine romance, but Mitsos was obviously the stereotypical man she had heard about; the type who would charm every female tourist in sight and see which ones were susceptible.

I'm not going to be one of them, she said to herself. She saw Mitsos give the girl something, and they started laughing. Eva felt stupid. He obviously handed his phone number out to anyone and everyone.

'What do you want to drink?'

Eva became aware the man behind the bar was talking to her. 'Nothing. Sorry, I have to go.'

The barman looked exasperated, but couldn't afford to waste time arguing about it and moved on to his next customer.

Eva saw Mitsos coming back into the bar and shrank back into the corner. As soon as he had his back to her, she made her way out as fast as she could.

As she walked back to the apartment, she tried to convince herself she had had a narrow escape. *I didn't need Tom, and I don't need Mitsos. I don't need anyone.* She wondered who she was trying to fool. She was certainly doing a poor job of fooling herself.

In the apartment, Millie was looking out of the window, her delicate silhouette a darker shade than the window behind her.

'How was your evening?' Millie asked, as she heard Eva come in.

'OK,' said Eva, trying to avoid any trace of emotion colouring her voice. 'Yours?'

'Here.'

Neither of them was inclined to try to make any further attempt at conversation, and Eva made her excuses and went to her room. Opening the doors to the balcony, she gazed down over the harbour. Somewhere down there, some of those glowing lights marked the Mimosa, where Mitsos was no doubt flirting with as many of his female customers as possible.

You idiot, she said to herself. She paced the room and reminded herself why she was there in the first place. It hadn't been to get tangled up with someone. She found her mother's emails and read them again, searching for any details she might have overlooked which could explain what had happened to her. Another line her mother had written caught her eye.

Perhaps it's better just to have dreams – that way they can never be shattered.

Eva gazed out of the window, wondering if she had been right. She was still sitting there, the emails on her lap, long after the last light in town had gone out and the harbour had descended into darkness.

* * *

Eva woke up to the sound of her phone ringing and scrabbled around for it. It was Mitsos. She felt a surge of happiness and then remembered what she had witnessed the night before. She ignored it and went to have a shower.

When she came back there were two messages waiting for her.

Eva, how are you?

I have to work all day and also tonight so can you come to the bar later?

She looked at the messages, growing more annoyed by the second. *Come to the bar like all the others. I bet you compare notes with the other barman. No chance*, she muttered to herself.

She spent the morning at the town beach and managed to get Millie to go as far as the Mythos for lunch. Back at the apartment, she realised she had left her phone there all morning. She checked it for messages.

Three from Amy, moaning about having to work; a few messages from group chats, which all seemed to concern the latest news about "poor Tom"; and another one from Mitsos.

Will you come to the bar later? I really want to see you.

You want to see me, do you? Eva said, looking at her phone. *Fine, but you might change your mind when you do.*

The hours until the evening dragged, and Eva became more indignant with every one that passed. By the time, she finally stomped into the bar, she was determined to let Mitsos know she would not be taken for a fool.

She saw him chatting to the same woman she had seen him with before. *I can do us both a favour if I confront him now*, she thought. Instead of hanging back as she had done the previous time, she walked straight up to them.

'Hello,' she said. She had aimed for conversational but

thought she sounded vaguely aggressive.

'Eva, hi,' said Mitsos, looking delighted to see her.

Unbelievable, thought Eva. *He doesn't even look embarrassed.*

'This is Niki,' he said.

'Hi. Good to meet you.' said Niki cheerfully, her American accent immediately apparent.

'Hello.'

'What would you like to drink?' Mitsos asked.

'A beer, please.'

'Sure. Niki, do you want another one?'

'No, I have to get going,' she said looking at her watch. She leaned across the bar and kissed Mitsos on the cheek. 'Bye.'

'Bye. Don't forget lunch tomorrow.'

Niki waved. 'As if I could! Bye, Eva.'

'Bye,' Eva replied, no longer sure what was going on. She wondered how Mitsos could be so brazen.

'I'll be back as soon as I can. Don't go away,' said Mitsos and went back to work.

Eva sat there for a while, feeling more and more foolish. Tom had frequently made her feel foolish, and now Mitsos was doing the same thing. She drained the glass, put enough money down on the bar to cover the cost and went outside. She stood there fuming, torn between returning to the apartment and going back into the bar to tell Mitsos exactly what she thought of him.

'Eva, wait.' Mitsos tapped her on the shoulder. 'Where are you going?'

'Back to the apartment.'

'Are you angry with me? I'm sorry I couldn't talk to you. It gets so busy sometimes.'

'I'm not angry about that.'

'What are you angry about then?'

Eva was taken aback. He had picked up on the unspoken point that she was angry about something. Tom would never have done that. She played with her necklace. 'I know how it works.'

'How what works?'

'The tourists come here and you charm them, and then they leave and some more turn up.'

'What are you talking about?'

'Niki. For example.'

'Niki?'

'Well, she's a tourist and you're meeting her for lunch tomorrow, and you even arranged it in front of me when you'd asked me if I'd like to go out and see the island with you. I know I'm not your girlfriend, but it's still weird.'

Mitsos started laughing.

'Don't laugh at me. It's not funny.'

'I'm sorry, Eva. I'm not laughing at you. I would never do that, but the situation is a bit funny. Niki is my cousin.'

'But she sounds American. I thought she was a tourist.'

'She lives in America, but she and her family come here every summer. When I see her for lunch tomorrow, it will be with all of my family and all of her family.'

'Oh.' Eva felt foolish and, worse, exposed.

'I'm not a – what's it called in English? I'm not what you think I am.'

'A womaniser?'

'Yes, that. It's true there are men who do what you said, but I'm not one of them.'

Eva looked at him, wanting to believe him.

'Meet me the night after tomorrow. I'm not working at the bar, and I'll take a night off from doing the portraits. We'll go out.'

'I …'

'Just here in town. You can leave anytime you want to.'

'I'm not sure.'

'Give me a chance, Eva.'

Eva found herself wanting nothing more than to give him a chance. 'OK, but only somewhere here in town. I'm not going anywhere else with you.'

'That's fine. I'll meet you here. At eight?'

'At eight.'

'Do you want to come back in for another drink?'

'No, I think I'll go back. Check on my friend.'

'OK, night, Eva.' Mitsos kissed her on the cheek, and Eva blushed.

'Good night, Mitsos.'

Chapter 11

Eva woke as usual to the sound of the rooster and looked at her phone; the fourth of August. She realised they had already been there for nearly two weeks and although she had seen the town and the Villa Iris, she had done nothing about trying to find her family, much less solve the mystery of her mother's disappearance. They had somehow slipped into August while she had been distracted. Now that the change of month had registered with her and she realised the holiday was already halfway through, it felt as though everything had changed. Suddenly, the end of the holiday felt much closer, and the prospect of returning home without achieving anything she had set out to do seemed all too possible.

Time was such an elastic concept on the island. It played tricks, and hours, even days, could disappear in the blink of an eye. And then there had been Millie's mood to contend with; and the breakup with Tom; and meeting Mitsos. She put her phone down and rolled over onto her back. Things hadn't worked out as she had planned. She had had visions of turning up and finding her grandfather, who had greeted her with joy and answered all of her questions while Millie stood by, smiling benevolently. She couldn't have strayed further from the reality of the situation if she had tried. She went into the sitting room, determined to take control of the situation and do something positive.

'Millie, I've been looking for trips round the island.'

'What have you found?'

'Only one. Look,' Eva sat down beside Millie, opened a website on her phone and started to read. '"See the best of Andraxos on this trip. After a stop at one of the island's lookout points, we will visit the Temple of Hera and then proceed to the village of Vathi for an olive oil tasting. After that, there will be free time in Vathi for lunch and the chance to enjoy the crystal-clear waters of this tranquil bay. In the afternoon, we will retrace our steps back to Andraxos Town. Pick up at 8 a.m. by the ferry terminal. Runs every day in July and August." What do you think?'

'It sounds like a good day out,' said Millie cautiously.

'I know you're worried about bumping into Dimitris, but he's not going to be on a tour bus going around his own island, is he? When have we ever been on a tour bus in London?'

'It does seem unlikely,' Millie conceded.

'I really want to go. One of the things I came here for was to see the island.'

'There's nothing to stop you going, dear.'

'No, I know that, but I'd like you to come with me. You've hardly been out since we've been here. Please?'

Millie hesitated. 'I suppose it can't do any harm, and I would like to get out.'

'Shall I book it then?'

Millie remembered again what she had said to herself when they had arrived about trying to retain a measure of control over events. She had failed dismally so far and considered the fact that the past two weeks had passed without incident pure luck. She had wondered more than once how long that luck would last. 'Yes, go ahead.'

'For tomorrow?'

'Yes, tomorrow.' Millie watched as Eva made the booking. She told herself Eva was right and that everything would be fine.

* * *

'Are you ready, Millie?'

'Yes, yes, I'm just coming.'

As they left, the courtyard was quiet and still, and the streets were only just starting to come to life as shopkeepers unpacked their wares onto the streets. They walked through the lanes, catching glimpses of the sea between the houses, a cooler blue in the soft light of early-morning and finally came to the staircase from where the view of the harbour started to open up before them. As they reached the bottom of the stairs, Millie caught Eva's arm.

'Eva, I'm not sure about this.'

'You'll be absolutely fine, Millie. As I said, nobody goes on tourist trips around the places where they live.'

'I suppose you're right.'

'I am. Once you're on the bus and you see it's only tourists, you'll feel much better.'

'I hope so,' Millie murmured.

They found the meeting point and introduced themselves to the guide. 'Welcome. My name is Vangelis. You're the first,' he said. 'British. Always early.' He smiled at them.

'How many other people are there? Millie asked, trying to peer at his list to see the names.

'Only eight more. Is this your first visit here?'

'Yes,' said Eva, determined, for once, to say something which would meet with Millie's approval.

A family of four from Germany appeared and introduced themselves and after another few minutes, two couples from Sweden joined the group.

As they got on the bus, Eva nudged Millie. 'I told you it would be fine. Now you can enjoy the day.'

'I do feel better now,' Millie admitted and finally managed a smile.

They set off, and Eva listened with rapt attention as Vangelis explained more about the island, its history and lifestyle. Millie watched Eva and marvelled that someone who had complained bitterly about history at school could now not learn enough.

'Here we are at our first stop. It's a lovely place to see the coast of our island and also our neighbouring islands in the distance.'

They all dutifully got off the bus and walked over to the viewpoint.

'It's breathtaking,' Eva said, reaching for her phone to start taking photos. She noticed that Millie had gone quiet. 'Isn't it lovely?'

'Yes, it is,' said Millie with her face turned away from Eva. She started to walk away, and Eva followed her. 'Millie, what's wrong?'

'Just go and take your photos, dear. I'll be with you soon.'

Eva retreated, sensing it was not the moment to push her to talk. She walked back towards the others, glancing over her shoulder, and saw Millie setting off down the road. She turned around, and Eva waved at her.

Millie returned the wave and then let the forced smile drop. She watched Eva return to the group and enjoyed the feeling of the breeze, which was constant at that altitude, cooling her down. She remembered the last time she had been to the viewpoint. Dimitris had taken her there. They had gazed out over the same scene together. She could almost feel his arms wrapped around her. She remembered that they had then taken a path through the woods. She wondered if it was still there and crossed the road to look for it. Everything was so overgrown, and at first she couldn't find it. She kept going, and finally she came across a slight parting in the trees.

She looked back towards the lookout point and judged the distance to be about right. Everyone was still off the bus, chatting and taking photos. She made her way through the trees and became lost in the world she tried so often to leave behind. The forest enfolded her, and she looked up at the soft canopy overhead. She could feel him beside her; the years had slipped away, and they were the two idealistic people of their youth. This was the path, she was sure of it.

Back by the minibus, Eva had started talking to Vangelis. 'Are there any other trips you would recommend? I couldn't find any.'

'This is the only one. You could hire a car, but it is only landscape and a few tiny villages. The boat trips are better.'

'Thanks.'

He turned, asked everyone to get back on the bus and then looked back at Eva. 'Where is your mother?'

Eva decided not to correct him, looked around her and then back at him. 'I don't know.'

'Can you phone her? We need to move on to our next stop.'

'Yes, sorry. I don't know where she can have gone.' Eva called her number and waited. 'Come on. Pick up.'

Millie heard her phone ringing. 'Hello.'

'Millie, where are you? We're all waiting for you.'

'I'm coming. Hold on.'

Eva heard the line go dead. 'She's on her way.' They waited and saw Millie emerge from the woods at the side of the road.

'What is she doing?' Vangelis asked.

'I have no idea,' Eva replied, as they watched her slowly make her way back up the hill towards the bus.

'I'm sorry,' Millie said, offering no further explanation.

'Right, let's go then,' Vangelis said, ushering them on board.

When they had settled in their seats, Eva turned to Millie and asked. 'What were you doing?'

'I was looking for something,' Millie whispered.

'What?'

'A place I went with him.'

'Oh,' said Eva. 'Well, look we're going to this temple next. 'Have you been there before?'

'No, I haven't.'

'You should be all right there then,' said Eva.

As the visit to the temple and olive oil tasting passed without incident, Eva started to feel more optimistic about the day, and Millie appeared to have cheered up as well.

'Now you have free time here in Vathi,' said Vangelis, as the bus pulled up on the outskirts of the village.

'If you go this way, you will be in the centre. There are some nice restaurants there and some good shops for souvenirs. In the opposite direction, you have the beach and also some more excellent restaurants. We will meet back here at 3 o'clock. Does anyone have any questions?'

The group shook their heads and drifted in different directions.

'Beach or village, Millie?'

'I'd like to do both. Let's go the village first and then have lunch at the beach.'

Eva had wanted to do that, but would have accepted any plan that Millie came up with if it made her happy. The village turned out to be no more than two streets dotted with a few shops which seemed to cater for tourists, and Eva and Millie soon gravitated towards the beach.

'I'd like to go for a swim before we have lunch,' Eva said, looking longingly at the water.

'You go ahead. I've got my book,' said Millie settling herself on the sand and wondering if her knee would permit her to get up again.

Eva, who was wearing her swimsuit under her clothes, slipped out of her shorts and T-shirt and quickly wrapped her towel around her.

'You can leave that here with me.'

'I'll take it with me,' Eva said, awkwardly, unwilling to admit to the fact she was too shy to allow herself to be seen in her swimsuit. She walked down to the water's edge, dropped the towel and slipped into the water, which was the perfect temperature.

The sun danced on the water, turning it into a million shards of light. She found herself thinking about everything that had happened since they had arrived: the links between her family and Violeta's; the tension with Millie and how they constantly came together and pulled apart again in a rhythm as predictable as the tide; the breakup with Tom; Mitsos. At the thought of him, her stomach flipped. She would be meeting him in little more than six hours. She turned on her back and floated, staring at the sky. Eventually, she reluctantly waded out and pulled the towel around her again.

She dried herself off and dressed quickly. 'Are you ready for lunch?'

'Yes, I'm quite hungry now.'

'Shall we eat there? Eva suggested, looking at a small taverna right on the beach.

They ordered, and away from the claustrophobia the

apartment had induced in her, Eva felt ready to tackle the subject of her family afresh.

'I know I've said it before, but I do understand that it's been difficult for you to come here. Not here I mean,' she said, looking around her. 'Andraxos.'

'I know what you mean.'

'I honestly didn't understand how strongly you felt about it. I thought everything would be fine once we got here, and we'd have a good holiday.'

'I can't help it. I can't pretend I'm happy here or that I feel relaxed. I know I haven't been good company, and honestly I doubt I will be until we're back at home.'

Eva nodded. 'There are only two weeks left.'

'Two weeks and four days.'

'Not that you're counting,' Eva said, attempting humour. Seeing it fall flat, she continued. 'And with that in mind, I want to know how you feel about me looking for my grandfather now.'

'I feel exactly the same as I felt when you mentioned it back at home and when you asked me about it after we'd arrived,' Millie responded.

'So I don't have your blessing to look for him?'

'You're making me sound unreasonable.'

'That's not my intention. It's just that coming here and seeing the island is only one part of the picture, but there's so much more. There's my grandfather and then there's what happened to mum. I've hardly done anything I set out to do.'

'And you blame me for holding you back?'

Eva wondered what to say. "Yes" would have been at least partially accurate although she recognised she had allowed herself to become distracted by Mitsos. 'That's not what I'm saying. How about if I could find a way to see him without telling him who I am?'

'And how do you think you're going to achieve that?'

'I don't know,' said Eva, threading her necklace between her fingers.

'And this thing with your mum ... how do you think you're going to find out what happened to her?'

'I don't know that either,' Eva mumbled.

Millie caught sight of Vangelis searching for his passengers. 'I think we should be getting back,' she said.

As they started to walk towards the bus, Eva heard her phone ringing. She looked at it. Mitsos. She couldn't answer in front of Millie, as much as she wanted to speak to him.

'Are you going to answer that?' Millie asked.

'It's Amy. I'll call her back later.'

They got back to the bus and discovered they were first again. 'Why don't we have a quick coffee?' Eva suggested, seeing her chance.

Millie agreed and as she ordered the coffee, Eva excused herself and retreated to the bathroom.

Sorry I missed your call. I'm on an excursion and I can't talk because the guide is explaining things.

No problem. Is tonight still OK?

Yes. I'll meet you outside the Mimosa at 8.

OK. I'm really looking forward to seeing you.

Eva stared at the words which had appeared on the

screen. She realised she felt the same, but she also sensed the situation was moving fast and was in danger of spiralling out of control. Despite her misgivings, she found herself replying with *Me too*. She hurried back to join Millie.

As they left Vathi, Vangelis started to speak again. 'And today I have a special treat for you. We have added a new stop to the tour, but I won't tell you anything else about it yet. It's a little surprise.'

Millie and Eva shrugged at each other and then started to doze, lulled by the heat of the afternoon and the hypnotic bends as the road switched back and forth through the wooded hills. They woke up as they felt the bus come to a stop.

'This is our final stop of the day. Our surprise. We need to get off here and walk for a few minutes as the road from here is not good for our bus.'

They obediently got off the bus and started to walk up the road. As they walked, they noticed the road becoming narrower. A car would be able to get up there but not a bus.

Vangelis stopped. 'Now I will tell you a little more about our stop. This is a local farm, and they make many delicious products here. You can try them, and if you like them, you can buy them too. Their speciality is honey. Do you all like honey?'

The group agreed that they did indeed like honey and proceeded to follow Vangelis through a gate. Eva and Millie trailed behind and were about to go through the gate when Millie stopped, grabbed Eva's wrist and gasped.

'What's the matter, Millie?'

'Look at the sign, Eva.'

Eva looked at it, but it was written in Greek and although she had been studying the alphabet, she needed a moment to work it out.

'Petrakis?' Eva said and her eyes widened. 'Petrakis.'

'Yes, this must be Dimitris's place,' Millie whispered.

'It could be another Petrakis,' Eva suggested, not believing it herself.

'For goodness' sake, how's it going to be another Petrakis? Dimitris's family had a farm up above the town, which is where we are now. Helena mentioned it in her emails as well and said she found it because someone thought she wanted to buy some local produce. This is their farm.' Millie started walking back down the road faster than Eva had ever seen her move.

'Millie,' Eva called out after her.

Vangelis hurried over, while the rest of the group hung back, watching them. 'Is there a problem?'

'My grandmother isn't feeling very well. I think it's the heat. I'm going to stay with her.'

'Very well. The driver is there so the bus is unlocked.'

'Yes, thank you. Sorry. I must go.' Eva hurried down the road to catch up with Millie, who had already got back on the bus and was sitting on the edge of an aisle seat, her back to the windows.

Eva noticed how pale she was, and as she sat down, she realised that she was shaking as well.

'Millie?'

Millie didn't respond. Eva found some tissues in her bag,

wetted them using the water from her bottle and handed them to Millie, who dabbed at her forehead and neck. 'I told them the heat had got to you. I didn't know what else to say.'

Eventually Millie spoke. 'I want to go back to the apartment. Now.'

'You're safe here Millie. Nobody's going to come down here from the farm.'

'How do you know?'

'Why would they?'

'To check on the person who has been taken ill?'

'I doubt it. They're probably busy with the group.'

'Perhaps,' said Millie, taking a drink of water and patting her face with the tissue again.

'We shouldn't have to wait too long,' Eva said, hoping it was true.

'I knew this excursion was a bad idea.'

'To be fair, we'd had a good day up until now.'

Millie didn't respond, and the minutes crawled by. Eva got up to stretch her legs and saw movement through the back window of the bus. 'There's a car coming.'.

'What have you got me into?' Millie looked as though she was about to have a panic attack, and Eva managed to resist the temptation to bite back at the accusation.

She sat down on the aisle seat opposite Millie and took her hand. 'It's all going to be fine,' Eva said, wanting to convince herself as much as Millie. Behind Millie, she saw the car slowing down and silently hoped the driver would keep going, but the car came to a stop beside the bus.

'Can you see the driver?' Millie whispered.

'No. The window frame is in the way.' Eva went to stand up, and Millie grabbed her. 'Sit down.'

They sat low in their seats as though if they could not see the driver, they would somehow remain invisible.

A brief exchange followed between the bus driver and the man in the car. They heard the soft thud of a car door closing. Eva ventured a glance and saw the top of a man's head. He was standing on the steps of the bus. The conversation continued, and they saw the bus driver indicate back down the bus with a movement of his head and then a shrug. They heard the other man respond. Millie and Eva looked at each other and held their breath. Seconds which felt like hours ticked by. There was complete silence and then they heard the car's engine come to life again, and the car pulled away.

Eva chanced another look. 'He's gone.'

Millie looked over her shoulder, needing her own proof that what Eva had said was true. She turned round in her seat and leaned back against the headrest.

'Millie, I get that you don't want to see Dimitris, but at the farm gate and just now ... that wasn't not wanting to see someone. It was more than that.'

Millie met her gaze. 'There was something I didn't tell you.'

'What?'

Millie shook her head, but before Eva could challenge her, she saw the group coming back down the road. They piled onto the bus, chatting and clutching packages.

'When we get back I want to know, Millie.'

The drive back to the town took no more than ten minutes. The group had grown sleepy and even Vangelis seemed to have run out of steam. Millie and Eva didn't say a word to each other until they walked through the door of the apartment.

Eva brought them cold drinks, and they sat down at the table. Millie took a gulp of her drink and stared out of the window.

'What didn't you tell me, Millie?'

'Oh, it's something and nothing. It doesn't matter now anyway.'

'I think it does. You weren't just worried back there Millie. You were terrified.'

Millie took another drink. 'I didn't think it would do any good for you to know.'

Eva waited.

'You remember I told you that after my last night here, I went back to the Iris and then my aunt drove me back to town to catch the ferry in the morning?'

Eva nodded.

Millie took a deep breath. 'I was waiting for Aunt Sylvia outside the Iris that last morning. I needed some time alone.'

'Yes.'

'While I was waiting, a man appeared. I thought he was just passing by, but he had come to speak to me. It was Dimitris's father. He ... he told me to leave and he threatened me and also Aunt Sylvia if I came back. Even now, I can feel his hands around my throat.' Millie's hands involuntarily moved to her neck as though she was checking the bruises she had seen appear a few days later. She remembered how she had suddenly taken to wearing scarves to conceal them from her parents.

'He hurt you?'

'Yes, and he scared me rigid. I said I was leaving, and I wouldn't come back, and then he let me go and disappeared.'

'You said Aunt Sylvia died the spring after you came here. You don't think …?'

'No, no, of course not. She died in Australia, and there was nothing suspicious about the circumstances. Besides, I didn't go back and nobody told her about my pregnancy. She had no reason to speak to his family, and he had no reason to hurt her.'

'Did you tell my mum about this?'

'Yes, I thought it would be enough to tip the balance in favour of her not coming here.'

'Do you think he did something to mum?'

'I don't know, Eva. I really don't.'

'But you told the police about that when mum disappeared so they must have cleared him.'

Millie realised Eva had made an assumption which she should correct, but she didn't have the energy to deal with the fallout. She got up and refilled their glasses.

'Why didn't you tell me what happened with Dimitris's father?' Eva asked.

'I didn't think it would stop you. Just as it didn't stop Helena.'

'No, it wouldn't have made a difference,' Eva admitted. 'How old would he be by now?'

'I'm not sure. I'd say he was in his early forties so I suppose he'd be in his eighties.'

'Unlikely to be quite as intimidating now then?'

'I suppose not. But now do you see why I reacted that way at the farm? It still feels like yesterday to me. All of it does now, being here again.'

'Yes, I do,' Eva admitted.

'And do you understand why I didn't want to come here but couldn't let you come alone?'

'Yes, I do understand, but nobody knows who I am.'

'At the moment. Unless you go digging and stirring the past up again.'

'I promised you that I wouldn't do anything without telling you first, Millie, and I still mean that. So you don't need to worry about me when I go out.' Even as she said the words, she wondered how much longer she would be able to keep that promise when the clock was ticking down.

'Thank you.'

'I'm going to have a shower,' Eva said, getting up.

'I'll see you later.' Millie watched as Eva walked out of the room. She had told her one of her secrets. She thought about the others and wondered how long she would be able to keep them from Eva.

Chapter 12

Eva thought about the day's events; Millie's fear when she had arrived at the farm and her confession back at the apartment. She thought she should feel angry with Millie for not telling her before, but she couldn't find it within her when she had already been through so much. Then the thought of meeting Mitsos started to overtake her other concerns. Their date was getting closer, and she could feel the nerves creeping up on her.

'Where are you going, Eva?' Millie asked as Eva emerged from her bedroom.

'Nowhere special,' she said, unsure if she would get the lie past Millie, who usually had the ability to detect an untruth at twenty paces. It had been the curse of her rebellious phase.

'I thought we could go to the Mythos together.'

'Actually, Millie, I don't feel very hungry. I'm going to give dinner a miss tonight. I think I'll just go for a walk.' Eva saw the disappointment on Millie's face. 'Why don't you go without me? Yiannis and Maria know you now. They'll look after you. You won't feel alone there.'

'I'm sorry I didn't tell you about Dimitris's father,' Millie said. 'I should have done.'

'It wouldn't have changed my mind about coming here, but at least I understand why you keep telling me to be careful.'

'Yes.'

'But I'm sure he's not a threat to us now.' Eva looked past Millie's shoulder at the clock. 7.30. 'Why don't you go down to the Mythos now? While it's quiet.'

'Are you trying to get rid of me?' Millie asked, eyeing her suspiciously

'No, of course not, but when we went there later in the evening, you said you didn't enjoy it as much because it got too busy.'

'I suppose so,' said Millie. 'Are you sure you won't come with me?'

'Yes. If I feel hungry, I'll get something down by the harbour.'

Eva watched as Millie left the apartment and saw her walk down the road to the Mythos. Millie cut a lonely figure and she felt bad, but there was no way she could tell her about Mitsos. She quickly finished getting ready, feeling the tension within her build further and further.

She slipped out of the apartment and took the other road down to the harbour, to avoid passing anywhere near the Mythos. She could feel her heart rate increasing although she wasn't sure whether it was deceiving Millie or going to meet Mitsos which was causing it. She stopped, took a few deep breaths and then went on to the Mimosa, where Mitsos was waiting outside for her.

He gave her one of his breathtaking smiles. 'Hello Eva.'

'Hi,' Eva said, overcome by shyness.

'I thought we could get something to eat and then see what's on at the cinema. What do you think?'

'Yes, that sounds good,' Eva said although she felt so nervous she was not sure if she would be able to eat anything.

Mitsos led her up some stairs and through quiet side streets, lined by whitewashed walls. She had lost her bearings but suddenly thought they seemed to be heading on the direction of the Mythos.

'What's the name of the place where we're going?'

'Taverna Lefteris.'

Eva relaxed again. At least there was no chance that they would run into Millie.

They rounded another corner and through a gate in the walls, Eva saw tables set out with crisp white tablecloths under trees garlanded with lights.

'This is it,' Mitsos said and stood back to let Eva go first.

'Thank you. What a gorgeous place,' Eva said.

'And the food is good too.'

Eva asked Mitsos to order for her and used the time to think about what she could say to him. Small talk had always been difficult for her.

'I really don't know anything about you,' said Eva, as the waiter disappeared with their orders.

'What would you like to know?' Mitsos asked. 'Ask me anything,' he said with a smile.

'OK, how old are you?'

'Twenty. And you?'

'Eighteen.'

'Are you still at school?'

'I've just finished. I'm supposed to start university next month to study architecture.' She paused. 'If I get the grades I need.'

'Supposed to?'

It occurred to Eva that Mitsos had picked up on the "supposed to", and she was impressed by that. 'All through school, I was sure that was what I wanted to do. I think I still do, but just recently I've been having a few doubts.'

'Why?'

Eva was forced to try to put them into words for the first time. 'I'm not sure really. I think it's because when I was at school, it was all about the next project I had to do or the next exam. Now, I'm here, and this is the first time I've had time to think about things. Get a bit of perspective.'

'Perspective is good. It's better to change your mind now than do something which doesn't make you happy.'

'Yes, that's true.'

'You told me you are from London.'

'Yes.'

'I have never been to London, but it's a big city and cities are all rush, rush, rush. It's not healthy. No time to think.'

'You're right,' Eva admitted. 'That's one of the things I love about Andraxos. There's time to stop and time to think.'

'It's the best place in the world.'

'Have you travelled a lot?'

'Not really. Only in Greece and that was mainly for military service.'

'You were in the army?' Eva could not hide her surprise. The army seemed totally at odds with Mitsos's character.

'Yes, it's compulsory here.'

'How long did you have to do that for?'

'Nine months, and I hated every day. I mean I love my country and if I had to, I would defend it, but it's not the life for me.'

'It must have been horrible, being forced to do it.'

'Yes, but it made me appreciate Andraxos even more.'

'So you don't want to travel? See the world?' Eva smiled. It was what everyone of her age said they wanted to do.

'What for? I have everything I need here. Well, almost.'

'Almost?'

'I work with my uncle a lot of the time. He's a fisherman. I don't like it much, but I'd never tell him that. I mean I love the sea, but I don't like the job. Times are changing, though. It's a dying industry. He'll probably have to give up the boat before long and that will break his heart. Nothing stays the same.'

It occurred to Eva that he suddenly seemed older than his years – not the cheerful barman or the quiet artist. This was another facet of a complex person; a thoughtful person.

'Anyway, that's another story. In the summer, I also work in the bar. It's OK, but what I would really like to do is something with art; more than a few portraits in the summer months.'

'You're good enough.'

'Maybe, but I think I would have to go to Athens or Thessaloniki to study and sell my work. I don't want to do that.'

'Perhaps there's another way. I mean I don't know anything about how things work here, but maybe you could do courses online if you needed to learn special techniques. And you could advertise your work on social media.'

Mitsos considered what she had said. 'You might be right. I will think about it. Thank you.'

'And if your uncle is going to have to give up fishing, it would be the perfect time to do something else.'

'Perhaps. My family are all wonderful, but they have never encouraged me to be an artist. They don't think it's a proper job and sometimes that makes me sad.'

'I think they should.' Eva blushed. 'Sorry, I shouldn't say that.'

'No, it's OK. I wish they would too. But what about you? Tell me more about yourself.'

And Eva found herself telling Mitsos about her life; an edited version in which both her parents had died when she was young but in which she avoided mentioning any connection with the island. She hated the omission, but her loyalty to Millie prevented her from telling him everything although every time she met his eyes, the only thing she wanted to do was tell him the complete truth.

* * *

'That was so good,' said Eva as she put her knife and fork down.

'Do you want anything else?'

'No, I can't move now.'

Mitsos laughed. 'Could you move as far as the harbour?'

'I'll try,' said Eva.

They said good night to Lefteris and walked back down to the harbour. Mitsos stopped in front of the cinema and consulted the programme. 'Have you been to an open air cinema before?'

'No, never.'

'It's a Greek film tonight, but there are English subtitles.'

'That's fine,' said Eva. 'It sounds like fun.'

They bought tickets and took the stairs up to the rooftop. A huge screen and rows of chairs had been set up and behind the screen, the upper town rose above them. 'Even if you don't like the film, it's worth coming up here for the view. Look.' Mitsos guided Eva to the balustrade.

Below, the lower part of the town stretched before them. The sea had become a swathe of grey silk brushed by the last light of the sun, the final diamonds of light skimming the surface of the water. The distant mountains were now an indistinct purple haze. The lights were flickering on in town and the occasional isolated light twinkled out on the headland.

'I could look at this view forever.' Eva said, transfixed.

'I know, but for now we should probably get some seats. It's starting to get busy.'

They reluctantly dragged themselves away and sat down. The buzz of voices around them started to subside as the lights went down, and the film started. Eva concentrated intently on the film. It was a good chance for her to learn more about Greece.

'Are you enjoying it?'

'Yes, I am.' Eva said, not taking her eyes from the screen as she followed the subtitles.

'Good. I thought it might be boring for you being all about Greece.'

'No, not at all.'

One of the actors started to sing, and the subtitles disappeared. 'I can translate, but I don't think it will make much sense if you don't know the history of the song.' Mitsos whispered.

'You don't always need to know the words to understand, do you?' Eva said, and as he looked at her, she felt the connection she had always longed to feel with someone.

Mitsos took her hand in his, and they turned back to watch the end of the film.

* * *

'Did you have a good evening?' Mitsos asked her as they queued to leave.

'Yes, I really did. Thank you.'

'I'm happy. I enjoyed it too. Can I see you again?'

'Yes,' Eva said without hesitation. 'I would like that very much.'

'I can walk you back to your apartment.'

'That's not necessary,' Eva said, thinking of Millie.

'I would like to.'

'Yes, I know but … it's just my friend.'

'What about your friend?'

'If she sees me with you, she'll have a million questions, and I won't get a moment's peace until she has decided she knows every last detail.'

Mitsos laughed. 'Well, I don't want to put you through that. I'll call you.'

'OK.'

He moved closer to her and gently touched her face. As he left, Eva realised just how much she had hoped he was going to kiss her and wondered why he hadn't. She walked back to the apartment, replaying every moment of the evening, and she was unsure whether she was more confused or elated. She was still torn between the two emotions when she walked into the apartment but felt elation was gaining the upper hand. As she caught sight of Millie, however, she realised she would have some explaining to do.

'Hi,' she said to Millie, who was making a drink in the kitchen.

'Hello.'

Eva picked up on her tone of voice immediately and felt her happiness starting to evaporate. 'What's happened?'

'You could check your phone occasionally.'

Eva looked in her bag and found her phone, which she had put on silent mode. Two missed calls and three messages from Millie. 'Sorry. I forgot it was on silent.'

'You know how much I worry about you here.'

'Yes, I do.'

'And…' Millie started but broke off.

'And what?'

'Nothing. Absolutely nothing.'

'Millie? It's obviously not "nothing".'

'Nothing is part of the problem.'

Eva looked at Millie, waiting for her to explain.

'Do you remember what you said about why you wanted to come here?'

'Yes. I said I wanted to learn more about the island.'

'What else?'

'Find out about my family.'

'And?'

'What happened to mum,' Eva mumbled.

'And what have you done since we've been here?'

'I've read loads of stuff about Greece and Andraxos.'

'You could have done that in London.'

'And I've finally got to see the town and the Iris, and we've been on an excursion around the island. I feel I know more about the place now. I couldn't have done all that if I hadn't come here.'

'You seem to have spent most of your time on the beach and in bars, judging by what you tell me. Not that you tell me much anymore.'

'What's that supposed to mean?'

' 'Where did you go tonight?'

'To the harbour.'

'But you didn't want to join me at the Mythos,' Millie remarked.

'I told you earlier that I wasn't hungry. I just wanted some air.'

Millie looked at her.

'Anyway, what if I do go to the beach or a bar? It's supposed to be a holiday too.'

'Oh yes, a great holiday stuck in here.'

'You don't have to be "stuck in here", Millie. You could go out.'

'Really? Look what happened today.'

'That was just bad luck.'

'Was it?' Millie gave her another one of her looks.

'I don't know what to say, Millie.'

I just don't know what we're doing here. You – or we – could have gone anywhere.'

Eva dropped her bag on the floor. 'What is that you want me to do, Millie? You told me you didn't want me to look for my grandfather or try to find out about mum. Now you're angry that I'm keeping my promise.'

Millie fell silent. She hated herself for being angry with Eva. The situation was not of Eva's own making, and she knew Eva was dealing with all the revelations which had come at her in the best way she could. She sat down wearily. 'I'm sorry. I'm not handling any of this very well. I shouldn't blame you.'

Eva sat down opposite her. 'I didn't think coming here would be this bad. You must hate me.'

'Eva, I might be angry with you, but there is nothing that could ever make me hate you.' Millie got up, picked up her book and headed in the direction of her bedroom before turning to add, 'If you think I could, you still have a lot to learn about me.'

Eva retreated to her bedroom and as she got ready to go

to bed, she thought about the evening: the connection she had felt with Mitsos; the conversation with Millie. The earlier elation had given way to confusion. She had achieved her aim to see Andraxos, but she had done nothing about trying to locate her family, much less solve the mystery of her mother's disappearance. What had seemed plausible at home, seemed so much more difficult now that she was actually there.

She got into bed and read her mother's emails again. As she drifted off to sleep, she found herself in a forest, which grew more impenetrable the further she ventured into it. She was looking for someone or something, but she had no idea who or what it was. She suddenly realised she was no longer alone, and she was now the hunted instead of the hunter. She felt someone's breath on her neck and then hands close around it. She gasped, opened her eyes and fought to get her breath. She found the light and the warm glow filled the room. *There's nothing to be afraid of. It was just a dream*, she told herself as she looked at the emails scattered across the floor.

Chapter 13

Eva slipped quietly out of the apartment and walked down to the harbour where Mitsos was waiting for her. It was still early, too early for Eva normally, but the purity of the early morning light and the thought of meeting Mitsos had given her a shot of adrenaline.

'Where are we going?' Eva asked.

'I want to show you a very special place.'

'Where is it?'

'Do you trust me?'

'Yes,' said Eva, realising that even if he had asked her the question as a joke, she really did trust him.

'Let's go then.'

They walked to the end of the harbour, where the buildings started to thin out, and Mitsos guided Eva to a car.

They set off and as they rounded the bend in the road, they were suddenly out of town and in a landscape which was rich and green despite the heat of high summer. Mitsos took the winding switchbacks as if they held as much challenge as a smooth motorway. Eva saw the road running perilously close to the cliff edges, where sheer rock faces tumbled into the turquoise shallows far below.

Feeling slightly dizzy, she forced herself to stop looking at the drop so close to the car and looked instead at Mitsos. She tried to identify what it was about him that drew her to him beyond the physical attraction. She had been touched by a degree of sensitivity and perceptiveness she hadn't previously encountered in the men she knew.

Mitsos turned and smiled at her. 'Are you OK?'

'Yes,' Eva said, realising she had been staring at him.

He turned off the road and parked. 'I hope you're ready to walk.'

'Where are we going?' Eva asked, as she tried to evade the brambles which scratched at her legs.

'To the pool.'

Mitsos seemed to have springs in his legs and Eva, who wanted to impress him, felt herself falling short. She found herself telling him she wanted to take photos to give herself a moment to catch her breath, hoping he wouldn't notice.

Her hopes were dashed, however. 'I don't mind if you need to stop. I'm used to this countryside and this heat. You're not.'

Eva wasn't sure whether she liked the fact that he had noticed or not.

'We're nearly there. It's just down here.'

Mitsos helped her down the hill and over the rocks, and Eva looked at the scene which unfolded in front of her. It was a place from a magical fantasy world; a pool almost completely surrounded by vertical rock walls apart from the approach path they had taken. At the far end, a waterfall cascaded into the pool. The early rays of soft, silver light slipped between the leaves and warmed the ground.

'Did you bring your swimsuit?'

'No, I forgot.' Eva lied. Ever since Mitsos had told her to bring one, she had known that she would conveniently forget. If she could barely face being seen in a swimsuit by strangers she would probably never see again, she certainly couldn't face being seen by Mitsos.

Mitsos's face fell. 'That's a shame. This is the perfect place to swim.'

'You go ahead. I'm happy just to sit here.'

'Are you sure?'

Eva nodded.

Mitsos pulled off his T-shirt and shorts. Stripped down to the swimming trunks which he had on under his shorts, he walked to the edge of the pool. Eva stared at him, a million thoughts flooding through her mind. She had experienced teenage crushes on actors and singers she would never meet, but passion had been absent from her relationship with Tom. This was the first time she had experienced desire for a man who was right in front of her.

He turned and smiled at her and then waded into the water. The tessellated patterns playing on the surface drifted apart as he plunged in. She moved closer and watched him cut through the pale green water. He broke the water's surface and shook his head, like a dog shaking the water off its coat.

'You should come in.'

'I can't,' said Eva, indicating her clothes.

'You could come in anyway.'

'With all my clothes on?'

'Why not? They'll dry in minutes.'

'I don't think so,' said Eva, wishing she was brave enough to do as he had suggested. But then she thought of revealing so much of herself; a soaked T-shirt would be totally unforgiving.

'Please?'

Eva hesitated and then remembered Tom asking her if she had put on weight. 'No, really. It's my fault. I should have remembered, but you enjoy your swim.'

'Are you sure?'

'Yes, really. Go on.'

Eva watched Mitsos. She was surrounded by the beauty of the pool, the waterfall and the glade, but the only thing she could look at was Mitsos. He emerged from the water, his shorts clinging to him, and Eva forced herself to look away.

He reached for a towel and retrieved some drinks from his backpack.

'I really wish you could have joined me. Will you next time?'

'Yes,' said Eva. She would think about how to get out of that later.

Mitsos put his drink down and lay down on his back. 'I think this is one of my favourite places on the island.'

Eva settled down beside him and stared up at the trees. 'I can understand why. It's so beautiful and peaceful.'

'It can get busy later on in the day in the middle of summer. That's why I suggested coming here early. That and the fact I have to go to work later. We don't have to share it with anyone.'

Eva felt something turn in her as Mitsos referred to them as we. Almost as if he considered them to be a couple. She thought again of the image of him in the pool. She gave herself a mental shake and sat up.

Mitsos reached across and stroked her back. 'What is it?'

Eva felt shivers down her spine at his touch. 'Nothing.'

'I think it's because you are from London.'

Eva looked at him. 'What do you mean?'

'In the city, there is always noise and there are always people. Without those things, people from a city feel on edge.'

'Perhaps,' Eva admitted. There was some truth in it, but the feelings she was experiencing were so much more than that and so much more than she could admit to Mitsos.

'You know, this is the perfect place for a sleep.'

'What now?'

Mitsos nodded. 'Lie down. Close your eyes and relax.'

Eva laughed. 'I don't know.'

'Try it.'

'Are you serious?'

'Yes.'

Eva did as Mitsos suggested, and they lay down side by side again. Mitsos reached for her hand. 'Don't be afraid of the peace.' Eva listened to the waterfall and found herself drifting to sleep.

When she woke up, she saw that Mitsos was still asleep. She glanced at her watch and realised she had been asleep for about half an hour. Eva noticed Mitsos stir, and he turned to face her.

'Did you sleep?'

'Yes, and I feel better now than after a whole night's sleep.'

'I told you. There's something special about this place.'

'There really is. I can't remember the last time I felt this relaxed. Thank you for bringing me here.'

'It's my pleasure. The only problem is we have to go back, and I have to go to work.'

'I wish we didn't have to leave yet.'

'So do I.' Mitsos stood up and helped Eva to her feet. It suddenly occurred to her that perhaps she could confide in Mitsos about the real reasons she was there and enlist his help. It would mean admitting to a lie about her mother, but she thought she would be able to explain that. Time was passing and the urgency to do something was becoming ever more important than worrying about how Millie would react if she took the initiative.

'Mitsos, I want to ask you something.'

'Sure, anything.'

Eva heard her phone ringing and silently cursed it. Of all the times she should have put it on silent mode, this was one of them.

'Do you want to get that?'

'No.'

'You should. It might be your friend.'

Eva was about to ask which friend he was referring to when she remembered her lie about who she was there with. She pulled her phone out. It was Millie.

'Hello.'

'Hello dear. I woke up and you'd gone. I was worried.'

'No need,' Eva replied, looking at Mitsos.

'Where are you?'

'Just out and about.'

'You're not doing anything are you?' Millie asked.

'What do you mean?'

'You know what I mean. Trying to find a certain person.'

'No, I'm not.'

'All right. I'll see you later then?'

'Yes.'

Eva shoved her phone back in her pocket.

'Problems?'

'No. Everything's fine.'

'What did you want to ask me?'

Eva looked at him, and her nerve failed her. Millie's intrusion could not have been more perfectly timed if she had tried. 'Nothing. It'll keep.'

Mitsos led her back along the path to the car. They reached the road, and she realised he had not let go of her hand and she was in no hurry for him to do so. He looked at her and hesitated. Eva thought he might finally kiss her, but then the moment was gone, and he turned back towards the car.

As they drove back, Eva felt that familiar sense of happiness and confusion. She couldn't understand what was going on or even think how to frame a question to ask Mitsos. She was still thinking about it when, in front of them, she noticed a shape on the side of the road.

'Mitsos, did you see that?' Eva asked as they passed it.

'What?'

'There was something on the side of the road.'

'What was it?' Mitsos asked.

I don't know, but can we go back and have a look? I'm sorry; I know you need to get to work.'

'It's OK. Let's take a look,' said Mitsos, reversing.

Eva was out of the car before Mitsos had turned off the engine. He found her cradling a dog in her arms, both of them covered in blood. She looked up at him, tears in her eyes. 'He's in a bad way. I don't know what to do.'

Mitsos crouched down and gently stoked the dog's head. 'I have a blanket in the back of the car. We'll wrap him up and take him to Pantelis. He's the vet,' he added by way of explanation.

Eva stayed with the dog and when Mitsos returned, they managed to put the blanket around him and carry him to the car. Eva sat in the back with the dog while Mitsos drove and made phone calls. Eva wished she could understand what he was saying, but it was impossible. Back in town, they carried the dog into the surgery.

Pantelis conducted his examination, and Eva stood watching in frustration as Mitsos and Pantelis had a long discussion.

'What did he say?' Eva asked when there was a pause in the conversation.

'He says it looks worse than it is, and he's pretty sure he can help him.'

'Thank goodness for that,' Eva said, relief hitting her. She looked up at Mitsos, whose top was covered in blood. 'You can't go into the bar like that. Are you going to get into trouble?'

'No, I phoned them when we were in the car. The bar isn't busy at the moment. They'll survive without me while I go home and change.'

'That's good. Mitsos, thank you so much for helping him.'

'Why wouldn't I?' He looked astonished, as though helping the dog had been the most natural thing in the world.

Eva thought back to Tom's dog, Dylan, crawling out from under the bed. 'Not everybody cares as much as you.'

Mitsos looked embarrassed by the compliment. 'Come on, we should go.'

'And what about him?' Eva asked, looking back in the direction of the dog.

'I'll come back and check on him, and Pantelis has my phone number.'

'Don't we have to pay?'

'Don't worry about that.'

They walked back to the car. 'I have to go home and wash and change. I'm sorry about how our morning ended.'

'You have nothing to apologise for. You were amazing,' Eva dropped her head, feeling infuriated at the fact she could feel herself blushing.

'When can I see you again?'

'Whenever you have time. I'm not working. You are.'

Mitsos touched her face, and Eva thought the moment she had been thinking about had finally come, but he dropped his hand and simply said. 'I'll call you.'

Eva watched him drive away. He obviously thinks I'm lonely, she thought to herself, and he's just being kind to me. She had sensed it was more, but then she thought she just wanted it to be more.

She wondered about the life which awaited her back in England. As she thought about the doubts she had mentioned to Mitsos a few days before, she realised there was more to it than having a chance to get some perspective; it was the thought of the endless hours of study, the pressure of exams, being mired in debt. A simpler life had its allure. And in Andraxos everything really did seem so simple and so clear in some ways. And then there was Mitsos.

Eva looked down and for the first time, noticed her own blood-soaked clothes. Aware of how she must look, she stopped at the first shop she came to and bought an inexpensive scarf to wrap around her. As she was about to leave the shop, she saw her. The woman was looking through the books in the stalls outside the next shop. She looked so much like her mother in the photos she had seen of her.

The woman turned away and Eva moved towards her, trying to see her face again. She edged closer to the shop and started to look at the books, alternating between glancing at them and the woman who still had her back to her. Eva circled round to the next stand, glimpsing the woman's profile through the metalwork of the stands holding postcards. Her heart was thumping, all reason lost. The woman moved on to the next shop, and Eva followed her, any pretense at window shopping abandoned.

The woman stopped and was greeted by the shop owner as an old friend. A conversation followed in Greek. Eva wished yet again that she could speak Greek and speak it well enough to tell if she had a foreign, English accent. While they were engaged in conversation, Eva saw her opportunity and moved round to where she could finally see the woman's face. She broke off her conversation, and Eva became aware that the woman was staring at her with a puzzled look on her face. She said something to Eva.

'I don't speak Greek,' Eva mumbled, glad they would not be able to communicate further.

'Do I know you?' The switch to English caught Eva by surprise.

'No,' Eva said, looking at her. She looked so much like her mother had, but then Eva realised her mother would be in her forties by now, and this woman was around the age her mother had been in the photos she had seen.

'So?' The woman looked at her, curious more than angry.

'Nothing. I thought – it's nothing.' Eva pulled the scarf more tightly around her. 'Sorry,' she said and hurried away, shivering in spite of the warmth of the day.

* * *

'You're back early,' Millie remarked, her back to the door, bent over the fridge.

'What? Oh yes. Back in a moment.'

Eva rushed into her bedroom, changed into clean clothes and ran a brush though her hair. She had just about stopped shaking. She took a few deep breaths.

'Eva, do you want a drink?' Millie called.

'Yes, please. On my way.'

Eva came back into the kitchen and threw her bundled-up top into the washing machine before joining Millie at the table. Millie watched her. Eva was doing nothing more than sipping her drink, but she was fizzing with pent-up energy.

'You were out early this morning. What did you do?'

'I went for a walk.'

'You look well for it. You're glowing.'

'It was quite a strenuous walk. Good exercise.' Eva thought of Mitsos and watching him swim. Her mind wandered to the image of his body cutting through the water, and how she had wished she had had the courage to join him. She thought of how gently he had helped her carry the dog to his car. And then her thoughts switched to the woman she had seen in town.

'Any plans for later?' Millie looked at Eva, who was a million miles away. 'Eva?'

'Sorry?'

'Do you have any plans for this evening?'

'Not really. I thought we could do something together.'

'I'd like that. The Mythos?'

'If you like. Or try somewhere else. I'm happy to do anything you want,' Eva said.

'In that case, let's try that other place. The one when you

come out of here and turn left.'

'That sounds great. I think I might go and have a shower,' said Eva, wanting to be alone with her thoughts.

'We'll have a quiet afternoon here then and leave at seven o'clock?'

'Yes, I'll be ready.'

Eva walked towards her room, and Millie thought about their exchange. Eva had said nothing out of the ordinary, but Millie recognised the signs. She had had her suspicions before and had dismissed them, but now she knew. She had seen the dreamy look on her face, the flush of excitement. Eva had met someone.

Eva went to her room and looked out over the town. Her meetings with Mitsos had started as a delicious secret, but had turned into something more than that. She thought again about the woman she had seen; she was a reminder of what Eva had failed to do. Another day had passed, and she had done nothing about finding her family. Mitsos had continued to distract her, and there was still the intractable problem of Millie's absolute resistance to her doing anything. Something would have to give, but she was not yet sure what that would be.

Chapter 14

'Hi,' said Eva, answering her phone and experiencing the familiar nervous excitement she felt when she heard Mitsos's voice.

'Hello Eva. How are you?'

'Fine. And you?'

'I have good news and bad news.'

'Start with the good news.'

'The dog we found is out of danger. '

'I'm so relieved.' Eva paused. 'But what will happen to him now?'

'I'll bring him home. We've got plenty of space.'

'I'm glad he's going to be with you. But what's the bad news?'

'I have to go to Athens for a few days with my dad.'

'OK,' Eva replied, trying to conceal her disappointment.

'I don't want to go, but I can't get out of it. Can we meet when I get back?'

'Of course.' Eva could hear a man calling out to Mitsos.

'That's my dad. I'm sorry, I have to go, but I'll see you

soon. It will only be two or three days at most. Bye.'

'Bye.' Eva looked at the phone and realised how deflated she felt.

She thought about the plan which had been starting to form and decided that in the absence of Mitsos, it was the perfect time to put it into action and finally find out about the Petrakis family. She thought about it all day and came close to telling Millie. She had promised to tell her before she did anything, but she didn't feel equipped to deal with her reaction. She convinced herself that her idea walked a fine line between doing what she wanted and keeping Millie happy and, after sleeping on it for another night, and a further morning of contemplation, she announced she was going out after lunch.

'Where are you going? You're not dressed for the beach,' Millie remarked, looking at Eva, who was wearing walking boots.

'I thought I'd go for a hike.'

'Again? Are you going alone?' Millie asked, thinking of Eva's recent behaviour. She was so sure she had met someone, but could not find a way to work it into a conversation. Andraxos seemed to have drained her of her normal capabilities.

'Yes,' said Eva, surprised. She wasn't sure what Millie was getting at.

'Do you think that's a good idea?'

'Why not?'

'You could get lost.'

Eva waved her phone. 'Maps. I'll be fine.'

'Have you got water with you?'

'Yes. Don't worry, Millie.'

Millie watched her go and cursed her knee. She couldn't have gone with Eva even if she had managed to persuade herself to leave the apartment. Everything was slipping further out of her control. They had been lucky so far, but Millie was not sure how long that luck would hold.

Eva walked down to the taxi rank and got dropped off close to the Petrakis farm. She watched the taxi circle round, kick up the dust at the side of the road and then disappear round the bend.

She stood there for a moment, rehearsing again what she would say. She took a deep breath. It was all clear. She walked up to the gate and paused. She thought of how Millie would react if she could see her and took a step back. Then she thought of her mother and her grandfather and slipped through the gate with her heart pounding. Her life up to that point had culminated in the simple act of walking through that gate.

She looked around, wondering which direction to go in. To her left, the pine forest stretched into the distance. There was a path straight ahead and another one to her right. It had all seemed easy in her mind, but now she wasn't so sure.

She ventured a little further past the gate and turned to look back at it. It wasn't too late. She could go back.

Behind her, she heard a woman's voice saying something in Greek.

Eva turned and saw Yiannis's wife, Maria. 'Eva!' she exclaimed.

'Maria.'

'What are you doing here?'

Despite her surprise, Eva came out with her carefully rehearsed line. 'I heard this was the best place to come to buy local products like honey so I thought I'd come and have a look.'

'Would you like to come to the shop with me?'

'Yes, yes, I would. Thank you.' The pounding in Eva's heart started to slow although the questions in her head continued to buzz around frantically.

Maria led her up the path in front of them and through some olive trees. A small wooden cabin was set in a clearing. 'Come in.'

Eva followed her in to the shop.

'Now what are you interested in?'

'I'm not sure. I'd like to take something home to remind me of Andraxos. Could you show me what you have?'

'Yes, of course.'

Maria started showing Eva all of the products in the shop, complete with full explanations. Eva murmured and added "yes" and "really" at what she hoped were suitable moments, but she was barely listening. She was thinking about how to turn the conversation round to finding out more about the Petrakis family and also to finding out why Maria was there.

'What do you think?' Maria asked.

'Oh, I don't know. Everything looks lovely.' Eva picked up a couple of bars of honey soap. 'I'm a bit limited for space, but I could fit these into my bag. Could I take these?'

Maria nodded. 'Of course. How did you get here?' she asked.

'I took a taxi.'

'How will you get back?'

'I thought I could walk. It's all downhill on the way into town.'

'If you can wait, I'll take you.'

'But what about the shop?'

'It closes at five and it's half past four now. I'll go past you in the car if you start walking now. Unless you'd prefer to walk?'

'No,' Eva said, seeing a possibility opening up to learn more. 'That's very kind, thank you.'

'Let's sit down and have a drink. I don't think there will be many more customers at this time of day.'

They went outside, and Eva sat down at the small table by the door. Maria disappeared and returned with some orange juice.

'So you work here as well as doing all the cooking at the Mythos?'

'Not usually. I'm just helping out here today. This is my father's farm so I can't really say no when he asks me to help,' she said, smiling.

Eva felt her heart rate ramp up again. She tried to think of an intelligent question which would not sound suspicious but was saved by Maria's chatty nature.

'The farm has been in my family further back than anyone can remember. Dimitris, my father, must be the fourth or fifth generation, I think.'

Dimitris, Eva thought. There could no longer be any doubt about whether this was the right place. She took a long drink, which saved her from having to say anything for a few precious moments. 'Could I possibly have another one?'

'Yes. I think I'll join you. It's a hot one today.'

Maria disappeared again and Eva tried to collect her thoughts. *Get a grip*, she told herself. *You won't have another chance like this.*

Maria set down another couple of glasses. 'Thank you,' Eva said. 'Growing up on a farm must have been fun.'

'Sometimes. I liked helping out when I was a child. When I got older and I had more school work, it wasn't as much fun, but I still had to do it. I have two brothers though, and they do most of the work.'

'What are their names?'

'Nikos is the eldest and then there is my younger brother Vasilis.'

Nikos – that name again. It was hard for her to reconcile the fear he had instilled in her mother with this place of tranquility. If Nikos was only half as affable as Maria, she couldn't imagine how the events of fourteen years ago could have played out.

'Eva?'

'Sorry, what did you say?'

'Would you like more juice?'

'Oh no, no thank you.'

'I'll take these back and lock up. Give me five minutes.'

Eva sat back in her chair and assessed what she had learned. This was definitely her grandfather's farm. Any doubt about that had been eliminated. Nikos was still around so perhaps she could find a way to meet him although she couldn't imagine how she would be able to engineer that. Maria was Dimitris's daughter. And then it hit her – Maria was her aunt, or half-aunt.

She saw Maria appear and watched as she closed the windows and locked the door. She wished she could tell her and give her a hug, but the reality of the situation intruded, and she resisted the impulse.

They walked down to where Maria had parked her car. Eva was quiet on the way back, preoccupied with what Maria had told her. She felt there were so many more questions she wanted to ask but none that would not seem inquisitive at best or strange at worst.

'Are you feeling all right?' Maria asked.

'Yes. It's just the heat. I always feel sleepy at this time of day.'

'Where shall I leave you?'

'By the harbour if that's OK.'

'Yes, no problem.'

Eva got out of the car and waved as Maria pulled away. She walked past the mounds of yellow fishing nets piled up by the edge of the harbour and sat down on a bench. She watched the boats float on the clear, calm water and breathed in time to their movement, searching for peace.

* * *

Back in the apartment, Millie noticed something in the washing machine. She frowned; she was sure she had emptied it after the last wash. She went over to it and pulled out Eva's top. It was dry and had not been washed. She vaguely remembered Eva throwing something in there a few days before. She turned it round and saw that the front was drenched in blood. She threw it back in the machine and closed the door. Her stomach clenched into a knot of fear. *Eva is fine. She is not in danger,* she repeated to herself over and over again, but another voice inside her head wondered about her granddaughter's frequent outings, her changed behaviour and now clothes covered in blood. The thought she might lose Eva too was beyond contemplation.

* * *

Eva started to drift into a daydream. She heard the creaking of the ropes as the boats occasionally strained against them and the sound of the tackle hitting the masts. Eva had always loved the water and boats, and she found the sounds restful. She looked round and took in the town, bathed in the sunlight of late afternoon. From that angle the rise on which the town stood was dwarfed by the hills which rose behind it

She started to feel calmer and then other thoughts intruded. If Millie saw Maria the next time they went to the Mythos, she might mention Eva's visit to the farm, and Millie would be furious with her. Even Yiannis might mention it. And how would Millie react if she found out that Maria was Dimitris's daughter? By trying to dig for information, she had given herself a whole new series of problems.

She heard her phone vibrate and fished it out of her pocket. Mitsos.

Hi. I'll be back tomorrow. Can you meet me in the evening?

Yes. Where are we going? Eva replied.

The beach?

Eva thought about the prospect of Mitsos seeing her in a swimsuit. *How about another walk?*

It'll be too late. The beach would be better.

Eva sighed. She'd have to come up with something by tomorrow. *OK.*

Meet me in the main square at 8?

Yes. See you then.

Eva sat, phone in hand, tapping it against her palm as she contemplated what to do about Millie. She was bound to find out what she had done so it would be better to tell her. But then again, another voice said, she might not find out and then there would have been more conflict for no reason.

She pulled herself away from the tranquil waterfront and walked back to the apartment, stopping on the way to pick up some food.

'Did you enjoy your walk, dear?'

'Yes, it was very enjoyable.'

'Is everything all right?'

'Yes, of course,' Eva replied.

'I thought we could go to the Mythos a bit later.'

Eva indicated the bag of shopping in her hand. 'I thought I'd cook.'

Millie took off her reading glasses and examined Eva. 'You? Cook?'

'I know how to cook. You taught me.'

'Yes and I also know that although you are perfectly capable, it's not something you normally choose to do.'

Eva shrugged. 'I felt like a change. I'll have to start getting used to it when I go to university.'

Millie watched as she put everything away and thought again about Eva's blood-soaked top.

'Dinner at eight?' Eva asked.

Millie nodded.

'I'm going to have a shower first.'

'Eva?'

'Yes?'

Millie looked at Eva and thought of all the things she wanted to say and ask, but it didn't seem to be the right moment for any of them. 'Nothing.'

Chapter 15

Eva spent the day with Millie, counting the hours until she could go to meet Mitsos.

'Where are you going?'

'Just for a walk, a bit of window shopping. Nothing specific,' Eva said, as casually as she could.

'I thought we might have dinner together.'

'I'm not really hungry, but don't let me stop you.'

'I might go the Mythos.'

Eva imagined the conversation Millie might have with Maria. 'You could try somewhere different.'

'Why?' Millie asked, giving Eva a look that made her feel as if Millie could see right through her.

'No reason. Just for a change.'

Millie continued to give Eva what she always thought of as The Look. 'We'll see.'

* * *

Eva finally headed out, leaving Millie alone again, and found Mitsos waiting for her.

He kissed her on the cheek. 'I missed you.'

'I missed you too.'

'What have you been doing?'

Eva thought about her visit to the farm. She was starting to regret it now, but she couldn't tell Mitsos about it without explaining why she had gone there in the first place.

'Not a lot. Sunbathing and shopping,' she replied truthfully. After all, she had been shopping at the farm. 'How was your trip?'

'Horrible. All that big city stress.'

'You wouldn't like London then,' Eva said with a smile.

'I might like it more if you were showing me around.'

Eva felt her stomach flip over and changed the subject. 'You said you wanted to go to the beach?'

'You don't want to?'

Eva shrugged. She had spent the previous night considering different excuses as to why she couldn't appear in a swimsuit in front of Mitsos and playing out different scenarios in her mind to explain away her visit to the farm to Millie, but she had come up with the sum total of nothing on both fronts.

'I suppose it's boring if you go there every day. How about going out on the boat?'

'The boat?'

'Yes, my family has a boat. I mean another one apart from the fishing boat. You won't have to sit among the fishing nets.'

Eva laughed. 'I'd love to do that.'

'Come on then.'

Eva followed him to the boat and watched as Mitsos

expertly manoeuvred it out of the harbour. She could see how he came alive when he was at sea, just as he did when he was talking about art. They rounded the headland, and Eva saw the Villa Iris and the beach below come into view.

'I'm going to moor the boat over there,' Mitsos said, pointing to a small jetty at the far end of the beach.

They got off the boat and watched as the sun set and drew a path across the water. 'I don't think I'd ever leave if I lived here,' Eva said.

'I'm happy you love my island.'

My island too, thought Eva. *If only I could tell him.*

They walked the length of the beach. They didn't talk much, but Eva felt they didn't need to. There was a quiet contentment in being there together. As they arrived back at the jetty, Mitsos looked up and saw the clouds passing across the moon, finally covering it completely. He smiled and motioned to Eva. He leaned over and put his hand in the water. It turned blue and flashed with electricity.

Eva gasped. 'What is that?'

'It's bioluminescence.'

'Is it dangerous?'

'No, not at all. Do you want to swim?'

Eva hesitated. Now it was dark she thought she might be brave enough.

'I'll go in first, and you can see what it is like.' He got into the water and it lit up around him. 'You have to come in.'

'I'll be there in a moment. I'll catch you up.'

'OK.' Mitsos started to carve a path through the water,

making it shimmer blue and when Eva judged that he was far enough away, she removed her shorts and slipped off the side of the jetty. The water sparkled around her. She started to swim towards Mitsos, and he stopped to wait for her.

'It's like swimming through stars,' she said.

'Isn't it beautiful? You are very lucky. We don't see this too often.'

Eva looked around her, and watched in wonder as she lifted her arm and it traced an arc of blue lights through the darkness.

'They used to call it the burning of the sea,' Mitsos said.

The sparks streamed over them, and Eva looked up and saw a sky full of stars reflected back at them. She looked across at Mitsos, and the perfection of the moment was almost too much. She had a sudden urge to ditch her old life and stay there forever. She would be brave and tell him everything.

'We should head back to the boat,' Mitsos said.

'Why?'

'I have to work the late shift at the bar, but also the wind is picking up. I think there's going to be a storm. The boat will be safer in the harbour than here.'

'They swam back, and Eva managed to wriggle into her shorts while Mitsos was occupied with the boat.

As Mitsos guided the boat back round the headland, Eva's fantasy of abandoning her old life started to evaporate. For a wonderful moment it had seemed possible, but she realised it had been nothing more than a ridiculous flight of imagination.

'Did you enjoy that?' Mitsos asked as they pulled into the harbour.

'It was wonderful. Thank you so much.'

'Next time we take the boat out, we'll go to Agios Stefanos,' Mitsos said, indicating the islet on the horizon. 'If you'd like to?'

'Yes, I really would.'

'But before that, we have a big festival tomorrow. Will you come?'

'I haven't heard anything about it.'

'It's one of the biggest celebrations of the year here. You have to see it. I'll meet you down by the harbour. I'll send you a message as soon as I can get there. I'll have to do a few hours at the bar first.'

Mitsos and Eva walked back to the Mimosa. 'I should go in,' Mitsos said.

'I suppose so,' Eva said, wishing he didn't have to.

Mitsos was still holding her hand. She heard someone shout, and they turned to see a man standing outside the bar, beckoning to Mitsos.

He sighed and let go of her hand. 'I'm sorry. I really have to go.'

'I know.'

'Do you want to come in for a drink?'

'No, I'm going to go for a walk, and then check on Mi –, my friend.'

'Just as well, you'd distract me.'

Eva waited until he had gone into the bar and then walked to the waterfront. She sat down by the boat. She thought back to the perfect moment in the sea with Mitsos, reliving every moment, and then she heard the first crack of thunder and it was gone.

* * *

After Eva had left, Millie had managed to read a few more pages before finally giving up. Even as an ardent reader, she was beginning to run out of steam. She had got up and paced round the apartment. The walls were closing in. She had checked her phone. As usual there were no messages from Eva.

She had let herself out and walked down into the courtyard.

'Good evening, Millie.'

'Hello, Gus.'

'Would you like to join me for a drink? I'm making coffee, but I can offer you something else.'

'Do you have any of that lemonade?'

Gus smiled. 'Yes, of course.

He returned, and they settled into chairs in the courtyard.

'Are you enjoying your stay?'

Millie thought that enjoying was one of the last words she would have chosen. Enduring would have been closer to the mark. 'Oh yes. It's been very relaxing.'

'Good. It's just that I often see Eva going out but not you. I thought perhaps you didn't like it here.'

'No, not at all. You know how young people are – always dashing about. They can't sit still.'

'Whereas we have learned the value of slowing down a

little and observing what goes on around us?'

'Perhaps.' Millie sipped the lemonade. 'Although I think I spend too much time observing and not enough time doing.'

'And what – or who – specifically are you observing?'

'Eva, mainly,' Millie admitted.

'Why?'

"I worry about her. She was always so focused on what she wanted, but I think she's losing her way.'

'Maybe her way has changed. You have to trust that she will find it.'

'That's true. I just don't want her to make the same mis –,' Millie stopped herself.

'Mistakes? We've all made them, haven't we?'

'And we all want our children and grandchildren to avoid them.'

'Yes,' Gus conceded. 'But life doesn't work like that. They have to make them all over again, and we have to stand by and watch.'

'It's not much fun, though, is it?'

'No, no, it isn't.' Gus paused. 'Have you had dinner?'

'Not yet.'

'I thought I might go to the Mythos for dinner. Would you care to join me?'

'Oh, well, yes, that would be lovely.'

'Shall we go, then? Gus asked, offering Millie his arm.

At the Mythos, Yiannis brought them a bottle of wine, and Gus poured Millie a drink.

'Have you seen much of the island?'

'We went on an excursion out to the temple and Vathi.'

'That's a lovely place.'

'Yes, it is. It feels a million miles away from the real world.'

'Always an advantage,' said Gus with a smile. 'Given that the real world gets crazier by the day.'

'Or we aren't keeping up with it.'

'Also a distinct possibility.'

'Mainly, though, I've just stayed in the apartment, reading. As you know, Eva is out most of the time.'

'Perhaps we should allow the younger ones to have some fun?'

'Perhaps we should,' Millie replied.

Maria appeared with the menus and greeted both of them. 'Where's Eva this evening?'

'I'm not sure,' Millie replied. 'Out and about in town, I think. I wish she'd let me know what she's doing.'

'Don't worry about her. She's safe here on Andraxos,' Gus said. His words were reassuring yet Millie saw something in his expression which was at odds with that. She thought about Helena.

'Gus, what is it?'

'Nothing. Really.'

'Please tell me.'

'There was an incident,' Gus said, reluctantly, 'but it I was many years ago.'

'What sort of incident?' Millie asked, sitting up in her chair.

'Oh, it was all a very long time ago and nothing has ever

happened here since. I shouldn't have mentioned it. You're going to be even more worried now. Please forget I said anything.'

'What happened, Gus?'

'It was up at the Villa Iris. Do you remember, Maria?'

'Yes, I do. The English woman. That was a strange business.'

'The English woman?' Millie asked, in a voice she didn't recognise.

Gus took his glasses off and pinched the bridge of his nose. 'There was a young woman who stayed at the Villa Iris and one day she disappeared.' He saw the expression on Millie's face and added. 'I'm going back years.'

'What happened to her? Did the police try to find her?'

'Of course. They questioned the staff at the Villa Iris and asked around in town but that was about it. No body was ever found, and then they concluded she had left the island and gone to Athens. I'm not sure why.'

Millie thought about that. A body. Her beautiful daughter reduced to a body. She took a deep breath and tried to get control of her emotions. 'It doesn't sound like they took her disappearance very seriously.'

'I think they did. But you have to understand that nothing like that had ever happened before – or has since. It was almost impossible to believe that anyone here had hurt her.'

'And what do you think?'

'I really don't know, but there has never been a serious crime here so I'm inclined to think they were right.'

A silence fell across the table. 'I'm sorry, Millie. What a topic for dinner. I'm hardly lifting your spirits, am i?'

'Millie, please don't worry about Eva,' Maria said. 'I've lived here all my life and I've raised three children here. I've never once felt afraid for them or me. I don't know what happened to that poor girl, but I am sure whatever it was didn't happen here. And Eva is sensible. A lovely girl. We had such a nice conversation yesterday.'

'Did you? Where?' Millie said, looking at her in surprise, torn away from her thoughts about Helena. Eva hadn't mentioned anything to her about meeting Maria.

'When she came to the shop.'

'Sorry?'

'Eva came to the shop yesterday to buy some souvenirs, and we had a chat.'

'I didn't realise you had a shop as well as the taverna. That must keep you busy.'

'I don't normally work there, but I've been helping out there for the last few days. When it's family you have to, don't you?'

'Yes, of course. I'd like to have a look around your shop too. I'm surprised Eva didn't mention it to me. Where is it?'

'It's out of town up in the hills. Eva got a taxi there, and I drove her back.'

'What did you say?' Millie asked, unsure whether she had heard correctly.

'Don't worry. It's perfectly safe to take a taxi here, Millie. We all know all the drivers,' Maria said.

'Yes, of course,' said Millie. 'Maria, what is the name of your shop?'

'Farm shop Petrakis. Not very original. It's just the family name.'

Gus caught the look on Millie's face. 'What is it Millie?'

'Nothing. I'm fine.' She turned her attention to the menu although she saw nothing of the options on offer.

* * *

After Gus had walked Millie back to the apartment, she had pleaded tiredness and the approaching storm as a reason not to have a drink in the courtyard and escaped to the apartment. To her relief, Eva was not there. She was not ready to face her yet. She paced the room, wondering how exactly Maria was related to the rest of the Petrakis family and why Eva had let her down so badly.

Tired of pacing, she slumped down on the sofa. She switched the light off and tried to calm herself down with deep breaths. Eventually, she heard the key in the door, and Eva walked in. She saw her shadow cross the floor as she walked quietly towards her bedroom, and Millie felt the anger rising inside of her.

'When were you going to tell me, Eva?'

Millie saw Eva's shadowy shape jump and freeze, and she reached across to switch on the lamp beside the sofa.

'Tell you what, Millie?'

'About Maria. About the shop. About the farm.' Millie could hear her voice rising.

'Oh. That.'

'Yes. That. What were you thinking Eva? You promised me you wouldn't do anything without talking to me first.'

Eva crossed the room and perched on one of the dining chairs. Her shorts still felt damp from putting them on after her swim, and she wanted to go and change.

'Well?' Millie asked.

'I didn't set out to go to the farm –'

'Don't give me that. Maria told me you took a taxi to get there.'

'Yes, that's true. What I mean is that when I left here I didn't intend to go there.' Eva tried to stay as close to the truth as possible, but she was conscious of her lies. 'Then I got to the harbour and … it was just a spur of the moment decision. Besides, going to a shop isn't suspicious, is it? We'd have gone in there on the excursion the other day if you –'

'If I what?'

'You know.' Eva said, looking uncomfortable. 'Anyway, my point is that I didn't know I was going until I was on my way. And then I thought it wasn't such a big deal.'

'Did you really?'

'Yes, Millie. For goodness' sake. It's a shop.'

Millie went quiet as she considered what Eva had told her. She wondered if she had overreacted. 'What happened when you were there?'

Eva heard the change in Millie's tone and felt the edge disappear from the tension which had filled the room. She related the outline of the events at the shop. 'And that was it. No harm done.'

'Is that why you steered me away from going to the Mythos for dinner last night and offered to cook?'

'Yes,' Eva admitted. 'I didn't think I'd done anything

wrong, but I wasn't sure you'd agree. I just didn't want another fight.'

Millie took a deep breath and asked the question to which she didn't want an answer. 'How is Maria related to the rest of the Petrakis family?'

Eva hesitated.

'Tell me, Eva.'

'Maria is Dimitris's daughter.'

'His daughter,' Millie said to herself as much as to Eva.

Eva nodded, afraid to say anything. She waited for the explosion, but Millie said nothing. 'You know what that means, don't you?' Eva continued.

'I'm sure you're going to tell me,' said Millie.

'Maria is my aunt and that means Violeta is my cousin. And Gus must know Dimitris. After all, his son married Dimitris's daughter.'

'I can't believe it. The only two places I've felt remotely safe since I've been here are in this apartment and at the Mythos. Now I don't even feel comfortable here or there. How am I ever going to look Maria or Violeta in the eye, knowing who they are?'

'I don't know, Millie.'

Millie stood up slowly, feeling a sharp twinge in her knee again. 'I'm going to bed.'

'That's it?'

'What more is there to say?'

'I don't know. I just thought … do you want to talk?'

'No.'

'Are you angry with me?'

'No,' Millie replied. 'I believe you didn't intend to deceive me, but you weren't honest with me either.' As she said the words, her conscience pricked her. Who was she to stand in judgement about that? 'I just need some time alone. I'll see you in the morning.'

Eva watched Millie leave and felt her heart break for her and for the relationship they had once had, which seemed to grow more fragile by the day. She got up and walked quietly to Millie's door and raised her hand to knock on it. She wondered what she could say to make things better. She normally seemed to make them worse. Her knuckles silently grazed the door's surface, and she realised there was nothing she could say. She dropped her hand and walked back to her own room.

Chapter 16

Eva found Millie on the balcony, cradling a cup of coffee and watching as the sun slowly started to flood the day with colour.

'Morning,' she said, wondering what reaction would greet her.

'Good morning, dear.'

The "dear" momentarily put Eva at ease, but the tone which underpinned her words was less comforting.

'Would you like to go for a walk?' Eva asked, unable to think of anything else to say.

'Yes, actually I would. I think I need to get out.'

They saw Violeta as they appeared in the courtyard, and Eva took a deep breath. Millie looked at her. 'Don't say anything.'

'Stop saying that. I know.'

Violeta greeted Millie and Eva. 'You're up early today. I'm happy I have seen you. Do you have a moment?'

'Yes, of course.'

'Good. I wanted to tell you that we will be leaving later

this morning, and we won't be back until the day after tomorrow. My friend Zoe will be here if there is anything you need.'

'I don't think we'll need anything,' said Millie, wanting to get away as quickly as possible, 'but thank you for telling us.'

'Where are you going?' asked Eva.

'Up into the mountains to celebrate. It's Dekapentavgoustos.'

'Deka what?' Eva asked. Mitsos had told her that he would meet her at the festival in town, but he hadn't mentioned the name of it. This had to be the same occasion.

Violeta laughed. 'It's a religious celebration, with the emphasis on religious in the morning and celebration in the evening. I would invite you, but all of our cars are full. I could ask around to see if anyone can take you.'

'That's very kind, but I'm sure we'll be fine here,' said Millie.

'You can still enjoy it in town,' said Violeta. 'There will be a concert by the harbour and lots of tables set out under the trees where people can eat. If you go down to the harbour now, you will see everything being organised. You'll also see the town at its busiest. Lots of people come home for this.'

'OK,' said Eva. 'Have a good time.'

After Violeta was out of earshot, Eva turned to Millie. 'I wish I could tell her we're related.'

'Well you can't. It's as simple as that.'

'I know.' Eva paused. 'Do you want to go to the harbour?'

'I don't know. She said there will be lots of people there.'

'That's a good thing. You can get lost in the crowd.'

Millie sighed.

'Millie, you've spent most of your time here hiding, and it hasn't helped at all. I wish you could just try to enjoy this festival if nothing else.'

'The only thing I'm going to enjoy is the flight home.'

Eva bit her lip. They were back to that again. She thought of a number of things she could say, but they all seemed likely to start an argument so she settled for, ' Are we going?'

'Yes, all right,' said Millie, putting on her sunglasses and pulling her hat down lower over her face.

They made their way through the winding lanes and down the staircase which opened out onto the main harbour road. As Violeta had said, the harbour was a hive of activity. Down by the port, a stage was being constructed; kiosks were being set up at regular intervals, and in the main square, large tables were being laid out under the mulberry trees.

They stopped at a bar, where they had a prime seat to watch all of the activity. A ferry docked and people, cars and motorbikes poured out.

'Violeta was right about it being busy,' Millie remarked.

'Tourists,' said Eva laughing. 'I wish they'd all go away again.'

'Quite.' A thought suddenly occurred to Millie. 'Shouldn't you receive your exam results today?'

Eva realised she had quite easily managed to forget about the significance of the day and also about her life back in England. 'Yes, they're due out today.'

'And Amy is collecting them for you?' Millie confirmed.

'It's 8.30 here so it's only 6.30 a.m. there,' said Eva. She wasn't sure she wanted the results or even what results she wanted any longer.

'Are you connected?'

Eva checked her phone. 'Yes.'

'Perhaps you should send her a message to remind her.'

'Not at 6.30. Besides, she won't forget,' said Eva, half-hoping she might. Amy was about the only person who hadn't completely taken Tom's side in their breakup and even though she had sent a few messages expressing her disapproval, Eva felt sure Amy wouldn't let her down. However, as soon as she had the results, reality would intrude, and she would be forced to make decisions for which she felt ill-equipped. 'Can we change the subject?'

'Yes, as long as you keep checking.'

'I will. Now, why don't we take one of those boat trips we've been talking about? The first boat leaves at 9.'

Millie looked over at the quay and the tourists gathering around to buy tickets. 'I suppose it would be safe.'

'Of course it will. We're not going to be stopping anywhere. It won't be like the bus.'

'I couldn't go through that again.'

'You won't have to. Come on. I think some fresh air out on the sea would be good for both of us.'

They bought their tickets and got on the boat. 'Check your phone again.'

'Nothing yet,' said Eva.

The boat set off and chugged through the serene waters of the harbour. The town receded until the buildings looked like dolls' houses. They rounded the headland and as they sailed along the coast, Millie's beach, as they both privately thought of it, came into view. The Villa Iris, standing proud above the beach, could be glimpsed through the trees.

Eva watched as Millie looked away. Every time they tried to do something, it went wrong. She was beginning to understand why Millie just wanted to stay in the apartment, and she thought perhaps she would too if she was in the same situation.

Millie stared out to sea, her eyes fixed on the islet of Agios Stefanos in the bay. Anything not to look back at the beach and the Iris. She felt claustrophobic, and her throat felt tight as though she might choke at any moment. She wanted to get off the boat and get away from the island. She fought to control the sensation and focused on Eva.

'Check your phone again.'

Eva complied. 'I haven't got a signal. I promise I'll check as soon as we get back.'

They sat in silence as the boat churned through the waters and rounded the next headland. As the Iris slipped out of sight, they both quietly breathed a sigh of relief. The rest of the trip passed uneventfully and as they came back into the harbour, Eva turned to Millie.

'Well that wasn't so bad, was it?' she asked, not believing the words even as she said them.

'I enjoyed the breeze,' Millie ventured. 'Now what about –'

'Yes, I know, my results. Hold on.' Eva waited to reconnect. 'I've got a message.'

'From Amy?'

'I don't know. I can't open it.'

'What do you mean? Isn't your phone working?'

'No, it's not that. I mean I'm too nervous to open it. I feel sick. I can't.'

'Yes, you can.'

'Will you do it?' Eva asked.

'No' said Millie firmly. 'You are an adult, and you are perfectly capable of doing it.'

Eva sighed although the flash of vintage Millie was welcome. 'Let's sit down first then.'

Settled on the nearest bench in the shade, Eva took a deep breath and prepared to open the message. She scanned it fast and then read it again slowly.

'Well?' Millie asked impatiently.

Eva couldn't speak and handed the phone to Millie.

'Is she sure?'

'I'm going to ask her.'

Eva tapped out a message and they sat and waited; every second stretching into minutes.

Amy's reply appeared – a photograph of Eva's results.

They looked at the message together; three A* grades and one A.

'Oh darling, congratulations. I'm so very proud of you.'

'Thanks,' said Eva, and she was not even ashamed when Millie gave her a hug in public.

'Check your university offer.'

'Hold on. I'll reply to Amy first.'

What did you get?
Two As and a B. Good enough for my first choice.
Well done. Going out to celebrate?

Yes. Party time! You?
I'm going to some sort of town festival.
Sounds dull.

Eva thought about Mitsos and the fact that couldn't be further from the truth, but she had no desire to tell Amy about Mitsos or argue the point with her. *We'll see*, she replied. She looked out over the harbour and realised she couldn't expect Amy to understand. She was about to put her phone back in her bag when another message from Amy appeared.

You going with Millie? That should be wild. Haha.

Eva felt anger rising inside her. Whatever their problems, Millie was off limits for ridicule. As she debated how to reply, another message appeared.

About Tom …
What about him?
He's seeing Isla.

Eva remembered the night of her birthday party. She hadn't been so far from the truth after all. She knew she didn't want to be with Tom, but the idea of him and one of her closest friends getting together made her feel uncomfortable. She thought of various things she could say but realised she didn't need the drama that would be caused by reacting. She started to type. *Good for them.*

You don't mind?
No. She's welcome to him.
Harsh

I have to check my offers. Later. Eva put her phone down, exasperated.

'What's going on?' Millie asked.

'I'm starting to think I don't know anyone.'

'Why?'

'It doesn't matter.'

'If it doesn't matter, could you check your offer, please? I want to know even if you don't.'

'OK,' said Eva. She found the page she was looking for. Her first choice university had updated to showing an unconditional offer. She was in. Everything she had worked for had paid off. She had dreamed about this moment and had expected to feel more excited, but that was before. Now she couldn't stop wondering whether the future she had planned so meticulously was still the one she wanted; GCSEs, A Levels, university, training to become an architect. It had all been so clear, this plan she had laid out for herself. Her future all mapped out. At one point, it had been comforting, but now it was suffocating. And now she was so close to the next step, she no longer knew whether she wished to take it.

'I've been accepted for my first choice.'

'That's wonderful. You don't look very happy, though.' Millie searched Eva's face.

'I am. Honestly. It's just a lot to take in.'

'I know, but now you can really celebrate tonight.'

Chapter 17

'I don't know what to wear,' said Eva.

'Why don't you wear that dress I bought you?'

'Oh yes, I meant to ask you how that got in my bag.'

'I can't imagine,' replied Millie, a trace of her old sense of humour resurfacing. 'Go on, wear that.'

Eva returned to her room and took the dress out of the wardrobe. She hadn't packed it because of what Tom had said to her about her weight on the night of the party. Perhaps she could give it another go. She put it on and examined herself from every angle she could twist herself into. Even though she was always brutally critical of her body, she thought she looked acceptable. She would take a chance and wear it. She remembered Mitsos promising he would see her that night and felt the butterflies in her stomach. She hadn't yet worked out what would happen if Mitsos and Millie met. Millie would not take it well, that much she knew.

They walked down to the harbour early in the evening. Without the anonymity afforded by her sunglasses and hat,

Millie felt exposed and looked around nervously.

'From what Violeta said, we could eat at one of those tables in the main square,' Eva said.

'I don't think so.'

'In case you see Dimitris,' Eva said.

'Yes and don't start sighing. You knew how it would be when we decided to come down here tonight.'

'Perhaps you're right,' Eva said, as it occurred to her that bumping into Mitsos was a distinct possibility. She suddenly felt as keen as Millie to get away from the harbour.

Millie looked at her in surprise. 'I thought you'd put up more of a fight than that.'

'No, let's just have a quick look round and then eat somewhere up in the back streets.'

'Not the Mythos,' said Millie.

'No, not there. Wherever you want to go.'

Millie looked at Eva. She had a feeling she was missing something. Eva wasn't one to give in so easily, particularly when she had seemed excited at the prospect of throwing herself into the festivities.

After a brief walk around, they wandered back up through the town and found a small place to eat with a balcony overlooking the harbour.

'I hope you don't mind,' Millie said.

'Mind what?'

'Eating up here. Not down by the harbour.'

'No, it's fine, honestly. It's more … peaceful.'

'I wouldn't have thought peaceful was what you were looking for.'

'I might go back down there later, but it's nice to have a meal together and to be able to chat.' Eva paused. 'Things have been so strained lately. And I feel terrible about all that business with Maria and –'

'Let's not talk about that. I agree things have been difficult, but once we're back home, everything will go back to normal. And now you've got university to look forward to. A whole new life. New experiences. New friends.'

'I suppose so.'

'Eva, what's wrong?'

'I don't know, Millie. I'm not even sure if anything is wrong.'

They lapsed into silence. 'If you want to talk to me, you can. You know that, don't you? About anything.' Millie thought about Eva's regular disappearances from the apartment, her new fondness for long walks and her conviction that Eva had met someone.

Eva thought about Mitsos and knew that was the last thing she could do. 'Of course,' she said.

As they finished their dinner and paid the bill, they heard the music start to drift up over the town.

'It doesn't sound like my sort of thing, dear. And with all those crowds and, you know… I think I might head back to the apartment,' said Millie.

'If you're sure,' said Eva, hoping she had disguised her relief, having spent the whole of the dinner wondering how she would be able to slip away to see Mitsos.

'Yes, it's time for me to call it a night.'

'Do you mind if I go down there for a while?'

'No.' Millie said. 'Enjoy yourself.'

'Are you sure?'

'Yes, quite sure. Just be careful.'

'I will.'

'Good night.'

They left the restaurant, and Eva watched Millie walking back up the stairs in the direction of the apartment. Her posture made her look older suddenly, and she noticed she was favouring one leg. Eva was torn. Should she go after Millie or go down to the harbour to meet Mitsos? At the thought of him, she found herself turning in the direction of the harbour.

Groups of people were starting to gather in front of the stage, and she threaded her way through them, getting as close as she could to the stage. She was glad that she had something to take her mind off everything. She felt her phone vibrate. It was from Mitsos.

Where are you?

Watching the concert.

Can you see the red kiosk? It's to the left of the stage.

Eva looked round, peering over the tops of people's heads. *Yes.*

I'm there. Will you join me? Eva felt the sense of anticipation she had felt when standing in her bedroom earlier; the butterflies fluttering in the pit of her stomach. She had a feeling that an irrevocable shift was about to take place.

On my way.

As she made her way through the crowd, she wished she hadn't worn the dress. She remembered Tom's comments when he had seen her in it. Finally she emerged to find Mitsos scanning the crowds, looking for her.

Eva saw Mitsos's reaction. 'Eva! You look so beautiful.'

'You like it?' Eva asked.

'Like it? You look amazing.'

Eva saw the way he looked at her and reflected again on the difference between Tom and Mitsos.

'I want you to experience everything that happens on this evening. Are you ready?'

Eva nodded, and Mitsos led her through the town, stopping at the kiosks to buy snacks and drinks. They arrived in another square set back from the main harbour road. Another stage had been set up, and there was a display of Greek dancing in progress. Mitsos started to explain the different dances and their history. A month before, Eva would have found it, as Amy would have put it, dull. Now, though, she listened with rapt attention. She needed to know everything about Andraxos and Greece, and being with Mitsos was anything but dull.

'Can we take part?' Eva asked, as Mitsos finished his explanation, and she noticed other people getting up to dance.

'I'm not the best dancer,' he said and Eva looked at him surprised. It was the first time he had seemed unsure of himself. 'You go ahead,' he said with a smile.

'I don't know what to do.'

'Join in and everyone will show you.'

'You won't come with me?'

'I'll think about it. Go on.'

Eva got up hesitantly and started to walk towards the crowds. She looked back, and Mitsos smiled at her and waved at her to join the group.

As she reached the dancers, they opened up to welcome her into the circle. They gave her instructions she could not understand, but she followed their feet as carefully as she could. They called out what sounded like encouraging comments, and she laughed along with them.

After weeks on a rollercoaster of emotions, she had found a moment of uncomplicated happiness. Her results were starting to sink in; she had passed her exams, even if she was no longer sure what she wanted to do with them. She had been welcomed into the community by everyone she had met so far and now this group of strangers had opened up to take her in. Her worries dissolved and even though a part of her knew they were bound to come back, for the brief period of time she was relieved of the weight of them.

Mitsos watched her as she laughed along with the group and danced with her hair flying around her face, her silver necklace glinting in the fairy lights. Eva saw him watching her, removed herself from the group and went over to reach for him. 'Come on.'

He took her hands and Eva felt the same electricity she did every time he touched her.

'You can dance,' Eva said as the dance finished, and they collapsed into chairs set out at the side of the square.

'I'm not sure about that, but you are very good.' Mitsos glanced at his watch. 'Do you want to see the fireworks?'

'I want to see everything.'

'Let's go now so we can get a good position.'

They walked down to the waterfront hand in hand, took their shoes off and sat with their feet dangling in the cool water. The crowds grew around them, an expectant hum in the air which matched the expectant feeling which was continuing to grow in Eva.

They watched as the fireworks exploded around them, illuminating the sky and the town, and Mitsos put his arm around her shoulders and drew her closer to him. 'Are you happy?' he asked.

Eva looked out across the water and thought about her problems with Millie and the range of feelings she had experienced since she had arrived there, but realised that at that moment none of it mattered quite as much as being with him. She looked at him, and watched the reflections of the fireworks dancing in his eyes. 'Yes, I am.'

He put his hand up to her face to brush her hair back. The feel of his hand against her face made her shiver.

'Eva,' he said quietly.

They hesitated and then his lips brushed against hers. He moved back a little, checking her reaction. Eva traced her fingertips through the five o'clock shadow which framed his lips, and they kissed again.

They broke the kiss to look at each other. They had no need to see anything. She put her head on his shoulder, and he held her close until the firework display had finished and the crowds had drifted away.

They walked back to the centre of town where there was another display of dancing.

'Do you want to watch?' Eva asked.

'Not really. Let's go,' Mitsos said.

'Where are we going?'

'Just round the corner there.'

They turned into a softly-lit street that felt a million miles from the celebrations.

'Why are we here?' Eva asked, looking around.

'Because I can't kiss you the way I want to back there.'

They kissed again and this time, with nobody else around them, the kiss was deeper and longer. She felt his stubble graze her, but the more they kissed, the more she wanted him. The longing that had built up had finally found expression, and the world faded away.

As the kiss ended, she felt as though her vision had blurred and everything had become hazy. She could not focus and that seemed to represent her life in general. Everything was spiralling and she no longer felt she had any measure of control. More than that, she no longer felt as though she cared as long as she could keep kissing Mitsos forever.

'I didn't think you liked me. Well, not like this.'

'I like you very much, but you thought I was a womaniser. I wanted to show you that isn't true. I didn't want you to think I was just trying to …. but I have wanted to kiss you since the first night I met you. You're so beautiful.'

Eva blushed and dropped her head.

Mitsos gently took her chin in his hand and raised her eyes to meet his. 'Why are you embarrassed?'

Eva cast around for an answer. She opted for honesty and felt vulnerable as she admitted the truth. 'I've never really felt pretty, let alone beautiful.'

'But why?'

Eva had no wish to bring Tom into the conversation, but it seemed unavoidable now. 'I had a boyfriend. He was very … critical.'

'Then he is an idiot.'

Eva laughed despite herself.

'You said "had"?'

'Yes, we split up.'

'Good. He is definitely an idiot, you know that?'

Eva laughed again, and Mitsos pulled her close to kiss her again.

'You know I am serious, don't you? Mitsos asked, still holding her.

Eva looked up at him. He had a way of making everything so simple. He didn't play the games which she had seen friends play or endure.

'I know.'

'Because you didn't trust me at first.'

'I wanted to.' Eva paused. 'And now I do.'

'I'm happy. When can I see you again?'

'Whenever you're free.'

'I'm working tomorrow, and then I have a family dinner. How about the day after tomorrow?'

'The seventeenth?'

'Yes. Why?'

Eva fell silent.

'Eva?'

'Nothing. I've just realised how quickly my time here is going. I leave on the twenty-third.'

'One week.'

'Yes.'

'Then we must make the most of the time while you are here.'

'And then what? We'll have to say goodbye.' Eva looked up at the stars.

'No, not goodbye. I don't want that. Do you?'

'No. It's the last thing I want.'

'Then we will find a solution,' Mitsos said and kissed her again. He sighed. 'I don't want to leave, but I have to work tomorrow. We have to take the boat out just after dawn.'

'I know you have to go. Maybe I should kidnap you so you have a good excuse not to turn up.'

Mitsos laughed and put his arms up in mock surrender. 'And I would be very happy to be kidnapped by you. Come on, I'll walk you back.'

Eva reached out and ran her hands up his chest and around his neck. Mitsos responded and kissed her again. 'You are making this very difficult for me.'

'Are you complaining?'

'No, I'm definitely not. Let me walk you home. We'll have a few more minutes together.'

'I'll go alone.'

'It's late.'

'I'll be fine. '

'Let me walk you back, please.'

Eva relented and allowed Mitsos to walk her as far as the church. 'You can leave me here.'

'Why don't I take you to the door?'

Eva thought about Millie's reaction if she happened to see her appear with a man. 'Honestly. I'll be fine. You know I don't need the third degree from my friend. Especially not tonight.'

'If you're sure.'

'I am. Remember I live in London.'

'OK,' said Mitsos, reluctantly. 'So I'll see you on Saturday.'

'Definitely,' said Eva, kissing him again.

'I don't want to go.'

'And I don't want you to, but you must. You have to work tomorrow. Go!' Eva said, smiling at him.

Mitsos gave her a final lingering kiss and disappeared into the night.

Eva walked back to the apartment. The lights were out and for that she was grateful. If she couldn't be with Mitsos, she wanted to be alone with her memories of the night without anyone intruding upon them. She stepped out onto the balcony, and the night wrapped itself around her, holding her in its embrace as Mitsos had done. Somewhere in the night a dog barked and someone called out to it. The stillness resumed. The lights framing the harbour reflected in the still water until, one by one, they blinked off, and the town surrendered to the night.

Millie had heard the door close quietly and felt the relief wash over her. She knew she had to let Eva live her life and in England it had been easy – or at least as easy as it was for any parent or grandparent. On the island, everything was so much more complicated. Even though Eva had promised not to do anything without talking to her first, she hadn't quite managed to live up to her promises and fate kept twisting the path and leading them back to the past.

Millie found her phone and looked at the date: the early hours of the sixteenth of August. They had survived just over three weeks. Perhaps with a little luck they could survive one more.

Chapter 18

The next day Eva asked the taxi driver to leave her some way down the road from the gate to the Petrakis farm, and she paused when she reached it. She knew how Millie would react if she found out that she had gone back to the farm, but she could not help herself. Even the thought of a furious row with Millie was not enough to deter her. Time was growing short, and she had to act.

She saw the path straight ahead leading to the shop. To the right was the pathway leading, she assumed, to the farmhouse. There were no tracks to the left, just thick pine forest so Eva decided to head in that direction first and see if she could circle round and get closer to the farm that way without revealing herself. After all, she didn't plan to go the farm and announce herself. She just wanted to see it. She sprinted across the open ground between the gate and the trees and stopped to catch her breath. Her clothes were already stuck to her in the late afternoon heat.

She moved quietly through the trees; the clean scent of the pine trees and the smell of herbs suffused the air. She couldn't see any buildings, but she was sure that if she just kept bearing right, the farmhouse would come into view. She heard a branch crack somewhere behind her and jumped. She looked around but saw nobody and carried on walking. The silence became absolute and started to unnerve her; she remembered Mitsos saying it was because she was from a big city, and she thought he had been right. It was too quiet.

She heard a rustling sound and as she turned, she saw a swatch of bright red flash between the trees. There was someone there. Her heart started to hammer, and she remembered the nightmare she had had of being caught in a forest.

In the split second she allowed herself to think, she decided to keep moving; the reaction of the hunted. She picked up her pace and then she saw a house ahead of her with a grove of olive trees to the left. That had to be it. She glanced behind her, but didn't see anybody.

She crept closer to the house, driven to do something which went completely against her better instincts. She knew she was trespassing on private land and perhaps also trespassing in areas perhaps better left alone, but the compulsion to know about her family swept every other consideration aside. She could only imagine how much stronger that need must have been in her own mother.

Another branch behind her cracked underfoot and the snapping sound was like a gunshot. Eva froze, waiting to feel a bullet hit her. When it didn't she continued to wait, expecting to hear someone shouting, a dog barking, but the silence resumed and held steady. She felt rivers of sweat pouring down her back and tugged at her top.

She waited until her heartbeat had slowed and as she regained her nerve, she moved a little closer to the house. She was so focused on it that she didn't notice the rocky incline in front of her. She slipped, lost her footing on the dry, crumbling ground and found herself at the bottom in a heap of dust, stones and pine needles with pain shooting through her foot. She clutched her foot, lips pressed together, willing herself not to shout to release some of the pain. Gradually, the worst of it started to subside, but she knew she had done some damage.

She managed to manoeuvre herself towards a tree and tried to use it as a support to help her get to her feet. She stood up, but as soon as she put any weight on her foot, she collapsed again. As she was trying for the second time, she heard a voice from behind her. She didn't understand a word, but the tone did not sound too friendly. She lowered herself to the ground again and turned round. She found herself sitting at the feet of a man wearing a red T-shirt and a battered pair of jeans, who had advanced towards her while she had been occupied with trying to stand up.

She looked up at him, unable to think of anything to say. She backed away and felt the solidity of the tree trunk behind her. He advanced slightly towards her. Even if she had not been injured, there would have been nowhere to go. She continued to stare at him, robbed of the power of speech.

He spoke again, and she thought he sounded a little less

angry although the way he was standing over her was intimidating enough to compensate for that. She had always prided herself on being streetwise and capable of looking after herself and had managed to stay safe in London. Now, though, she was at the mercy of a stranger on a supposedly safe Greek island.

'I'm sorry, I don't speak Greek.'

He switched to English. 'What are you doing here? This is private land.'

'Is it? I'm sorry. I was out walking, and I got lost.' She realised she could have said she had been looking for the farm shop, but it seemed too late to add that now.

He studied her for a moment. 'What did you do?' he asked, gesturing in the direction of her leg.

'I fell down that slope. I've done something to my foot or my ankle. I'm not sure. It all hurts.'

'Here. I will help you. Try to stand.' His abrupt tone was at odds with the offer of assistance.

With the man's support, she managed to get to her feet, but could put no weight on her ankle. He sighed.

A stiff breeze suddenly broke through the heat of the afternoon, covering Eva's shoes in another layer of dust. The olive trees shivered and were transformed into the flutter of a thousand silver wings. He looked around. 'The Meltemi is on its way.'

'What's the Meltemi?'

'The wind. You can't stay here, and you can't walk. Come, I will take you to the house. We will look at your foot there.'

Eva looked at him and at the house. It seemed she was to see it after all. She hesitated. Her instincts told her she should not be going anywhere with a complete stranger. She tried to move her ankle, flinched as the pain hit again and realised she had little choice in the matter.

'Thank you. What is your name?'

'Nikos.'

Eva felt a jolt of fear. He could only be the Nikos that her mother had referred to her in her emails. He was the right age. He had to be her half-uncle. She remembered how her mother's emails had changed in tone after she had met him and wondered if she should be afraid of him rather than reluctantly grateful that he had come to her rescue.

'Did you hear me?' Nikos asked.

'Sorry. What did you say?'

'What's your name?'

'Eva.'

Nikos helped her up, and they edged towards the house, progress hampered by Eva's injury. He opened a gate and helped Eva into a garden where nature had not been completely tamed, but had been kept in check. Eva sat down on one of the chairs with relief and took in her surroundings while Nikos searched for his key. Flowers burst from brightly coloured pots and cans and above them, a canopy of vines provided shade.

'You have a beautiful garden,' said Eva.

'I'm not the gardener,' he said gruffly. 'Come on.'

The cool was welcome after the burning sun outside, but the immaculate interior only served to make Eva conscious of how dishevelled she was. They went into the kitchen, and he sat her down again. 'Take off your shoe. Let me look at it.'

Eva sat obediently, quietly squirming in discomfort, as Nikos examined her foot and ankle.

'Nothing broken. Wait here.' He put her leg up on a chair.

He left the room, and Eva looked around her. She had wanted to see the house but now wondered why. It was just a house. What had she thought she would learn by seeing it?

'Eva?'

She turned slightly and saw Mitsos standing in the doorway. The dog they had rescued was by his side and bounded over to greet Eva. She patted his head absent-mindedly while staring at Mitsos, feeling that something had shifted, but she could not quite comprehend what it was.

'Mitsos?'

'Eva! What are you doing here?' Mitsos asked, looking surprised and happy in equal measure.

'I went for a walk, and I fell.' The embarrassment had returned and was biting into her, compounded now by confusion at seeing Mitsos and the awareness that she was looking far from her best.

Mitsos pulled another chair out from the table and sat down next to her. Eva started to ask Mitsos why he was there but was distracted by him pulling a twig from her hair. 'What happened to you? You're in a bit of a mess.'

'Thank you.'

'But a lovely mess.' He smiled at her. 'Are you OK?'

Eva was saved from saying anything by the return of Nikos.

'You've met our guest then,' he said, sitting down in front of Eva and proceeding to bind her ankle expertly. 'Are you allergic to anything?'

'No.'

'Good. Then take these.' He handed her some tablets and a glass of water. 'You should rest here for a while. Mitsos will stay with you. Later we will see if you can walk. We will take you back to town this evening.'

'Thank you. You've been very kind,' said Eva, and it occurred to her that despite his manner, he had been.

Nikos said something to Mitsos in Greek, turned and left the room. She heard the front door shut, and the sound echoed through the house.

'What did he say to you?'

'I have to make sure you don't get into any more trouble.' He leaned across and brushed his hand across one of the smudges on her face and then looked at her ankle. 'Does it hurt a lot?' he asked, the concern in his voice clear.

Eva nodded and closed her eyes. She sensed him move and felt his mouth against hers. She broke the kiss and forced herself to ask the question which now urgently presented itself. 'How do you know Nikos?'

'He's my father.'

'Your father?'

Mitsos nodded.

'Eva, what's wrong?'

'Your father?'

If Mitsos was confused by the repetition of the question and her tone of voice, he let it pass. 'This is my grandfather and grandmother's house. We live over there,' he said, indicating vaguely in the direction beyond the olive grove.

'We?'

'Yes, me, my parents and my brother, but we're all in and out of each other's houses all the time.'

'Oh,' said Eva. She wanted to dig further but couldn't think how to frame any of her questions without them sounding odd. She suddenly thought about something Gus had said on their first night on the island and saw the faintest glimmer of hope. She seized it.

'So your father is Nikos and your grandfather is Mitsos? Isn't that the way it works with names here?'

'Well, my father is called Nikos and so is my great-grandfather.'

'So your grandfather is called Mitsos?' Eva repeated, feeling relieved. Not Dimitris. There had been some sort of mix up after all although she couldn't make any sense of it yet.

Mitsos smiled. 'My grandfather's name is Dimitris, and it's my name too, but everyone calls me Mitsos. It's a nickname really, but it saves a lot of confusion. Nobody calls me Dimitris.'

Eva felt the stark truth being revealed to her in a few innocent sentences. She and Mitsos were related. She reached for her phone, thinking she could distract him for long enough to search the Internet to find out how their relationship would be termed. Half-cousins? Second cousins? She had no idea. She realised her phone was not there and started patting all her pockets although she knew it had gone.

'What have you lost?'

'My phone.'

'You probably lost it when you fell. I'll go and look for it later.'

'I really need it now,' said Eva.

Mitsos shook his head. 'I have my orders. I have to look after you. Nobody will steal it. It'll be fine.'

It occurred to Eva that everything would be far from fine, but there was no way she could tell Mitsos why. She searched around for something, anything, to say to break the silence. 'I had no idea you lived round here,' said Eva. That much at least was true.

'It must be fate that brought you here. It's a good opportunity to introduce you to my family. I thought it would be easier for you if you didn't meet them all at the same time, but now you're here…'

'Introduce me?'

'Yes. As my girlfriend.'

'Is that how you think of me?'

'Of course.'

'We've never discussed it.'

'What is there to discuss?'

Eva thought again how everything was so uncomplicated in Mitsos's world. He was happy to call her his girlfriend and introduce her to his family without long, tortuous conversations about whether they were dating or not. There was no anguish over whether it was too soon. Except now everything was far from simple. She could not be his girlfriend. Eva forced herself to focus.

'If you say that, they'll have a lot of questions. I don't really feel up to that at the moment. Perhaps you could just say we've met a few times in town.'

Eva saw a hurt expression cross his face, but before she could say anything else, a man about the same age as Millie appeared in the doorway. He addressed Mitsos in Greek, and a rapid exchange took place. Eva couldn't determine whether the exchange was angry, curious or friendly and looked from one to the other, wondering what would happen next.

Mitsos turned to her. 'Eva, this is my grandfather, Dimitris.'

Eva gazed at the man she had come so far to see. Her grandfather; her mum's father; Millie's great love.

'Are you in pain, Eva?' Mitsos asked.

'Yes, I'm sorry. It just got really bad for a moment then.'

Dimitris had advanced towards her and was looking anxiously at her. 'Don't worry. We will look after you,' he said to Eva, in slow but correct English.

Eva looked up into her grandfather's eyes. 'You're very kind.'

Dimitris patted Eva on the shoulder and sat down. 'We will eat, and you will be our guest. Then we will see if you can walk. For now you must rest and relax.'

Mitsos brought them drinks and started setting the table.

'Nikos told me you fell,' Dimitris said.

'Yes, it was stupid of me. I was just out walking and then,' she gestured at her ankle, 'this happened.'

'Where are you staying?'

'In town.'

'You are a long way from home.'

Strange words thought Eva; a long way from home and yet in her grandfather's house. The urge to tell him was almost unbearable.

'I suppose I am. I've been trying to get fit so I've been walking a lot.' She shrugged. 'I'm sorry. I didn't realise I'd walked so far or that I was on private land.'

'No damage done. It is better that you had the accident here where someone found you.'

Before Eva could reply, other members of the family started arriving, and she was surrounded by people speaking Greek to and over each other. She was aware she seemed to be the object of most of the conversation, judging by the looks and gestures in her direction, and she wanted the floor to open up and swallow her. She would rather have been anywhere else at that moment; even the hot, uncomfortable hall where she had done her exams would have been a preferable option. She suddenly wondered if Maria would walk in but couldn't deal with anything beyond that moment.

The conversation started to subside. 'Right,' said Mitsos. 'Let me introduce you. You know my dad, Nikos. This is my mum ,Katia, and this is Loukas, my very annoying younger brother.' For that Mitsos received a friendly punch on the arm. *My half-uncle and aunt and my other cousin or half-cousin or second cousin*, thought Eva. She still couldn't work out the last part.

This is my uncle Vasilis and my aunt Stella, their daughter Elektra and theirs sons Stefanos and Andreas. And this is my wonderful grandmother, Angelika, one of the best cooks in Greece, along with my mum of course.' He turned and said something to her in Greek and received a reply. 'She doesn't speak English so I was just telling her what I said, and she said you're very welcome here.'

Eva had built up an image of the woman who had married Dimitris. She had pictured her as a cruel, man-stealing woman even though she knew from Millie that had not been the reality of the situation. The woman standing in front of her, smiling down at her and welcoming her to their home, was about as far away from that image as it was possible to get. She was sure this was a woman she would not be able to dislike even if she tried.

Eventually everyone settled themselves around the table. Eva was assured she should not move and ended up sitting next to Mitsos at one end of the table, opposite Dimitris at the head of the table. Angelika and Katia started bringing plates to the table, and Loukas disappeared from the room with a plate of food and a drink.

'It's for my great-grandfather, Nikos. He can't get out of bed. He's very old,' Mitsos explained.

Eva thought back to what the older Nikos had done to Millie and could find no compassion for him.

As the drinks were poured and the food was handed round, Eva felt her mouth go dry. What would under any other circumstances have been a wonderful occasion, had turned into the last place she wanted to be. She had never felt less inclined to eat anything. She pushed the food round her plate and tried to smile politely.

Mitsos was very attentive and kept trying to translate the gist of the conversations which seemed to be conducted with the volume turned to maximum. 'Are they having an argument?' she asked Mitsos quietly at one point.

Mitsos laughed and placed his hand on her arm. 'No, they are talking about honey.'

Dimitris looked down the table at them and thought that somehow Eva reminded him of someone he had once known. She didn't look exactly like his Em, but there was something in her manner which reminded him of her. He watched the way Mitsos looked after her and the way he touched her arm when he spoke to her. Memories were coming back to him; memories which he thought he had safely packed away.

Mitsos said something to him and woke him from his reverie. 'Our honey is famous, isn't it?' he said speaking in English.

'What's that?'

'Our honey is famous.'

'Oh yes, yes it is.'

The conversation continued around Eva, mainly in Greek and occasionally in English. The buzz of voices and the heat of the room started to get to her. She felt her head start to hurt as much as her ankle and, abandoning any pretence at eating, put her knife and fork down.

Angelika said something to her, and Eva turned to Mitsos, looking for a translation.

'She's worried. She thinks you don't like the food.'

Eva had read enough to know that refusing food was considered an insult. 'No, I love the food. It's delicious. It's just the pain in my ankle is making me feel a bit sick.'

Mitsos said something which evidently solved the problem as Angelika nodded sympathetically and Katia, who was sitting on the other side of Eva, patted her hand. 'Don't worry. You must rest.'

Eva looked around the table and felt her heart aching. Millie had been everything to her, but she had always sensed she had missed out by not having any other family. Now they were all here and the kindest people anybody could have wished to be related to. And she couldn't say a word. And then there was Mitsos.

The conversation continued, punctuated by laughter at something which Eva could not understand.

'My dad is talking about the time he caught someone breaking into the shop,' Mitsos explained.

'I'm sure that didn't go down too well,' Eva said.

'No, it didn't. He happened to have his shotgun with him. He'd never seen anyone move so fast. That's what everyone was laughing about. My mum and grandmother saw the thief making a run for the gate.'

Across the table, Nikos interrupted them. 'He deserved to be scared. He was trying to steal from us and who knows what he would have done next? I would do anything to protect my family.'

There was a momentary silence before the chatter resumed, and Eva assumed that they had moved on to other topics, but she chanced a few glances across the table at Nikos and wondered just how far he would go to protect his family.

* * *

'You've all been so kind to me,' said Eva and although it was true, she was relieved the meal was drawing to a close, and she would be able to leave soon. Keeping her emotions under control in such circumstances had been something she had not thought herself capable of doing.

'You are welcome. It is always a pleasure to help someone,' Dimitris said.

'Thank you.' Eva wished she could give her grandfather a hug and felt a tear starting to sting her eye.

'Eva, what's the matter?' Mitsos asked.

'Nothing. I'm just tired, and my ankle is hurting again.'

'I want to see if you can stand,' Nikos said.

Mitsos helped her up, and she gingerly put her weight on her ankle, grimacing as she did.

'You should drive her home, Nikos,' Dimitris observed.

'I could take her,' said Mitsos.'

'No, you should stay here. Nikos will take her.' Dimitris said.

'Come on,' said Nikos and helped her to the door.

Eva turned awkwardly and looked back at her family gathered round the table, and Mitsos giving her that smile. She felt as if her heart was going to break out of her chest but managed to mumble her thanks. The only thing she wanted was to be alone.

Nikos helped her down the path and manoeuvered her into the car. There was absolute silence, which at any other time Eva would have found uncomfortable, but a pain that was as much physical as emotional consumed her, leaving little room for any other consideration.

Eventually she noticed that Nikos kept glancing in her direction. It was not sinister, more curiosity mixed with something she could not define. She ignored it at first, but then it began to annoy her.

'What are you looking at?'

'Nothing.'

He glanced at her again, and Eva snapped. 'There is obviously something.'

'You just remind me …'

'Of?'

'Forget it.' Nikos kept his eyes on the road. 'Where are you staying?'

The last thing Eva wanted was for him or any of his family to know. You can leave me at the church at the top of the town. Agios Georgios, I think it's called.'

'Yes. You can manage from there?'

'Yes,' Eva said, thinking she would rather crawl than be delivered to the door by Nikos.

The car drew to a stop outside the church. Eva thought about the previous night, the night of the festival. It now seemed as though a lifetime had passed since that night.

Nikos helped her out. 'Wait.' He went round to the back of the car and produced a walking stick. 'I kept it in the car for my grandfather. He has no use for it now.'

'Thank you. How can I return it to you?'

'Leave it at Thanos's bar when you can.'

'Where's that?'

'It's by the monument in the main square. But you can ask anyone. They will know.'

'I dropped my phone earlier when I fell. Could you try to find it?'

'Someone will leave it at the bar if we find it.'

'Thank you – and I am very sorry about everything.'

Nikos made a gesture which was indecipherable to Eva and then unexpectedly said, 'Take care, Eva. See a doctor tomorrow.'

Eva looked at him, unable to say anything and slowly hobbled away, sensing that he was watching every painful step. Only when she had turned the corner, did she hear the engine start and the car pull away.

She let herself into the apartment building and considered the stairs up to the apartment. They looked like an insurmountable obstacle from where she stood. She realised the walking stick would be of little use so she tucked it under her arm and started to make her way up the stairs on her hands and knees, hoping nobody would see her. In that much at least, she was fortunate and, at the door, she managed to scramble into an upright position with the aid of the stick. She turned the key and opened the door as quietly as she could. If only Millie was asleep, she might get away with it and have the night to come up with a story Millie could accept.

As she opened the door, she caught Millie mid-pace. She swung round. 'Where on earth have you been?'

Eva limped into the room. 'I'm sorry. I would have called you, but I lost my phone.'

Millie took in Eva's filthy clothes, her bound ankle and the walking stick, and her anger started to fade.

She went over to her and helped her to the sofa. 'What happened to you?'

The events of the afternoon and evening caught up with Eva. She thought about her family, Mitsos and the pain in her ankle. The enormity of it all suffocated her. 'I can't.'

'I think you can. I've been worried sick about you.'

Eva shook her head and started to cry and shake uncontrollably. 'I just can't. Please don't. Not now, Millie.'

Millie put her arms around her and let her cry until her top was soaked with Eva's tears, and Eva had cried herself out. 'Do you want to talk now?'

'No. I will but not yet. Please.'

'Just tell me one thing.'

'Eva waited, and Millie gently turned her face towards her. 'Has anyone done anything to you? Physically?'

'No, I promise you. It's nothing like that.'

'If anyone has hurt you …'

'No, nobody has hurt me.'

'You can tell me, Eva. You can tell me anything, you should know that.

Eva thought about the events of the previous few hours and was no longer sure if that were true, but she nodded.

'In that case, let me help you to your room.'

Millie put Eva's arm around her shoulders and, once in her room, sat her on the bed.

'Thanks. I can manage from here.'

'We'll talk in the morning,' said Millie, in a tone which was kind but suggested no argument would be accepted.

Millie closed the door behind her, and Eva looked out of the window. Out there, in the darkness beyond the headland, was her family. And Mitsos. She felt a dagger of pain shoot through her ankle and found she was still not out of tears after all.

Chapter 19

As the hours ticked by, Eva's thoughts of Mitsos were only punctuated by her attempts to dream up a plausible excuse to satisfy Millie, and the vain attempt to find a position in which she didn't feel uncomfortable. Every time, she thought she might have succeeded and she closed her eyes, memories of the evening appeared before her. She realised she must have fallen asleep eventually because she was woken by a dream in which Mitsos kissed her in front of his family, and they all said how happy they were for the two of them.

Eva stood up and tested her ankle. It was less painful than it had been, but when she undid the bandage, the bruising was already spectacular. She managed to shower and dress, bandaged her foot again and, grabbing the walking stick, hobbled into the main room.

'Coffee?'

'Yes, please,' Eva replied, trying to judge Millie's mood. She appeared perfectly calm, but lately that calm veneer was capable of shattering quite easily.

She limped across the room, leaning heavily on the

walking stick, sat down at the dining table and pulled another chair across to rest her leg on.

Millie brought coffee and croissants across and sat opposite her. They both sipped the coffee and waited for the other one to say something.

Eventually Millie took the initiative. 'Do you know what the date is?'

'The seventeenth?'

'Yes. The anniversary of the day I last heard from your mum.'

'Oh.'

'That's another reason I was so upset last night.'

Eva could find nothing to say.

Millie changed tack. 'How's your ankle?'

'It hurts, but it's not as bad as it was last night.'

'We'll ask Violeta to get a doctor over here to take a look at it.'

'No, I don't need –'

'You are going to see a doctor. If it's broken, it must be set correctly.'

'OK,' said Eva meekly. She could hardly say that Nikos had reassured her it was not broken.

The silence resumed. 'When are you going to tell me what happened?'

'There's not much to say. I went for a walk, as I said I would, and I fell.'

'And then?'

Eva swallowed and came out with the story she had rehearsed, hoping Millie would accept it although she had her doubts.

'A local man found me and helped me back to his house. He bandaged my ankle and let me rest. After he had had dinner, he drove me back here.'

'You went to a total stranger's house and then got in a car with him.' Millie spaced out each word, making her disbelief apparent.

'Yes, I know, I know, but I didn't exactly have much choice, did I? I'd still be stuck out there now if he hadn't come along.'

'I suppose so. And how did you lose your phone?'

'I think it fell out of my pocket when I had the accident. He said he would look for it and hand it in at some place in the main square called Thanos's bar if he found it.'

Eva looked at Millie, wondering if she had got away with it. She had stuck to the truth as far as she could, which she had once read somewhere was the best way to avoid getting caught out. She told herself she had not really lied to Millie. She chanced a weak smile.

Millie held her gaze. 'You're not telling me everything.'

'I haven't lied to you.'

'Maybe not, but you certainly haven't told me everything.' As she said it, she reminded herself again that she had still not been completely honest with Eva and was on shaky moral ground.

'I don't know why you think that,' Eva responded defensively.

'When you came home last night, you cried and cried. I don't think I've ever seen you like that before. No, don't get embarrassed. You don't need to be, but I can't understand why you would be crying like that over a twisted ankle – or even a lost phone.' Millie suddenly added, 'Are you sure he didn't touch you?'

'Millie, please, he didn't do anything to me, apart from bandage my ankle and bring me home.'

'So why were you in floods of tears?'

'I don't know. It had just been a long day, and I was hot, tired and in pain. And I thought you'd be angry about the phone. It cost a lot of money.'

'I'm not buying it, Eva.'

'Why can't you just leave it be?' Eva asked.

'Like you did when I said we shouldn't come here?'

'We're back to that, are we?' Eva muttered.

'We are when you won't tell me the truth.'

'Like you have?'

'What?'

'You haven't told me everything, Millie. I already know that. You didn't tell me about Dimitris's father before we came here, and the longer I spend here, the more convinced I am that there's other stuff you haven't mentioned.'

'I've told you everything I know,' Millie snapped back, trying to ignore her conscience, which refused to stop nagging her. 'I've shared everything with you – all my most personal moments and feelings. I even agreed to come back to this bloody island. What the hell more do you want?'

Eva looked at her, stunned into silence. She had never heard Millie sound so angry before. She could not have been more shocked if Millie had hit her.

The silence reverberated around them as they eyed each other warily. Millie was already bitterly regretting her outburst while Eva wondered if she would ever be able to make amends; if they would ever again be Millie and Eva against the world.

'If I tell you, you'll hate me and if I don't tell you, you'll hate me so what am I supposed to do?' Eva looked utterly miserable, and Millie reached out to take her hand.

'I could never hate you. I'm sorry for what I said. I shouldn't have shouted at you. It's just that this whole thing is getting to me. I want us to go home and get on with our lives.'

Eva wrapped her hands around both of Millie's and slowly looked up at her. She took a deep breath. 'I met them.'

'Met who?' Millie responded, trying to catch up.

'I met all of them. The whole family. Including Dimitris.'

Millie stared at Eva, who clutched her hands even tighter, refusing to let her pull away.

'I don't understand,' Millie said.

'I went back to the farm yesterday.'

'What?' It was Millie's turn to look shocked. 'You promised you wouldn't, and I thought after the first time – .' Millie broke off and shook her head.

'Yes, I know, but I had to find out more about them. I was running out of time, and I knew you'd get angry, but I had to.'

'Go on.'

'I don't know what I was thinking, but it was like I couldn't stop myself. I didn't plan to go to the house and introduce myself or anything like that. I just wanted to see the house, and I thought I might get to see my grandfather from a distance. I set off through the trees, and I sensed I was being followed. I got scared, and I slipped and fell. That's when I did this.' Eva stopped and chewed on her lip. 'The man who found me was Nikos.'

They looked at each other, and Eva saw Millie struggling to stay calm. 'Nikos?'

Eva nodded, dropped her gaze and studied her lap.

'And after that?' Millie managed.

'What I told you was true. I did lose my phone, and Nikos did help me to the house, but there's more to it than that. Loads of people turned up, and I was invited to stay for dinner. I asked them about the phone, but they just said not to worry, and that they'd get it back to me. Oh, Millie, it was so awful. I sat there being welcomed as a stranger while I was trying to work out how I was related to everyone.'

Eva started to cry again, and Millie's anger started to crumble. 'That must have been terrible.'

'It was. I just had to sit there and try to smile as if everything was fine. And they were so kind to me. Obviously I couldn't say who I was. And I knew you'd be worried because you'd be thinking something had happened to me, but there was nothing I could do.'

Millie squeezed her hand, and then a thought occurred to her. 'Was Maria there?'

'No.'

'Just as well. It might have been awkward to explain why you had gone back there again.'

'But the thing about the family – that's not all.'

Millie waited.

'I haven't told you everything. I met someone not long after we got here. He's Greek, and I didn't tell you because I thought you'd think history was repeating itself and you'd get angry and … anyway, his name is Mitsos. I was so happy, but Mitsos is Dimitris's grandson so we're related.' At that Eva started to cry harder, and Millie moved round the table to comfort her. She had so many questions of her own, but they would have to wait.

* * *

'Thank you, doctor.'

Millie saw him out and reassured Gus, who had come with him, that they would be fine. As she went to close the door, Violeta appeared. 'How is Eva?'

'She's going to be fine. It's just a sprain.'

'That's good. May I see her?'

Millie hesitated. She wanted to talk to Eva further about the events of the day before, but she could not think of a way to put Violeta off. 'Of course.'

'Hello,' said Eva.

'Hi. Can I come in?'

'Sure,' said Eva, glad of any opportunity to avoid a further post-mortem of the day before with Millie.

Violeta sat down beside Eva who was on the sofa with her leg up on a chair, an ice pack on her ankle and a packet of painkillers by her side.

'I'll leave you to it then,' said Millie and disappeared into her room.

'Does it hurt a lot?' Violeta asked.

'It comes and goes.' Eva looked at Violeta properly for the first time since she had come in and saw that she had been crying. She pushed herself up in her seat. 'What's the matter?'

'Nothing,' said Violeta, rubbing at her face as though she could brush away the red patches.

'That's not nothing.'

'You have your own problems.'

'It'll mend, but in the meantime, I'm not going anywhere. Do you want to talk about it?'

'I've been longing to talk to someone, but I can't tell any of my family about it.'

'So talk to me,' Eva suggested, thinking as she spoke that she was also family.

'You're my guest.'

'I could also be your friend.'

Violeta smiled at her sadly.' I would like that.'

'Come on. Please tell me.'

'OK, but you mustn't tell anyone.'

'I promise.'

'Do you remember I told you about that boy I liked?'

'Yes,' Eva replied.

'I decided to talk to him. I was fed up with all the wondering and waiting.'

Eva nodded.

'He said he was very fond of me but not like that.'

'Oh.'

'He was very kind about it, but I'd always thought we'd

end up together and …' Violeta broke off. 'I was stupid to think it could come to anything.'

'Did he say anything else?'

'He said he'd never thought of me like that, and he couldn't imagine thinking of me like that because we're cousins.'

'Cousins?'

'Yes.'

Eva fell silent as she thought about that. Violeta was Maria's daughter. Maria was Dimitris's daughter. Violeta's cousin might have been at the dinner the night before. Or he could be a cousin on her father's side of the family. She wondered how to ask for his name, but Violeta did the work for her.

'I've always had a crush on Mitsos.'

'Mitsos?'

'Yes, that's his name.'

'I'm so sorry, Violeta,' Eva said, not trusting herself to say anything more.

'And then he said…' Violeta stopped and shook her head as though wanting to deny what he had told her.

'Go on.'

'He said he'd met someone. Someone special. He said he didn't mean to be unkind but that it was better if I heard it from him.'

Eva felt her mouth go dry. 'Who?'

'He didn't tell me her name. I hate her, whoever she is,' Violeta said.

Eva saw her raw anger and could no longer look her in

the eye. 'I really am very sorry,' she said, realising she was sorry in more ways than Violeta could imagine. 'I wish I could help you.'

'Thank you. You're very kind to listen to my problems.'

'I don't mind. I'm sorry I can't give you any advice.'

'That's OK. It just helps to talk to someone. You can understand why I can't tell my family.'

'Yes, I can see that would be very difficult,' said Eva.

'It would be impossible.'

'What are you going to do?'

'What can I do? It's helped me with one decision, though. I'm going to go to university in Athens. Make a fresh start. See the world. Make lots of money. Then come back here and make him realise what he's missed out on.' Violeta laughed, but it was hollow.

'Sounds like a plan,' said Eva, joining in with the false jollity.

'And you?'

'Stay here for a few days and go crazy until I can get out and about again.'

'I should leave you to get some rest,' said Violeta getting up. She walked to the door. 'Thanks for listening Eva. It's helped a lot.'

'I don't think I've helped you very much.'

'You have. Just by listening.'

'You're welcome,' said Eva. She watched Violeta leave and as the door closed, the dam broke and she started to cry inconsolably. Mitsos had rejected Violeta because she was his cousin. She was also his cousin. There was no way they could have a future together. She had never before felt that everything was so utterly hopeless.

In her room, Millie heard Eva crying. Her initial instinct was to comfort her and then as she reached the door, her nerve failed her. She was so drained that she had no idea what to do for the best. Her hand rested on the door handle. She heard the crying start to subside, waited for Eva to compose herself, found her courage and walked into the room.

'How was Violeta?' Millie asked.

'OK. She just wanted to talk about something.'

'Perhaps she's not the only one.'

Eva rubbed at her eyes.

'Please let me help you.'

'I don't think you can. I don't think anyone can.'

'Why don't we find out?'

Eva shrugged.

'I think we should start by talking a little more about what happened yesterday.'

Eva shifted in her seat and repositioned the ice pack. 'I don't know where to start.'

'Talk me through what happened.'

'I've already told you everything'

'Humour me.'

'Nikos found me and took me to the house. He disappeared, and then Mitsos came into the room. I couldn't understand why he was there.' Eva relived the moment of confusion and then the dawning of understanding. 'Then everyone else started arriving, and it was really confusing because everyone was talking at once and speaking Greek, and Mitsos was translating some of the things they were saying but not everything …'

'Slow down. Take your time.'

'As I said, Dimitris was there.'

'How does he look?' Millie tried to keep the tone light but heard the break in her voice.

'Well.'

'And who else?'

'Nikos and his wife, Katia, and Loukas. That's their other son, Mitsos's brother. Then there was Nikos's brother and his wife and their children.

'Anybody else?'

'You remember Dimitris's father, the one who threatened you?'

'How could I forget?' Millie's eyes opened wide in alarm. 'He was there?'

'He's still alive, but I didn't see him. Loukas took some dinner to him in his room. It seems he's really frail now. He's past being able to hurt anyone, Millie.'

'I'm glad about that at least. Was anybody else there?'

Eva concentrated on moving the ice pack around again to avoid looking Millie in the eye. 'Angelika was there.'

'Dimitris's wife?'

Eva nodded, still not daring to meet her gaze. She heard Millie take a deep breath, and time seemed to stand still.

'What's she like?' Millie asked, eventually.

'She doesn't speak English so I could only speak to her through Mitsos.'

'Don't be evasive.'

'Millie, please –'

'Just tell me.'

Eva sighed. 'From what I could tell she seemed very pleasant. Mitsos told me that she said I was welcome. She seemed quite concerned about me.'

'I'm glad she's a good person.'

'You are?' Eva finally met Millie's eyes.

'Yes, I would have hated Dimitris to be married to someone who was unkind.'

'I thought you'd be angry that I didn't dislike her. I wanted to.'

'Why? None of this is her fault.'

'No. It's Nikos's fault. The older Nikos, I mean.'

'Exactly, not Angelika's, and when you love someone you want the best for them, don't you?'

'I suppose so,' said Eva, unsure if she would have been as generous as Millie.

'What happened after dinner?'

'Mitsos offered to drive me home, but Dimitris intervened and said Nikos should bring me back me instead.'

'Why?'

'I don't know.'

'Do any of them know about you and Mitsos?'

'No. I managed to think clearly enough to tell Mitsos I didn't think it was the right moment to introduce me as …'

'As his girlfriend?'

'Yes,' Eva said quietly.

'And did Nikos speak to you on the way back?'

Eva told Millie about the conversation she had had with Nikos in the car. 'He started to say I reminded him of someone, and he sounded, I don't know, kind of sad. Then he went really quiet again, but when he said goodbye, he told me to take care. Like an uncle might.'

'He is your uncle. Your half-uncle at any rate.'

'Yes, so Mitsos is my cousin. Or my second cousin. Or my half-cousin. We're related whatever the term is. No, no, no.' Eva thought about what Mitsos had said to Violeta, grabbed a cushion and hugged it to her.

Millie wondered just how seriously they had become involved. She had watched Eva coming back to the apartment, glowing in the way she herself had done as a young woman after her meetings with Dimitris. She kicked herself; she should have followed her instincts and tried to intervene. But then she thought back to her relationship with Dimitris, and she knew no intervention would have done any good.

Millie brushed Eva's hair back from her face. 'You really do have feelings for Mitsos, don't you?'

Eva looked at Millie and nodded. Her eyes were glassy with tears. 'Yes, and now I don't know what to do.'

Millie had always prided herself on being the one who would provide Eva with a safe harbour and answers, but for once she had nothing to suggest. 'I don't know either darling. We'll have to work it out together.'

'Just like it used to be? You and me against the world?' The faintest flicker of hope appeared in Eva's eyes, and to Millie she looked like a little girl again for just the briefest of moments.

'Yes, just like it used to be.'

They both fell quiet. Eva tried again to work out exactly how she was related to Mitsos and kept reaching for her phone to try to find out, before remembering she no longer had it.

For her part, Millie was preoccupied with thoughts of Dimitris. Eva had not said much about his family and, in truth, she was not sure how much she wanted to know. The thought that he had gone on to marry and have a happy family life, having forgotten all about her, was something she had long ago accepted intellectually, but now that it had been presented to her as a cold, hard truth, it still hurt. It was not that she wished him unhappiness, anything but … she sighed. Her thoughts were still so tangled after all those years.

Millie finally broke the silence. 'You've met Nikos. What did you make of him?'

'I don't know. He wasn't very friendly at first, but he wasn't scary. Well, maybe just a little bit to start with, but when he found me, I was trespassing on their land. He had every right to be annoyed.'

They both lapsed into silence again before Eva continued. 'I'm sure I reminded him of mum. I look like her, don't I?'

'Yes, you do.' The sadness in Millie's voice was tangible.

'I want to find out what he knows.'

'I don't think that's a good idea. Nothing good has come of this trip. I think we should leave it alone, lie low and go home as planned in a few days. Try to put it all behind us.

Nobody knows who we are, and I think we should keep it that way. Let's just get away from here before anything else happens.'

'Whatever happens, I can't put Mitsos behind me and, now we've come this far, don't you want to know what happened to mum?'

'Of course I do. More than you can imagine.'

'Then I have to speak to Nikos again. He's the key to everything. I'm sure of it.'

'But what are you going to say?

'I don't know.' Eva threaded her necklace through her fingers.

And how do you know you won't be putting yourself in danger?'

'I don't think he's dangerous. Quick to get angry, maybe, but not dangerous. Perhaps something else happened which made mum want to leave, and it was nothing to do with Nikos. Anyway I have an excuse to go back.' Eva tapped the walking stick by her side.

'I thought he told you to leave it at the bar?'

'Yes, but I could return it with a present to thank all of them for being so kind. That wouldn't be so strange.'

'I don't like any of this, Eva. I can't risk Dimitris recognising me, but I can't let you go alone.'

'Then we have to make a plan because I'm going to find out the truth one way or another.'

Chapter 20

Millie and Eva set off for the bar. After three days of rest and painkillers, Eva no longer needed the walking stick and her limp was barely noticeable.

They introduced themselves and were met with a friendly reply from Thanos. 'Yes, you are the girl Nikos told me about. You have come for your phone?' he added.

'Do you have it?' asked Eva.

'Yes, yes, wait here.'

Thanos re-emerged with Eva's phone in his hand.

'Thank you,' said Eva, sounding as relieved as she felt.

'I can take the stick?'

'Not yet. I need it for a little longer.'

Thanos shrugged. 'When you are ready. Have a good day.'

Millie and Eva wished him a good day in return and left the shop. Outside, Eva plugged her phone into her mobile charger and switched it on. She saw lots of messages waiting for her, but only one that held her attention. Mitsos.

I hope your ankle is better. Contact me as soon as you get your phone back. We've lost so much time. I miss you.

Millie had been watching Eva's expression closely. 'Problems?'

'Mitsos.'

Millie opened her mouth to say something, but Eva stopped her. 'I'm going to send him a quick message, and then we'll go.'

Hi. I've just got my phone back. Ankle still hurts, but it's getting better. I miss you too.

Mitsos replied immediately. *That's good news. When can we meet?*

I'm not sure. I need to rest it a bit more.

Let me know as soon as you can. I'll find a reason to get away. I can't wait to see you.

I'll be in touch, I promise.

'What was all that about?' Millie asked.

'I said I couldn't meet him today.'

'What if he's at the farm now?'

Eva looked startled. 'I hadn't thought of that.'

'Perhaps we shouldn't go.'

'No, we're going. I told you that I'm going to find out what happened to mum once and for all. If Mitsos is there, I'll have to deal with that when and if it happens.' Her stomach clenched tight at the thought of it.

'Nothing is going to stop you, is it?'

Eva shook her head and headed towards the waiting taxis where she asked for the Petrakis farm. Millie reluctantly got in. The journey took them over the headland with spectacular views down plunging cliffs to the Aegean. The windows were open and at any other time, Eva might have been preoccupied with the state of her hair or Millie with the casual, perilous way the taxi took the bends, yet all they could think about was what would come of their visit.

The taxi drew up at the gate. They paid, got out and looked at each other. They had made a plan, but it didn't feel like a particularly good one now that they were there.

'I'll go in and give them the present and ask to speak to Nikos. Wait for me over there,' said Eva pointing towards the pine trees.

'I don't want you to do this, Eva.'

'I'm not exactly looking forward to it, but I have to know about mum. I'll only be a phone call away if there's a problem.'

Millie sighed, but realised she was hardly in a position to criticise. She had raised a granddaughter as wilful as she had been at that age. She moved along the line of the fence and slipped into the shadows of the trees.

Eva took a deep breath and tried to ignore the trembling which had taken control of her legs. If her nerve failed her, she could just drop off the present and leave. I wouldn't seem odd. It would be fine.

She arrived at the end of the path, opened the latch on the gate to the courtyard and stepped into the shade provided by the vines. Deep breaths, she told herself. She knocked on the door and waited.

Just as she was about to give up and walk away, the door clicked open and she saw Katia, Nikos's wife, standing there.

'Hello,' Eva started hesitantly.

'Eva! This is a surprise. Come in,' said Katia and stepped forward to give her a kiss on the cheek.

'Thank you.'

Eva followed Katia into the kitchen, looking around for signs of any other members of the family. She seemed to be alone, but she wanted to be sure. 'It's very quiet today. Where is everyone?'

Katia flapped a hand. 'Dimitris is at the coffee house. Mitsos is out fishing with his brother and his uncle, and Angelika is at the shop. 'Would you like a coffee?'

'Yes, please.' Eva relaxed slightly at the thought that whatever else was about to happen, she would not run into Mitsos. 'And Nikos?'

'On the farm somewhere.' She motioned in the direction of the pine trees, where Millie was waiting. 'Inspecting the plants, mending fences, feeding the chickens; so many things to do every day. How is your ankle?'

'Getting much better thank you, and I also have my phone back.'

'Good. Nikos asked Mitsos to go to the bar with it.'

'Actually, in a way that's why I'm here,' said Eva.

Katia looked at her questioningly. 'Let's have our coffee, and you can tell me.'

They settled at the table, and Eva sipped the thick, sweet liquid. It had gone from being a shock to the system the first time she had tried it to a welcome taste. Katia said nothing more and seemed content to let Eva take her time.

'You were all so kind to me the other day that I wanted to bring you a present to thank you.'

'That is very nice, but it is not necessary. We believe in helping people. It is an honour for us to do it. We keep the old traditions here.'

'I'm not insulting you, am I?'

'No, but you did not need to bring a gift.'

Eva opened the bag on her lap and produced a beautifully wrapped box.

Katia opened it to reveal a selection of cakes from the shop Violeta had recommended to her.

'They look delicious. We must try some with our coffee.'

They finished the coffee and cakes in a comfortable silence, and then Katia noticed the walking stick.

'Shall I take that?'

'I thought I might give it to Nikos and take the opportunity to thank him as well.'

Katia looked surprised. 'It's a long walk to the farm. You have to follow the track through the forest. Are you sure you want to go? It might be too much for your ankle.'

'Yes, I want to thank him personally.' Eva suddenly felt restless, anxious to get on with what she had come to do. 'I should go now before it gets too hot. Thank you so much for everything.'

'You are always welcome to come and see us again. When do you leave?'

The thought of leaving Andraxos provoked a visceral reaction in Eva, which went beyond anything she could have anticipated. The thought of going back to her old life or even going forward into her new one, lacked any attraction.

'On Friday, but I don't want to go.'

Katia smiled at her. 'Andraxos has that effect on people who take the time to get to know the place. We don't have the glamour of some of the islands. We still have a simple life here. It appeals to some people.'

'It certainly appeals to me. I wish I could stay.'

'Perhaps you will return, and when you do you can visit your friends here.'

Eva swallowed hard. 'You are very kind, but I must go now.'

'Remember to take the path through the forest. Keep the sea on your left and eventually you will come to a clearing and you will see the farm buildings. Nikos will be around there somewhere.'

Katia saw her to the door.' Good bye, Eva.'

Eva took a last look around the room. 'Good bye, Katia.'

Eva heard the door close behind her but remained where she was, collecting her thoughts. After she had calmed down, she headed to the forest to meet Millie.

'You've been ages,' Millie whispered.

'Katia wanted me to have coffee with her. You were the one who taught me to slow down here and accept Greek hospitality.'

It was a point with which Millie could not argue so instead she asked, 'Who did you say Katia was?'

'She's Nikos's wife. Anyway, Katia said Nikos is over on the farm. We need to follow the path through the trees to get there.' Eva looked around. 'Where is it?'

'I saw a path earlier while I was waiting for you. Over there.'

'I can't see another one so I suppose this must be it,' Eva said. 'Come on then. And look where you're going. You don't want to end up like me.'

They made their way through the forest. In the quiet hush of the morning, the day waited expectantly for the heat of the afternoon to engulf everything in its path. Even the cicadas were silent. They crossed sun-dappled glades and patches of forest so dark they still felt cool and damp. Between the trees, they saw flashes of the sea, far below them on their left. Eva finally saw a clearing ahead and came to a halt. Millie stopped just behind her.

'Look,' Eva said, pointing to the right at cultivated land and some small outbuildings. 'That must be it.' She started to move but felt Millie's hand on her arm.

'Darling, it's still not too late to stop all this. We could turn back, even now. No harm done.'

'Do you remember you told me about the "what if" moment? The agony of wondering if you'd done the right thing? This is one of mine and if I turn back now, I'll regret it forever.'

Millie watched helplessly as Eva broke the cover of the trees, leaving her to do what she had always been obliged to do since they had arrived – watch and wait and hope.

Eva emerged from the forest, blinking in the blinding white light. She pulled her sunglasses off their perch on the top of her head and put them on. She looked around, trying to get her bearings. Behind her was the pine forest. In front of her was rough scrub land with some cultivated land and farm buildings to the right and, to her left, the cliffs which fell away to the sea. In the stillness, she could hear waves breaking on the rocks below. She moved closer, peered over and instantly recoiled. She wasn't frightened of heights, but the earth was crumbling away, and she was afraid of losing her footing.

She headed back to the area from which she had come but instead of returning to the safety of the trees, she moved towards the farm. The land was broken up into small parcels, each growing a different crop, bounded by rough stone walls. She followed the narrow, dusty path which ran down the middle of the lots.

There was nobody in sight, but the further she walked into the heart of Nikos's territory, the more nervous she became. She felt her hair grow damp and start to cling to her neck and her heart rate increase. She tried to draw strength from the fact she was doing this for her mum and that Millie was not far away but nothing helped. She stopped at the end of the path, debating which way to turn. As she was deciding what to do, Nikos appeared from round the corner of the building in front of her. He flinched at the sight of her, and they stared at each other.

'Hello,' said Eva, desperate to break the silence.

'What are you doing here?'

'I, er, I went to the house.' She added quickly, 'I saw Katia.' She thought that if Nikos knew she had been seen there, it might buy her some safety.

'Why?'

'Why what?'

'Why did you go to the house?'

'I bought a present for all of you to thank you for looking after me, and to thank you for returning my phone.'

'What did you talk to Katia about?'

'Nothing in particular. Just how beautiful Andraxos is and how sad I feel about leaving.' Eva thought she saw Nikos relax marginally, but was unsure; his reactions were hard to read.

'When do you leave?'

'Friday.' Eva paused. 'I'm sure you're pleased.'

Nikos snorted. 'It makes no difference to me.'

'Even so, I can imagine that perhaps you don't like sharing your island with tourists.'

'They don't normally come up here. Well, only to the shop. They don't walk about all over my farm.'

'No, of course not.'

They eyed each other as Eva tried to think how she could broach the subject she had gone there to talk about. There was no subtle way to introduce it.

Nikos broke the silence. 'I understand why you went to the house, but why are you here?'

'Katia told me you'd be here, and I wanted to thank you personally for helping me. And I have a question.'

'What?'

Eva took a deep breath. This was the moment of no return; the moment at which everything would escape from her control; the moment when words would be spoken, which would never be able to be taken back.

'Who do I remind you of, Nikos?'

The cicadas started to rasp, vibrating like the tension in

overhead electricity cables. The noise surrounded them, sucking the oxygen from the air. Eva felt as though the buzzing had invaded her brain. Nikos continued to stare at her.

'The other night in the car, you told me I reminded you of someone. Who?'

Nikos remained silent, but Eva saw something change in his expression and sensed she had gained the upper hand although she had no idea why. Without stopping to think further she said, 'I remind you of Helena, don't I? Helena, your half-sister.'

Nikos took a few steps backwards as if Eva had physically attacked him. 'Who are you?'

'I am Helena's daughter – and your niece.'

Nikos shook his head and tried to retreat further but found his back against the wall of the outbuilding. 'I don't know who you are talking about,' he said.

Eva took a step towards him. 'You know who Helena is. I am here because she came here years ago, and she met you. But she never came home again. I've been waiting all my life to come here and find out why.'

'You're crazy. This Helena you're talking about may have come to Andraxos for all I know, but I don't know anything about her. I've never heard of her.'

'I'm not crazy. My mum wrote emails to her mother, my grandmother, and I've seen them. She said she'd met you and by what she wrote, she got very upset after meeting you. Why do think that would be, Nikos?'

'What emails?'

'I don't carry them around with me, but I have them.'

'I don't know what you're talking about.'

'You might not know about the emails, but why would I be here if it wasn't true?'

'There's nothing for you here. Go away.'

'No.'

'You heard me. Leave.'

'No.'

'Get off my land.'

'No.'

'This is just like …'

'Just like what, Nikos?'

'Nothing.'

'Just like when my mum came here? That's what you were going to say, isn't it? You told her to go away too.'

Nikos eyed her and appeared to weigh up his options. 'What do you want?'

'I told you. I want to know what happened to my mum. I don't want anything else – just the truth.'

'Just,' Nikos laughed; a short, bitter laugh.

Eva stared at him defiantly, and Nikos assessed her. 'Come,' he said reluctantly.

'Where?'

'Let's sit down.'

Nikos led her back down the path between the lots and towards a stone bench in the scrub land between the farm and the forest. Eva realised that if Millie had not moved, she would be able to see them and the thought reassured her.

'Sit.'

Eva complied, and Nikos sat down beside her. He lit a cigarette and offered Eva one, which she declined.

'Helena did come to see me. 2005, wasn't it? Not that I could forget.' He paused and ran a hand through his hair. 'I met her in almost the same way I met you. She came up here, and I found her creeping about.'

'Is that why you were so hostile towards me?'

'I don't like people wandering around uninvited on my land. But it didn't help that you looked so much like her. It was like she had come back again.'

Eva let him contemplate that and said nothing.

'You really do look so much like her,' he said.

'What happened, Nikos?' Eva asked quietly.

'She came here to find my father – her father. I didn't know that at first, but he wasn't here anyway.'

'Why?'

'He was in Thessaloniki. His uncle had died and he had to go to the funeral and help out.'

Eva recalled her mother's emails, and remembered that Nikos had told her the same story. 'So you told her the truth about him not being here?'

'Yes. It was a bad time. He was there more than he was here that summer and autumn.' Nikos caught Eva's questioning look. 'The problems with my uncle's house and business were never ending.'

'And you weren't curious as to why some stranger from England was so interested in your family and farm?'

'Being curious always leads to problems. I've found it's better in life not to ask too many questions. And I had a bad feeling, and I hoped if I ignored it – her – she would just go away.'

'But she didn't?'

'No. She came back the next day and told me who she was. I ... I didn't react well.'

'What did you do?' Eva asked.

'I didn't believe her at first. I told her she was lying, but somehow I knew she wasn't. What reason would a stranger have to come to a remote Greek farm and claim someone was her father?'

'So once you believed her, what happened?'

'I got angry but, in the end, I agreed to listen to what she had to say. She told me that her mother was from England and had met my father when she was on holiday here. They had some sort of holiday romance,' Nikos sounded disgusted as he said the words, 'and then she had found out she was pregnant when she returned to England.'

'Why were you so angry with her?'

'Because if Helena had met my mother and told her, it would have broken her heart to know her husband had had another woman.'

'It was before they married.'

'But not before their families had decided they would marry.'

'I've spoken to my grandmother. They really loved each other. It wasn't a holiday romance. I mean it was but not in the way you think.'

Nikos took a long drag on his cigarette, realised it was almost down to the butt, and ground it into the stone bench.

'That doesn't make it better, does it? Stirring all that up again. Anything could have happened. I am the eldest son, and it is my responsibility to protect my family.'

'And how did you protect them, Nikos?' Eva asked, remembering the story of the thief and the shotgun.

Nikos looked around the farm and then fixed his sights on the horizon far out to sea, a smudge of blue and purple shimmering in the haze. In the distance, Eva heard goat bells clinking. A gentle wind ruffled the trees and the scent of wild herbs drifted on the breeze. Time slowed. Still she said nothing; she was learning the value of patience and could wait for as long as it took.

'I told her I needed time to think, and I said I'd meet her here again a few days later. But it was on the condition she didn't go to the house again or talk to anyone else.'

Eva thought back to the emails. His story of the events which had played out there matched her mother's version.

'I cancelled it once. I couldn't go through with it, but then I decided I had to see her and make sure she understood she couldn't come back. This is the exact spot where we met.'

'She sat here with you?'

'Yes.'

Eva ran her hand along the bench as if through it she could somehow reconnect with her mother. 'And then?'

'We argued. She told me she had the right to meet her father, and I told her she didn't have the right to destroy all of our lives. We were screaming at each other.' Nikos bit down hard on his lip. 'She got up and started pacing up and down, shouting at me, calling me selfish and cruel. I told her she was the selfish one. Why did she need to destroy a family just to meet someone she had been without her whole life?'

Eva willed herself to stay quiet.

'She started to walk away, and I got up and asked her where she was going. I was afraid she'd go to the house.'

'She yelled back that she hadn't decided yet. We started shouting at each other again, and then I realised how close she was ...' Nikos looked at the cliff edge stretching away in front of them and gestured slightly towards it.

Eva followed his gaze and thought of the jagged rocks below.

'It was an accident, Eva. I didn't push her. I wasn't even that close to her. She just lost her footing.'

Eva felt tears start to form. 'What did you do?'

'I couldn't see her so I ran back to the house, drove down to the harbour and took the boat out. I searched for her until dark but ...' He shook his head. 'I've lived with this for so many years. I thought it was all behind me, but it never really was and then when I saw you, I knew.'

Eva hunted around in her pocket for a tissue while Nikos lit another cigarette. She looked up at him and said, 'I think you should meet someone.'

'Who?'

'Helena's mother.'

'What?'

'She's here with me.'

'Where?'

'Close by.'

'No, I don't want to. I can't meet her.'

'Please, Nikos. Wait here.'

Eva got up and walked slowly towards the pine trees, turning around every few steps to make sure he had not disappeared, but he seemed incapable of movement.

Eva found Millie and told her Nikos's story. She felt Millie's body start to shake as if it would break apart, and she pulled her close and held her. 'I always hoped perhaps somehow she would still be alive, but she's not, is she?' Millie said.

'No, Millie, she's not. I think you should meet Nikos, though.'

'Why?'

'I think it might help both of you.'

'I don't know, Eva.'

'I do.'

Millie looked at Eva and saw for the first time the adult rather than the child; someone who had taken control of the situation.

'I can't forgive him, but I think it really was an accident, and you need to believe that too. Come on.' Eva took her by the hand, and led her into the sunlight.

Nikos stood up as he saw them approaching him, stubbed his cigarette out and ran his hands down his trousers.

'Nikos,' said Millie.

'Helena's mother,' he said.

'Call me Millie.'

'Millie,' he said, awkwardly.

'Tell me what happened to Helena.'

'I've just told Eva.'

'Yes, and now I want you to tell me.'

Eva watched as Nikos told Millie everything that had happened. She saw the same expression on Millie's face that she had seen so many times before; scanning for even the hint of a lie. If there was one, Eva knew Millie would detect it.

Nikos finished his story, and Millie continued to look at him, her own loss competing with her compassion for the guilt of the man in front of her. Eva looked from one to the other of them, wondering how the sequence of events she had triggered would end.

The silence seemed to stretch into infinity. Eva waited. Finally Millie spoke. 'I believe you. I'm sure it was an accident so you don't need to be forgiven for that, but I forgive you for not helping Helena to get in touch with her father. It was for the best. It would have destroyed your family.'

Millie stepped forward and embraced him as a mother would a child in need of comfort as Eva looked on, stunned by the generosity of her grandmother's spirit.

* * *

The three of them sat in silence on the bench, Eva between Millie and Nikos, as they all wondered where they would go from there. Nikos lit yet another cigarette and offered Millie one, which she accepted, ignoring Eva's disapproving look.

'Didn't the police ever come to you to ask about my mum?' Eva asked.

'No. Why would they?' Nikos asked, looking genuinely surprised.

'Because of the emails. I told you that she talked about you in them, and she seemed scared of you. If I had been investigating her disappearance , I would have come to talk to you.'

Beside her, Millie squirmed awkwardly.

'What is it, Millie?'

'I didn't tell you absolutely everything, Eva.'

'What are you talking about?'

'I showed you all of your mum's emails, but I didn't show them to the police. Not all of them.'

'What? Millie, how could you not show all of them to the police?'

'I showed them the ones which proved she was here and the one in which she said was going to look into getting a ferry back to Athens earlier than planned, but I didn't show them the ones which mentioned Dimitris and Nikos.' Millie took a deep breath. 'And, while I'm confessing, I didn't mention to the police what happened when Dimitris's father came to see me all those years ago. You assumed I did, but I didn't.'

'What happened?' Nikos asked, but his question was lost as Eva asked, 'I don't understand. Why not?'

'I couldn't believe that any child of Dimitris's could do anything terrible.'

'Couldn't or didn't want to?' Eva shot back.

Millie shook her head. She thought of how convinced she had been of that fact at first and how, only much later, the doubts had started to creep in and by then it had felt too late to do anything.

Seeing the look of despair on Millie's face, Eva tried to modify her tone. 'But what about finding mum? Surely that was more important?'

'Of course it was, but I didn't know what to do. I thought the police would find her and then by the time I realised they wouldn't, I couldn't say I'd lied. It would have thrown doubt on everything else I had told them, all of which was true. And I would have put Dimitris into an impossible situation as well.'

'Did my father know about Helena?' Nikos asked.

'No,' Millie said sadly. 'I knew his life had been planned out so I thought it was better for him not to know. Ignorance is supposed to be bliss, isn't it?'

'Will you tell him now?'

'I don't think there's any point, is there? But how I wish I could see him just once more.' As she spoke the words, she wondered who had said them. She had spent the last month desperately hoping she would not see him.

Nikos hesitated and said, 'I will tell him you are here.'

'But you were terrified that if he met Helena, it would destroy your family,' Eva said. 'Why would you be happy for him to meet Millie?'

'Because I destroyed your family, and now I see Millie is a good woman, and she did not deserve that. She is not how I imagined her to be.'

Millie decided to let the remark pass.

He deliberated further. 'I will tell him and then … it is

my father's decision, not mine. Give me your phone number.'

'We leave in a few days,' Eva reminded him.

'Yes,' said Nikos. 'And there is another thing. Eva, I see the way Mitsos is with you. You must end it.'

Eva met his eyes. 'I know. I just don't know how.'

Nikos got up slowly. 'I can't help you with that, but I will speak to my father about Millie, and then we will all have to see what happens. I must go. You can find your own way back?'

'Yes,' said Eva.

'Thank you, Nikos,' said Millie.

'Be careful with that cigarette. Don't start a fire.'

They watched him trudge back towards the farm, and they were finally forced to confront each other.

'I'm sorry, Eva. I should have told you everything.'

Eva kicked at the dust. 'I don't have the energy to be angry, Millie. Besides, things aren't always straightforward. I used to think they were, but I see now life isn't like that. There is just one thing.'

'What's that?'

'Is there anything else you haven't told me?'

'No, you know everything now. There are no more secrets.' Millie stubbed her cigarette out on the bench and put it in her bag. She took Eva's hand, and they got up and edged closer towards the spot where Helena had fallen.

'Mum really didn't choose to leave us, did she?'

'No, darling, she didn't.'

The wind started to pick up, and the waves crashed

against the rocks with renewed intensity. Arms around each other, they stood and watched, hypnotised, thinking of their daughter and mother, and felt the sadness of a place where only ghosts remained.

Chapter 21

Their day started with coffee and croissants, which was a reassuring ritual despite the fact that neither of them had any appetite.

'Tell me more about Mitsos.'

'What about him?'

'You obviously care for him very deeply. I never got that impression when you were with Tom. I think that's something to talk about … if you want to.'

Eva saw only concern in Millie's eyes, and it was true that she wanted to talk about him. She lit up inside just thinking about him.

'We met down at the harbour, and he drew a picture of me.'

'Can I see it?'

Eva got up and returned with the cardboard roll from which she carefully pulled out a piece of paper.

'It's beautiful,' Millie said. 'He's really captured you. Not just the way you look, but you. He's very talented.'

'We started meeting regularly after that,' said Eva. 'I

couldn't tell you, Millie. I knew it would bring back all sorts of painful memories and worry you.'

'Is that why you broke up with Tom?'

'No, we broke up before I met him. Mitsos is so different to any of the boys I've ever met, Millie. He's warm and kind and artistic. He's sensitive. He's comfortable with himself. He doesn't play games with people. Does that make sense?'

Millie nodded.

'Are you angry?'

'I'm not really in a position to be angry with you, am I?'

'I suppose not, but even so…'

'I hate to say it, my dear, but Nikos was right. I can't quite work out if you're first cousins or half cousins or what you are, but you are related, and that's not a lie you can live with forever.'

'But would it be a lie? It's more of an omission, isn't it?'

'Lying by omission hasn't worked out very well on my part, has it? And what if he found out later?'

Eva remembered what Violeta had said to her. She had promised not to tell anyone, but now she felt compelled to share her secret with Millie. 'If I tell you something, will you promise not to say a word to anyone?'

'You should know the answer to that but, yes, I promise.'

'Violeta is Mitsos's cousin.'

'Yes, I know that. And?'

'When Violeta was here the other day, she told me she had had a crush on Mitsos and when she told him, he said he liked her but not in that way and besides they were cousins so nothing could ever happen between them.'

'So that's why you were so upset when she left. You see? If he ever found out – and worse if he found out that you knew and hadn't told him – how do you think he would react? I know cousins do get married in some places, but that's neither here nor there in this case. The only point that matters is that Mitsos has made his feelings on the subject very clear. I know it's terribly painful, but you have to end it.'

Eva looked at Millie, her eyes pleading for her to change her mind and say she had been wrong. 'It's not like we were brought up together, though. And we're not full first cousins.'

'Yes, but you'd still be keeping something extremely important from him. Besides,' Millie continued, 'think it through. Imagine you got married. I wouldn't be able to go to the wedding. Imagine you had children. It would be very difficult, impossible, for me to see them.'

'I'm not even thinking about marriage and children, Millie. I'm only eighteen.'

'Yes, but one day you won't be eighteen and those things might start to become important to you.'

'I don't know. I can't think straight.'

'And what about your plans to become an architect? It's all you have ever wanted to do.'

'I know. I know.'

'Even if there weren't all the other problems, I doubt Mitsos would be able to settle in the UK. You might be able to come here after you've qualified, but I can't see many opportunities for you here. In Athens perhaps if you could speak Greek.'

'Mitsos hates Athens. He hates all big cities.'

'You see?'

'You're being very practical.'

'And you must try to be practical too. I know only too well that it isn't easy, but you must think Eva. Not just feel. Think.'

They returned to the cooling coffee, and Millie's phone rang. 'Yes?'

'It's me,' said Nikos. 'I haven't told him about Helena and Eva. Only you. He wants to see you.'

'When?'

'Tomorrow at 8 p.m.'

'Where?'

'He said you'd know.'

'Yes, thank you,' said Millie, and the line went dead.

'What was all that about?' Eva asked.

'That was Nikos. I'm meeting Dimitris tomorrow night.'

'Where?'

'At our beach.'

'How do you feel?'

'I don't want to talk about it.'

'You wanted me to talk about Mitsos.'

'Yes, I did,' Millie conceded. 'I'm sorry.'

'What am I going to say to Mitsos, Millie?'

'When you see him, I'm sure you'll find the words. Just be –'

'Careful?'

'Yes,' Millie said, managing the slightest of sad smiles.

'And what are you going to say to Dimitris?'

'Like you, I haven't the faintest idea, but I hope I'll find the words too. That's all we can do, isn't it? Hope.'

'I suppose so,' said Eva.

Millie stood up. 'I think I'd like a few minutes alone if you don't mind. Arrange to see Mitsos, but please remember what I said. Think about the future. Think about the repercussions. The decisions you make now will last a lifetime.'

* * *

Eva sat out on the balcony. The bleached-out purity of the light, the lack of sleep and the thought of having to break up with Mitsos made her feel dizzy. She reached for her phone and sent a message.

Hi. Can we meet tomorrow?

I was hoping we could meet today. We only have today and tomorrow.

I know, but I don't feel great.

Is it your ankle?

Kind of. I haven't slept very well lately with the pain and thinking about leaving.

OK. Tomorrow then. What time?

The harbour at 5? Can you make it?

I'll make sure I can. xxxx

Eva put her phone down and wondered what she would say. She was still thinking about that when she heard movement behind her. Millie appeared on the balcony and sat down.

'I've contacted Mitsos. I'm going to see him tomorrow.

He wanted us to meet today, but I couldn't face it.'

Millie nodded.

'And there's something else. It's about mum,' Eva continued. 'I'd like to go back to where she ... well, you know.'

'Why?'

'I'd like to take some flowers. It's like a way for us to say goodbye . I know you don't want to go anywhere near the farm and neither do I, but this is really important to me and –'

'I think it's a lovely idea.'

'You do?' Eva said, surprised.

'Yes, I do.'

'The only problem is I don't want to run the risk of them seeing us at the farm again.'

'No, that wouldn't be a good idea. Perhaps we could get there by boat?'

'I don't think they run trips over there and besides, I don't want to share the moment with a load of tourists.'

'I was thinking that Nikos could take us,' Millie said.

'Nikos?'

'Yes, why not? He could do that much for us.'

'I suppose you could ask,' Eva said. She waited as Millie rang him and a short conversation ensued.

'And?' Eva asked.

'He said he'd meet us at the harbour in an hour. Will you be ready by then?'

'I'm ready now.'

At the florist's, Millie selected flowers , and then they went to sit by the harbour in a café shaded by mulberry trees.

'Tell me more about mum.'

'What do you want to know?'

'Everything. For example, in the florist's you were picking out flowers in mum's favourite colours. I wouldn't know. I still feel like I don't know anything about her.'

And so they sat there, and Millie told Eva all about Helena; the things she had loved and hated; the things which had made her laugh and those which had made her angry. Eva made a mental note of everything; she laughed at the anecdotes Millie told her and came close to tears when Millie told her how Helena had reacted when Eva's father had died.

'I'm so sorry you never got to know her or your dad.'

'So am I, but I had you, and I will never be able to thank you for everything you've done for me. I've thought it so often, but I think it's about time I said it. I know you must have made a lot of sacrifices for me.'

'If I did, they were worth it. You have turned into a wonderful young woman, Eva.'

'I don't know about that, but I will try to make you proud of me.'

Millie put her arm around Eva's shoulders. 'I already am.'

'I don't know how you can say that. I've made you so unhappy. I only cared about coming here and getting what I wanted.'

Millie sighed. 'For most of my life, Andraxos has shaped my life. First with Dimitris, then getting pregnant, the loss of Helena, caring for you, and the knowledge that one day you would demand the truth.

'Coming back here was, short of losing you too, my worst

fear. You have shown me I can look it all in the face rather than hiding and letting it stalk me from the shadows. I know Nikos, Dimitris's father, can't hurt anyone ever again. And now I know what happened to Helena. I need to thank you; I am not angry with you. I'm just worried about you.'

Tears blurred Eva's vision. 'I thought I'd messed up.'

'No.' Millie looked around her. 'This place has broken my heart over and over again, and now it's broken yours too, but we're still here and somehow we'll get through it.'

'Will we?'

'Yes, you have no idea what a strong person you are. You have risen above everything, and the best is yet to come for you. It's all right to feel sad and confused and to need some time to make sense of everything.'

'But –'

Nikos appeared before Eva could finish and led them to the boat. They sat at the back while Nikos steered the boat out of the harbour and around the coast. Finally, he brought the boat to a stop, and they floated on a translucent sea.

Millie and Eva looked up at the towering cliffs looming above them.

'We can't get any closer because of the rocks,' Nikos called out from the front of the boat.

'Nikos, come and join us,' Millie offered.

Nikos hesitated and then made his way along the boat and sat beside them.

They stayed there a while longer, Millie with her arm around Eva and Eva with her head on her shoulder, watching the pull and push of the sea; a tug of war between the land and the water. It was hypnotic. The breeze started to grow stronger, and Eva shivered.

'Have you ended it with Mitsos?' Nikos asked, breaking the silence.

'Not yet. I'm going to tell him tomorrow.'

'But you won't tell him the truth?'

'No, of course not.' Eva paused. 'Nikos?'

'Yes?'

'Will you look out for him?' Eva asked.

'Of course.'

Eva hesitated. 'There's something else.'

'What?'

'Mitsos is a really talented artist. Please would you and Katia encourage him? I know he has his responsibilities, but please … would you? But don't tell him I told you.'

'I will try.'

'No, promise me that you will.'

Nikos met her eyes. 'I promise.' He looked over at Millie. 'I will look out for my father too. If I had done things differently with Helena, maybe none of this would have happened.'

'There's nothing we can do now except try to make the best of things,' said Millie. 'I know you have suffered over the years, but you told us what happened, and you brought us here. I think that's atonement.'

She handed some of the flowers to Eva and some to Nikos and, one by one, they threw them into the sea, each lost in their thoughts and memories of Helena, a young woman who had touched or changed them all in some way.

Chapter 22

Eva walked along the harbour front. She remembered how enchanted she had been by everything during her first few weeks on the island. Now even the warmth, the light, the colours – none of them could lift her spirits.

She saw Mitsos waving at her in the distance. She was excited, and then her mood crashed as she remembered what faced her. There could be no happy outcome whatever happened now.

As she came face to face with Mitsos, he reached out to run his hand through her hair and kiss her. Eva sidestepped the move. 'What's wrong?' Mitsos asked.

'Nothing. I'm still tired.' She took a deep breath. 'Mitsos, I need to talk to you.'

'I need to talk to you too.'

'About what?'

'My parents have started to come round to the idea of me doing something with art.'

'That's wonderful news.'

'I don't know what happened. They still want me to help

out with the fishing, but they said they would give me time to devote to setting up a small studio here in town.'

Eva silently thanked Nikos. 'I'm so happy for you.'

'Come on. I want to show you the place.'

Eva followed him to a small building set back from the waterfront. It looked a little dilapidated, and the door was secured by a padlock. 'I know it doesn't look much yet. It belongs to my grandfather, but he said he hadn't been inside for years, and I could use it rent free.'

Mitsos unlocked the door, and they went in. It was little more than an empty, dusty space, but it had a huge skylight, perfect for an artist's studio. Eva was able to imagine what could be done with it. She had a fleeting image of herself drawing up the plans for it.

'It's great.' She swallowed hard, realising she would not be there to see any plans come to life. 'It's going to be great.'

'There's something else too.' Mitsos took her hand and led her through to the back. 'There's enough space here for a small apartment. Big enough for one – or two.' He looked at Eva and waited.

Eva looked around her, a sense of despair sinking into her bones. 'Mitsos, I think … I mean …'

'I know it's fast, but I've been thinking about it. You should go to university or at least try it. You will regret it if you don't. I can get this place ready and then you can spend your holidays here. I can visit you in between or if you hate university, you can come and stay here.'

'You've got it all planned.'

'I'm sorry. I thought you wanted us to be together. I

thought this was a way to make it work.'

'No, I mean yes. It's a good idea.' Eva started to feel claustrophobic. 'Do you think we could go outside? It's a bit musty in here.'

'Yes, sure.' Mitsos locked up and they stood outside, both waiting for the other one to make the next move.

'I really am very happy that your parents have come round. As for the apartment, you just surprised me. I didn't realise how serious you were.'

'I've always been serious about you, about us. You must know that.' Mitsos paused. 'My mum really likes you.'

'You've talked to her about us?'

'I didn't have to. She can read me like a book. So you've got the mum seal of approval.'

'What about your dad?'

'He takes time to warm up to people. By the way, what did you want to talk to me about?'

Eva's resolve started to falter. 'Let's get on the boat first. I'd like to see the islet. You know, Agios Stefanos.'

'OK.'

They walked along the harbour, past the men touting for tourists to fill their boats for late afternoon cruises. Mitsos jumped aboard and helped Eva on.

'Let's go,' said Mitsos.

'Do you need me to do anything?'

'Only enjoy the journey,' Mitsos said, with a smile that hurt Eva.

Eva heard her phone ringing. She pulled it out of her pocket and saw that it was Millie.

'Hi.'

'Hello dear. Are you with Mitsos?'

'Yes.'

'Have you spoken to him yet?' Millie asked.

'No, not yet.'

'You can't talk?'

'Not really.'

'But you are all right?'

Eva was not all right, and she could never imagine being all right again. 'Yes, I'm fine.'

'Good. Remember what I said.'

'I will. What's happening there?'

'Nothing yet,' Millie replied.

'Well, good luck.'

'Thank you. We'll talk later.'

'Yes.' Eva hung up and trailed her hand in the water, watching as the town started to recede from view. They moved further out to sea, and Eva could see Millie's beach and the Villa Iris, a white sugar cube amongst the trees above the beach. Millie would be meeting Dimitris there soon after a wait of nearly half a century.

She thought about the twists and turns of fate which had delivered them to this place. If John and Sylvia had not bought that house; if Millie had declined Sylvia's invitation all those years ago; if she had not met Dimitris ... if, if, if. It was endless. She reminded herself she would not have been born but for all those events, but found no solace in the thought.

'Eva, come here.'

Eva moved to the front of the boat and saw Agios Stefanos coming into view. From their angle of approach, it looked like an inhospitable hulk of rock covered with scrub and prickly pear. She couldn't understand why Mitsos had been so keen to take her there.

Mitsos caught her expression. 'Wait until we get there,' he said, and Eva noticed again how he seemed to read her thoughts.

They rounded the headland and started to follow the coast of the islet and suddenly a small inlet appeared. An old jetty sat adjacent to the most beautiful beach Eva had ever seen. The sand shimmered silver and the water was pure turquoise. It was backed by towering rocks and the only approach to it was by the sea.

'You see?'

'I see.' Eva said.

Mitsos tied the boat up and helped Eva ashore. He went back to the boat and reappeared with a big basket. 'I brought some food. Come on,' he said and sat down on the beach.

'Mitsos, you know I have to leave tomorrow.'

His face fell. 'I know, but I don't want to talk about it. Not yet.'

'Then when? We're running out of time.'

'I'd like to enjoy this place with you and have a picnic and pretend everything is fine and that you're not leaving.'

'So would I, but it's not fine, and I am leaving. We have to talk about it.'

Mitsos turned to face her. 'I know, and you're right. I'll make a deal with you. If we can enjoy the next few hours here, I promise you that we'll talk about it later.'

'Later as in before we leave here?'

'Yes. Now, let's unpack this picnic.'

And so they ate and drank, and Eva allowed herself to join in with Mitsos's fantasy that there were no problems, and that they had all the time in the world. They laughed and talked of nothing consequential. Eva almost convinced herself there was no need to have the conversation she had planned. They cleared everything away, and Mitsos kissed Eva as he moved past her.

She watched him take the basket back to the boat. The sun had started its descent. By the following night, she would be back in England, and Mitsos would be here. The thought broke her heart.

Mitsos returned and put his arms around her as they watched the sunset. Eva felt his kisses soft as summer rain on her neck.

'Tell me your deepest secret,' Mitsos said.

Eva went quiet. What was her deepest secret? The fact that they were related? The fact that her mother was his grandfather's daughter? The fact that she was here with Millie, his grandfather's first love, who was probably even now meeting him? The fact that his great-grandfather had once threatened Millie? Where would she ever start with all that?

'I wish I could remember my parents.' She could feel herself on thin ice, but it was better than the truths she could not tell him.

'You said they died when you were very young.'

'My dad died in a fire. He tried to rescue someone.'

'He died as a hero then.'

'I suppose he did,' Eva said. 'I'd never thought about it like that before. I've always felt angry with him for leaving us.'

'And your mum?'

Unable to bring herself to lie and unable to tell him the truth, she said, 'I find it difficult to talk about her. Do you mind if we don't?'

'OK, but I want you to be able to trust me and feel you can tell me anything.'

'I do. But it's … complicated. Anyway,' Eva continued, 'What about you? What's your deepest secret?'

Mitsos hesitated. 'For years I'd been angry with my parents for not allowing me to do what I love. Now, they've accepted it and they're trying to help me, and I feel guilty. They've given me a loving home, but it wasn't enough for me. I'm ungrateful. I have much more than so many people.'

'You have a great family, but you have a true gift too. I'm happy they've finally recognised that.'

'They are not the only reasons I'm lucky, Eva,' Mitsos said and leaned forward to kiss her.

As she felt their lips touch, she was filled with a longing for him and sense of hopelessness which was worse than physical pain.

'Eva,' he said and cupped her face in his hands. He saw a stray tear slip down her face and gently brushed it away with his thumb. 'Why are you so sad?'

'I can't. I don't know. It's …'

His mouth silenced her with a long, deep kiss.

Eva pulled away. 'Mitsos, I really have to talk to you.'

'What is it, Eva?'

'You know I'm leaving, and we won't be able to see each other again despite all your plans. That's why I couldn't get excited about the apartment at the studio.'

'But if you come here in the holidays, and I go to England sometimes, that could work until you finish university. Perhaps I could even work there for a while.'

'No, I think the rules are going to change. I don't think you'll be able to do that unless you earn a lot of money and you can do specific jobs. And besides, this is your home. You wouldn't be happy away from here. I can see how much you love this place. You even hated having to go to Athens for a few days so you really wouldn't like London.'

'But I love you.'

'What did you say?'

'I said I love you.' he repeated softly. 'But you know that, don't you?'

Eva stared at him. Here was the man she had dreamed of meeting, declaring his love for her; a love she returned, but could never give. She cursed the universe for handing her a set of cards she could not play.

'You do know that, don't you?' Mitsos repeated.

Eva shook her head. 'No, I didn't know that.'

'Well, I do.'

'I love you too,' she heard herself replying because although it was impossible for them to be together, what she said was true.

'You don't have to say it just because I did.'

'But I do. You just took me by surprise. I didn't think you would ever feel like that about me.'

'I wish you would believe in yourself. And believe in me.'

'I do believe in you.'

'And believe in us.'

'I want to.'

'Then if I can't go to England, you could come here after you finish university. We'll make do with holidays until then.'

'It's the same problem. I won't be able to come and live here just because I want to.'

'But when you are qualified you can work here, can't you?'

'I can't speak Greek.'

'You could learn.'

'I did years of French at school, and I can only just about manage to ask for a coffee. Languages aren't my thing, science is. Besides, I can't see how I could be an architect here on the island even if I could speak Greek.'

'So what are you saying?'

'I'm saying I can't see how we can be together.'

'You don't want us to be together?' Mitsos's tone was confused, rather than angry.

Eva realised she was arguing for something she didn't want. It was not surprising she sounded less than convincing.

'Yes, I do.' Eva said, taking his hand. 'But you must see it's impossible. How can we have a future together when we can't even live in the same country?' And she thought of all the other things she had not told him; secrets which would poison their relationship if she allowed it to continue. What could she say when the very reasons she could not be with him were the things she could not tell him?

Mitsos pulled her close. 'I don't believe there isn't a way for us to be together.'

'Please, you have to accept it,' Eva said. His every protestation weakened her will further until she almost believed him.

'If I thought it was what you really wanted, I would accept it. But I don't believe you.'

'That's because I don't want it, but I'm being realistic.'

'Don't be. Just for a while. Leave reality behind.' Mitsos kissed her, and she closed her eyes and let the sensations drown out everything.

The world started to disappear as his arms enfolded her. A desire beyond anything she had ever experienced before enveloped her. She tried to think, but there was only Mitsos and that moment. She fought to regain control over herself and the situation.

'I'm sorry, I can't.'

'Have I done something wrong?'

'No, no, you haven't. It's just that leaving you is going to be the hardest thing I've ever done and if we … it will only be even worse. Would you just hold me?'

'I will do whatever you want, Eva.'

They lay down on the beach , and Mitsos held her close to him. 'What do you know about the stars?'

Safe in his arms, Eva looked up at them. 'Not very much.'

'You know the light you can see now is from millions of years ago. That's why I like looking at them. It makes all the everyday stuff easier to cope with.' He turned and stroked her cheek. 'Well, almost all of it.'

'I need you to promise me something, Mitsos.'

'What's that?'

'You won't wait for me.'

'I can't promise you that. You know how I feel about you.'

'I do, and you know how I feel about you, but it's not meant to be.'

'Don't ask me to forget about you.'

'You should, though. You'll find a lovely girl here who can stay on the island with you and who will make you happy.'

'I might find someone, but she won't be you so I won't be happy. Anyway, if that's what you really want, why are you crying?'

'I'm not.'

Mitsos looked back at the sky again.

'Will you promise me something else then?' Eva asked.

'What's that?'

'I don't know if you were planning to or not, but please don't come to the ferry tomorrow. I told you that saying goodbye is the hardest thing I'm ever going to do. I won't be able to do it again.'

'I don't know, Eva. I want to promise you, but I can't because it would be a lie. And I still don't believe this is the end for us.'

'You have to,' Eva settled back into his arms. 'Just not for a few hours yet.'

Mitsos looked up at the stars with her. 'We'll see. I can wait. I will watch the stars and think of you and when you can return, I believe you will.'

Chapter 23

Millie had looked at all of the clothes she had pulled out of the wardrobe and spread across the bed. After trying on every combination, she had settled on a summer dress which hid the upper arms she hated but accentuated her waist, which had weathered the years and a pregnancy well.

She had taken more time over her hair and make-up than she had in years. She applied some lipstick and then wiped it off again. She examined her face in her small hand mirror. She looked at the crosshatch of lines around the corners of her eyes and the furrows between her eyebrows. She set the mirror down and brushed her hair, the threads of silver in her dark hair catching the light.

She looked at herself in the mirror on the dressing table. She supposed she was presentable, but she wasn't sure she wanted Dimitris to see her, marked by time as she was now. Surely it was better for them to remember each other as they had been – young, full of the future. It would only bring disappointment and reality crashing in. Or perhaps that would be a good thing and the spell would finally be broken, and she would be released from it.

She thought perhaps she would phone Nikos and tell him to pass on a message that she couldn't make it, but each time she picked up her phone, she put it down again. *I could just go to the beach and see him. I don't have to meet him or speak to him*, she said to herself.

She looked at her watch. She was too early, but she had to get out. She locked the door of the apartment and as she walked into the courtyard, she met Violeta.

'Millie, you look so beautiful.'

'Thank you, Violeta.'

'You must be going somewhere special.'

'Not really. I just felt like dressing up a bit.'

'And why not?' said Violeta, smiling at her. She looked around. 'Isn't Eva with you?'

'No, not this evening.'

'Where is she?'

'I'm not entirely sure.'

'Oh well, have a good evening.'

'Thank you, dear. And you.'

The shops had reopened after the afternoon siesta and the shopkeepers were calling out to passers-by to take a look at their goods. The tourists were all wearing shorts and T-shirts, and she felt overdressed. She hurried on her way to the taxi stand and asked the driver to take her to the Hotel Villa Iris.

At the hotel gates, she got out and looked again at the building. Towels were hung over balconies; through the gates she could see people in the grounds and the sound of laughter drifted from the direction of the bar. She realised she still resented the fact that other people were allowed to enjoy the place even though she knew it defied logic.

She turned off the main road and headed in the directions of the trees. She slipped her shoes off and edged downhill through the carpet of sand and pine needles. She stopped where the trees finally gave way to the sand and waited and watched in their shelter, the air heavy with the scent of pine and the sea.

The last of the tourists were packing up for the day and preparing to head back to their hotels and apartments. The beach emptied, and the bartenders at the shack on the beach put the chairs away and closed for the day.

Millie thought about Eva and wondered how she was getting on. She phoned her and was reassured to hear her voice. She put her phone away again. As she continued to wait, she saw a boat in the distance, heading towards the islet in the bay, the sails drenched in golden light. She wished she was there instead of on the beach. She was starting to wish she was anywhere else.

There was nobody left on the beach, and it occurred to her for the first time that Dimitris might have changed his mind. Why would he go all that way to see her when he could be in the comfort and warmth of his home with his family? He had no need to add any complications to his life.

She stepped out onto the beach, wanting to experience it once more on her own, without having to share it with anyone else. Her place; their place. She sat in the dunes, the place she had spent the night with Dimitris. She remembered every moment of that night – the tears, the fraught conversation, the love. Her heart was drowning in memories.

She grieved not only for what had been lost so many years ago but also for what had been lost in all the long years which had followed. She concluded that the good life she had had was not the same as the life she had wanted. She would have traded everything for that life. Except Eva. The thought stopped her in her tracks. She would have had Helena but not Eva.

Tired of sitting and waiting, she walked to the water's edge and watched as the shadows lengthened. The days were already starting to grow shorter. Although the autumn was still far away in Andraxos, in England a chill would be in the air before long. The thought of the long winter nights ahead tightened around her like a vice. The breeze stirred the air and she shivered; it was the first time she had felt cold since she had arrived on the island. She wished she had brought something with her, a protective layer.

She walked along the shore and convinced herself she was glad he had not come. She would say her goodbyes to him here alone, in her own way. She looked out to sea, remembering.

'Emily?'

She turned and heard her breath catch in her throat. Dimitris was standing only feet from her. She was rooted to the spot.

'Em?'

Still she could not move. He covered the remaining ground between them. 'Em.' Not a question anymore.

She faced him for the first time, and the air seemed to spark with static. 'Dimi.'

She took in the man who had been in her heart for so many years. She would still have recognised him even if she had not been expecting him. His black hair had turned to grey and his face bore the traces of a life fully lived, but his eyes were as dark and lively as they had always been. Neither time nor her memories had betrayed her.

She wondered what he thought when he saw her; whether he was surprised, disappointed.

'Em,' he said with wonder in his voice. 'You're really here.'

Millie nodded, robbed of the power of speech.

'I couldn't believe it when Nikos told me you were here.'

She continued to look at him, unable to trust herself to speak.

'What made you come back?'

Millie tried to think. She had told Eva she would find the right words, and she had to do the same thing. 'I wanted to see Andraxos one last time.'

'Last time? Are you ill?' She heard the concern in his voice.

'No, it's nothing like that, but I don't travel as much these days. I have a business, commitments …' Millie broke off. She had seldom felt less articulate.

'Life gets very busy.'

'Yes, it does.'

Dimitris paused. 'Your commitments … you are married?'

'No. I was, but it didn't work out.'

'Life rarely turns out as we planned – or hoped.'

'True.' Millie tried to think of something to say. 'You married Angelika?'

'Yes. We were married the year after you left.'

Millie nodded. She wanted to ask him if it had been a happy marriage, but she could not.

'She has been a good wife to me.'

Millie was quiet, every thought and every question which rushed into her head discarded as inane or inappropriate.

'Do you love her?' The words were out before Millie had had time to consider them.

'I grew to love her.'

Millie felt a tear roll down her cheek. It made her skin itch but she was desperate to avoid drawing attention to it so she let it tickle her skin and willed herself not to touch it. Perhaps it had gone unnoticed.

'But it's a different type of love. It's not what our love was.'

Millie looked up at him.

'You have always been in my heart, Em. I have never forgotten you. I thought you would forget me once you went back to your life in England, but I never forgot you.'

'I didn't forget you,' Millie said. 'I've thought of you so often over the years. You never left me.' Her first love had been able to inflict the deepest of wounds, which had continued to bleed under the surface.

Dimitris looked at her but seemed lost for the right words as well. 'It must be strange to be back here after so long.'

'Forty-four years.' Millie looked around her. 'It's a lifetime ago and in some ways, it feels like it because so much has happened, so much has changed, but in other ways, it's the blink of an eye.'

'Life is the blink of an eye. Only the young don't realise that.'

'I don't know if that makes them the lucky ones or not.'

'Neither do I.' Dimitris gazed out over the sea. 'Did you plan to see me when you came here?'

'No, I only planned to see the island again. I didn't want to risk making any trouble for you.'

'But you met Nikos?'

'Yes,' said Millie uneasily, wondering exactly what Nikos had told him. She should have asked, but she had been so consumed with the thought of meeting Dimitris she hadn't considered that.

'Nikos told me you decided to try to find me.'

'I had a change of heart after I got here. By chance, I found out about the farm shop – it's well-known in town. That led me to Nikos and … you. What did Nikos say to you about me?'

'He said an old friend was on the island and hoped to see me. He doesn't know about what happened between us.'

Millie thought about the web of lies which had been spun around all of them and now held them captive. Dimitris knew nothing about Helena or Eva and had no idea that Nikos knew about what had happened between the two of them all those years ago. He believed Nikos thought she was simply a friend from the past although even to Millie it seemed to stretch credibility that Nikos would have accepted that without question and simply passed her number on.

Perhaps everyone just believed what they wanted to because they suspected that questioning things would lead them to places they had no wish to visit.

'There is so much I want to say to you, but I don't even know where to start.' Millie thought of the lifetime of conversations they had never had. She had thought there would be so much to say and yet now she could think of nothing, and she understood there was nothing which needed to be said. They were both there and that was enough.

A vast, velvet sky strewn with stars stretched above them. Dimitris looked up at it and then at Millie. 'We don't have to talk, Em. We never did. We always understood each other without chatting all the time. You're here and that's all that matters.'

Millie nodded, but still needed to break the silence. 'Your English has improved.'

'I had to learn – to keep up with the times. I insisted on my children learning too.'

My children, thought Millie.

'They are a great blessing. Do you have any?'

'No, no, I don't,' Millie heard herself say. What good would it have done to tell him they had had a daughter, only in the next breath to explain that she had died? Then she would have had to explain the circumstances surrounding Helena's death and drag Nikos into it. Now the lie was told, and it was done. It would be Dimitris's truth, a better one than the real truth.

'That is a pity. You would have been a wonderful mother.'

'In another lifetime.'

'Or another universe. Some scientists say there are many. In another one, we are together, Em. You and I.'

When he took her hand, the decades melted away. They were Em and Dimi, the two young people who had longed to be together. She was grateful that he was such a good man; the years she had spent wishing that things could have been different had not been wasted on a man who did not deserve it.

The moon appeared from behind a cloud and lit a shimmering path to the horizon.

'You have always had a part of my heart and you always will, but I have a family and responsibilities.'

Millie closed her eyes, willing herself to remain in control. She concentrated on the feel of the sand beneath her feet and the sound of the insistent hush of the waves breaking on the beach and tried to anchor herself to the world through those sensations.

She felt the tears escaping and then her face cradled in his hands as he softy brushed the tears away. 'Don't cry, Em. Please. I hate to see you so sad.'

'I'm sorry,' Millie said.

'Don't be sorry either. Seeing you again is something I never dreamed of, and it has made me so happy.'

'Why?'

'I told you I have never forgotten you. You have no idea how often I have thought of you and wondered if you were happy and what you were doing.'

'I must be rather a disappointment.'

'No. Why do you think that?'

'Divorced. No children.'

'You think I would judge you for anything and especially for that?'

'I don't know.'

'I would never judge you. You made the decisions you needed to. All I can see is my Em. My lovely Em.'

Millie found a tissue and dabbed at her eyes. 'What a wreck I must look.'

'No, you are still as beautiful as you ever were.'

'I think perhaps I should go,' said Millie, feeling she could not take much more. 'I'm sure your family will be wondering where you are.'

'In a moment.' Dimitris hesitated. 'One last kiss?'

Millie looked at him and tried to memorise every line and angle of his face, to capture those final moments with him. 'Yes, but then you must go. I will keep my eyes closed because I can't watch you leave again. I can't say goodbye.'

Dimitris took her face in his hands, and Millie felt his lips against hers. A memory brought to life. Dimitris released her and took a step back to survey her. He had not expected it, but he found himself as overwhelmed by his feelings as he had been as a young man. How different things could have been if they had been born into a different time. He couldn't bear to go, but he had no choice, just as he had had no choice all those decades ago. Slowly, he turned and walked back across the sand and into the pine trees.

Millie waited and when she finally opened her eyes, he had gone for the last time.

* * *

Eva walked back through the quiet streets, lost in thought. As she neared the gate to their apartment, she looked up and saw Millie approaching from the opposite direction.

'Did you see Dimitris?'

'Yes.'

'Do you want to talk about it?'

'No. Did you see Mitsos?'

'Yes.'

'Do you want to talk about it?'

'Not really,' Eva replied, and Millie saw a new self-sufficiency about her; the transition to adulthood she had glimpsed before was continuing to develop right before her.

They saw their sadness reflected in each other. Nothing would ever make things right, but they found strength and consolation in each other as they had done so often in the past. It occurred to Eva that if nothing else, she had not lost Millie after all. And Millie, for her own part, wondered how she would ever convey to Eva how precious she was to her.

Chapter 24

Millie had watched every hour of the night tick by; the last night she would ever spend on the island. She had watched as the stars had faded from view and the inky night sky had mellowed to a soft, milky glow. It should have been a tranquil hour, she thought, but the silence sparked with a tension which told her that although their last night there was finally over, she could not relax yet. Even there, in the quiet shadowlands between night and day, there was no peace to be had.

Eva had also retreated to her room. She had been able to think of nothing but Mitsos, the feel of his arms around her, the pain of their final parting. The minutes had bled into hours, and the weight of the passage of time had pressed down on her. Then thoughts of her mother had come to her as well. She had solved the mystery of her disappearance but given herself a new burden in the process. Like Millie, she was awake to see the wrung-out colours of dawn appear on the horizon.

She got up and made coffee, thinking of the long day

ahead. As Millie emerged from the bedroom, she offered her a cup.

'Please. You're up early.'

'I couldn't sleep. Too much on my mind.'

Millie looked at her and waited.

'I was thinking about Mitsos, mainly, but everything is just so …' Eva stopped, unable to think of an adequate word. 'Nothing will ever be quite the same, will it?'

She suddenly looked so much younger and less self-assured than the adult who made fleeting appearances and then fled again. Millie had a sudden memory of a young Eva coming to her for comfort after she had scuffed her knees. She had had absolute trust in Millie's ability to make everything better. Now, as Millie looked at her, she was struck by the fact that she could no longer make anything better.

'Probably not.' Millie said and slumped on the sofa.

Eva glanced at her watch. 'I should pack. Have you finished?'

'Yes.'

Eva returned to her room, took the clothes out of her wardrobe and flung them on the bed. She returned to nursing her coffee while she reviewed the wreckage. Every item reminded her of something. The walking boots and blood-stained T-shirt from her her trip to the pool with Mitsos ; the sketch; the black dress she had worn on the night of the festival. Putting her coffee down, she picked the dress up, remembering that night and how Mitsos had made her feel.

She shoved all of her things into her bag, unable to bear looking at them any longer. She zipped up her bag and joined Millie, who was sitting out on the balcony, watching the boats plying to and fro in the harbour beyond the terracotta rooftops.

'If you're ready, we can go,' Millie said.

'Five minutes?' Eva responded, playing for time. The reality of leaving which had been weighing so heavily on her was now becoming something she was not sure she could face.

'Five minutes,' Millie conceded.

'How do you feel about Andraxos now?'

'It will always be a part of me – and you – but now I'm at peace with that. I will miss it, but I will never return. It's you I feel for.'

'The thought of leaving, of getting on that boat, of never being able to come back, of never seeing any of them again, of never seeing Mitsos again … it makes me feel sick.'

'Are you sure you don't want to talk about last night?'

'Quite sure. Do you want to talk about Dimitris?'

Millie took her point and cast around for a change of subject. 'Aren't you at least looking forward to seeing your friends?'

'They haven't been the best of friends over the last month. I've always felt a little apart from them and now even more so.'

'You never told me that.'

'Because it sounds stupid.'

'No, it doesn't. I've always felt a little apart from other people too.'

'Maybe it's a family trait.'

'It could be. I sometimes think Helena felt that way too.'

They sat and watched the day start to unfold before them as the town came to life, and people went about their business; another normal day for them on their beautiful island. Millie thought about the fact that they would continue to do those things day after day, long after she and Eva had left.

'Come on,' she said reluctantly.

Eva followed her inside, and they took a final look around the apartment which had been their home for the last month and which had witnessed so much. They went downstairs and found Violeta in the courtyard.

'Thank you for a lovely stay,' Millie said.

'It was our pleasure.'

Eva looked at Violeta; the person she had felt could have become a friend; the person who was her cousin but would never know. 'Good bye, Violeta. Thank you for everything.'

Violeta gave her a big hug. 'Thank you for listening when I needed to talk.'

Eva turned to Millie. 'Could you give us a moment?'

Millie nodded and wandered off to the far side of the courtyard.

'How are you really, Violeta?'

'A little better, I think. I've decided to finish school in Athens.'

'That's a big step.'

'Not really. I have relatives I can stay with there, and I know some people at the school I'll be going to.'

'What did your family say?'

'They were fine about it. They know I'll be with family, and Gus won't need much help here until next summer. The busy part of the season will be over by the end of the month. We don't get that many visitors here in September.'

'I'm glad you're OK.'

'I think now it might have been for the best. Mitsos is a wonderful person, but he's a dreamer. I'm a doer. And he could never leave Andraxos, even for Athens. I want to see the world. What happened … it's pushed me to make a decision. Set out on my own path.'

'Good for you.'

'I would like it so much if we could stay in touch, Eva.'

'So would I,' Eva said, knowing they would never be able to do so.

'You have my phone number, don't you?'

Eva nodded and was saved from saying anything else by the arrival of Gus.

'Have a safe journey. Remember you're welcome back at any time. We'd be delighted to see you again.'

'Thank you,' Millie said, joining the group. 'Please say goodbye to Yiannis and Maria for us.'

'We will.'

Violeta and Gus waved them off, and Millie and Eva walked through the quiet back streets for the last time. They took their time with Eva stopping every now and again to take a photo, trying to delay the inevitable.

Eventually they made it to the quayside, and Millie thought one more time of the day she had first met Dimitris while Eva remembered the night she had had her portrait drawn by Mitsos. Their ferry appeared around the headland, and they watched as it drew closer. Eva willed it to turn around and leave before it docked, but the moment to depart could not be postponed any longer.

'Eva.' She heard him call her name.

She turned and saw Mitsos, moving through the crowds, running towards her. Behind her, she heard Millie's intake of breath, and she felt her heart start to pound.

'I had to see you before you left,' he said, as he reached Eva.

'I asked you not to come here.'

'I know, but I told you I couldn't promise not to come.'

'We said everything last night.'

'No, no, we didn't. I have something for you.' Mitsos became aware that other people were staring at them and drew her to one side. Eva realised she had lost sight of Millie, who had been carried along on the tide of people waiting for the ferry.

'This is for you,' he said and gave Eva a small box.

Eva opened the box and found a silver star on a bed of dark blue velvet. 'You never take your necklace off so I thought you could put this on the chain to remind you of me. After our conversation about the stars and how they give us perspective.'

Eva looked down at it. 'It's lovely, Mitsos, but I can't accept it.'

'Please Eva. Take it and wear it and think of me.'

Eva hesitated. She wanted something tangible to remind

her of him and, at the same time, she wanted to wash all her memories away.

'Please.'

Eva accepted it from him with a muffled thanks.

'Promise me that you won't forget me.'

'I don't need to promise you. You know I won't forget you, but it doesn't change anything.'

'There is always a solution.'

'No, there isn't. I want to believe there is, but that's not enough.'

'Eva,' Mitsos said, closing his hands around hers, 'We will keep in touch, and we will find a way.'

Eva shook her head, trying to dismiss the pain of the goodbye. She knew it had to be final even if Mitsos could not.

'I'm not ready to give up on us.' Mitsos released her hands. 'Trust me.' He raised her face to his and kissed her. For one moment, Eva allowed herself to forget everything except Mitsos.

The ferry's horns started blaring, and the clanking of chains and the grinding of machinery filled the air as the car ramp was lowered. 'I have to go,' she said through her tears.

'I know.'

'Please don't say anything else.'

Eva turned away and joined the throng of passengers. She looked for Millie but couldn't find her. She looked back for one final glimpse of Mitsos but could no longer see him either over the heads of the crowd closing in behind her. She was adrift on a sea of strangers and was relieved when she finally found Millie in the crowd.

'Are you all right, darling?'

'No, Millie, I'm really not.'

Millie had seen Eva cry, she had seen her angry, she had seen her sad, but she had never seen her like this. Her face was pinched and strained. They said no more until they had found their seats, and the ferry had pulled away.

'You won't believe me, but I do know how awful this is for you.'

'I should have told him the truth. He's going to think I've just walked away, and I don't care about him, about hurting him.'

'And then what? Do you think that would make everything better?'

'No. Maybe.' Eva thumped the arm rest in frustration. 'I don't know.'

'It doesn't help now, but think about this; you can't build your happiness on someone else's sadness. Think how many lives you would have to wreck to try to get what you want. Even if Mitsos still wanted to be with you after you'd told him you're his cousin and thrown a grenade into his family.'

'I know and that's why I walked away, but I love him. All I want is to be with him. It's so unfair.'

Millie put her arm around Eva, remembering the day she had left Dimitris behind. She knew no words, no reasoning, would have comforted her then either.

'And that's not the only thing.'

'What is it? Tell me,' said Millie, gently turned Eva's face towards her.

'I can't say it.'

'Why not?'

'I don't want to hurt you.'

'Eva, tell me.'

'I'm scared I won't ever be able to love anyone again. You didn't or you wouldn't let yourself. Not after Dimitris. What I felt – feel – for Mitsos is so powerful, and now I feel empty. It's so hard. I just want it to go away, and I don't want to feel like this ever again. Love frightens me now, but I don't want it to. I'm going to be like you. It's the past all over again.'

'Darling, love scares all of us. It rushes in to fill a void we didn't even know existed. It's only when it leaves that you feel the emptiness.'

'It's not just that, though. I thought if I knew about this side of my family and the island, and if I could find out what had happened to mum then everything would be sorted out. I would have answers to my questions, and my curiosity would be satisfied. But it's left me with a longing for more – to know them better, to know Andraxos better – and to be with Mitsos. All my old problems have just been replaced by new ones, worse ones.'

Eva saw the look on Millie's face. 'You see, now I've hurt you. You think I don't care about you, that you're not enough, but that's not it at all. I just thought I could have more.'

'Stop worrying about hurting my feelings.'

'I just want to shut it off.'

'You can't, but you can live with it. And you can survive it.'

'I don't think I can.'

'You can do anything. Look what you have managed to achieve. You got me to come here and confront the past. You met your family even if they can never know. You found out what happened to your mum. I never believed I would get to find out what really happened, and I can only thank you for that. I only wish it hadn't caused you so much pain in the process.'

At the mention of her mother, Eva fell silent. She wished yet again that she could remember something about her; that she had the slightest precious memory to hold onto. And then Mitsos consumed her thoughts again.

Millie hesitated and then added, 'The only consolation I can take from my mistakes are that they gave me you and Helena, and perhaps I can prevent you from repeating my mistakes. I don't want you to live a life full of regrets, and I don't believe the future is written.'

Eva looked out of the scratched window and over the deep blue of the Aegean. She remembered how full of happiness and hope she had been when they had arrived, hanging over the railings, eager to arrive, full of confidence.

'I was the one who wanted to come here. You warned me, but I wouldn't listen. And now I hate what coming here has done to me. I'm not the person I was when I came here. Something has shifted inside me, and it's like the pieces don't fit together.'

Eva heard Millie start to say something and stopped her. 'I don't want to talk about it anymore. Not yet anyway.'

* * *

Outside Heathrow airport, the rain hit the street; the type of rain which fell so hard that the tarmac spat it back up again.

Millie ushered Eva into a taxi, feeling the cold rain soaking through her summer clothes, and gave the driver their address. The journey home had been harder than even Millie had expected. Eva had withdrawn into her own world, drifting through the stages of the journey in a dream and all Millie wanted was to get her back to the sanctuary of their home.

In the back of the taxi, Millie watched the windscreen wipers working furiously to keep the windscreen clear. She looked at Eva, so close to her and yet unreachable. Somewhere along the way, they had switched places. She had made peace with her past while Eva was now tormented by hers, and Millie would have done anything to switch back again.

Eva watched the rain slamming against the window, the rivulets of water distorting the world beyond, the neon lights painting the water in primary colours. She remembered Mitsos diving into the pool, his body cutting through the water and causing ripples to echo out to the edges. She felt a hand reach for hers and closed her eyes. Mitsos. But this hand was small and delicate. It closed around hers, a single gossamer thread tethering her to the world, and she felt her own respond although she had nothing more than that to give.

* * *

Eva dumped her bag on the floor by the door. The house looked different to her, smaller and jaded, as though she was seeing it through different eyes.

'I keep wondering if I could have done things differently.'

'Darling, there was nothing else you could have done, but show me someone who hasn't thought that at some point, and I'll show you a liar.'

'I think I'll go to bed.'

'All right.' Millie watched as Eva retreated upstairs. She made coffee and roamed the downstairs, trying to process the events of the past month. Eva's birthday seemed now a distant, fragile memory. Upstairs she heard footsteps, but eventually the floorboards ceased to creak.

She tiptoed upstairs and paused at Eva's room. The door was ajar and Millie cautiously peered round it. Eva was sitting on the edge of the bed, with the lights out, staring at her phone.

Millie knocked on the door frame. 'What are you doing?'

Eva looked up, her face hollow in the glow from her phone, which lit her from below. 'I've just deleted all of my social media accounts. Now I'm resetting the phone.'

'Why?'

'This is my attempt at a fresh start.'

Millie watched as Eva finished what she was doing and then took the back off of the phone to remove her SIM card and memory card.

'I couldn't bring myself to wipe these. Will you take them?'

'Are you sure about this?' Millie asked, as Eva pressed them into her hand.

Eva nodded.

'What about your friends?'

'As I said, they were never really the best of friends. I'd rather be alone than have friends like that.'

'Even Amy?'

Eva hesitated. 'Even Amy.'

'You can make a fresh start, but you can't deny your past, Eva.'

'I can try.'

'No you can't. It's a part of you. The sadness, the pain, the regrets are just as much are part of you as all the good things. You can move on, but you can't deny them. I know that only too well.'

'I need to try to start again. At least this way, Mitsos can't contact me.'

Millie started to say something, but Eva stopped her. 'I don't trust myself, Millie. If I speak to him again, hear his voice … I know what I have to do, but doing it once, twice, was too much. I don't think I could do it again. Whatever the consequences.' Eva hesitated and then gave Millie the star which Mitsos had given her. She looked down at her hands and pulled off the ring she had bought back in those first, happy days on the island. She handed it to Millie.

Millie looked at the collection of small objects in her hands which represented such a huge part of who her granddaughter was and what she cared about. 'What do you want me to do with them?'

'I don't know. I just know I don't want to see any of them again.'

'Do you want to talk?'

'No. Sorry.'

'You don't have to apologise. Just try to get some rest.'

Millie went back to her room and the world grew silent. Time hung in the balance, heavy and watchful.

In the still hours before dawn, Millie quietly opened Eva's door. She finally seemed to have fallen asleep. Returning to her room, she found a small jewellery box she had not used in years, gathered up Eva's memories and carefully put them inside. She took down the box of her own memories and found the photograph of Dimitris. She traced the outline of his face, and for the first time she could look at him and remember the happy times rather than the pain of their first parting. She gently placed his photograph on top of her aunt's letter, took both boxes to the wardrobe and put them in their place at the back of the shelf.

In the space between where they were and where they would be lay uncharted territory, but she was determined that they would find a way to navigate it together. She believed in Eva in a way her own parents had not believed in her. What was lost could never be reclaimed, but a reconciliation with that loss could be made.

Millie made a vow to herself to stand by Eva until she was ready; ready to find her own path again and ready to take the jewellery box from her and decide what to do with the contents. Until that day, she would be her protector and the guardian of her memories.

About the Author

Alex Milan was born in England but has spent the last twenty years living and working in other countries. Her first novel, The Last Carriage, was published in April 2020. You can find out more about Alex at alexjmilan.com.

CPSIA information can be obtained
at www.ICGtesting.com
Printed in the USA
BVHW071154719042I
605294BV00006B/879